MORE DIXIE GHOSTS

More Haunting, Spine-chilling Stories
from the American South

Edited by
Frank D. McSherry, Jr., Charles G. Waugh,
and Martin H. Greenberg

Rutledge Hill Press
Nashville, Tennessee

Published in Nashville, Tennessee, by Rutledge Hill Press, Inc., 211 Seventh Avenue North, Nashville, Tennessee 37219

Typography by D&T/Bailey Typography, Nashville, Tennessee
Cover design by Harriette Bateman

Library of Congress Cataloging-in-Publication Data

More Dixie ghosts : more haunting, spine-chilling stories from the American South / edited by Frank D. McSherry, Jr., Charles G. Waugh, and Martin H. Greenberg.
p. cm.
ISBN 1-55853-299-4
1. Ghost stories, American—Southern States. 2. Southern States—Fiction. I. McSherry, Frank D. II. Waugh, Charles. III. Greenberg, Martin Harry.
PS648.G48M67 1994
813'.08733083275—dc20 94-7992
CIP

Printed in the United States of America
2 3 4 5 6 7 8—98 97 96 95

Table of Contents

Acknowledgments

"Lost Boys" by Orson Scott Card—Copyright © 1989 by Orson Scott Card. First appeared in *The Magazine of Fantasy and Science Fiction*. Reprinted by permission of the author.

"What Say the Frogs Now, Jenny?" by Hugh B. Cave—Copyright © 1983 by Stuart David Schiff for *Whispers IV*. Reprinted by permission of the author.

"First Dark" by Elizabeth Spencer—Copyright © 1959 by Elizabeth Spencer. From *The Stories of Elizabeth Spencer*. Reprinted by permission of Doubleday and Company, Inc.

"The Tree's Wife" by Mary Elizabeth Counselman—Copyright © 1950 by Popular Fiction Publishing Co. Reprinted by permission of Weird Tales Ltd.

"The Chrome Comanche" by Alan Dean Foster—Copyright © 1990 by Thranx, Inc. Reprinted by permission of the author and the author's agent, Virginia Kidd.

"Toad's Foot" by Manly Wade Wellman—Copyright © 1979 by Mercury Press, Inc. First appeared in *The Magazine of Fantasy and Science Fiction*. Reprinted by permission of Karl Edward Wagner, literary executor for the estate of Manly Wade Wellman.

"The Jabberwock Valentine" by Talmage Powell—Copyright © 1988 by Talmage Powell. Reprinted by permission of the author.

"Sleeping Beauty" by Robert Bloch—Copyright © 1958 under the title "The Sleeping Redhead" by Male Publishing Co. First appeared in *Swank*. Reprinted by permission of the author.

"The Burlap Bag" by Davis Grubb—Copyright © 1967 by Davis Grubb. Reprinted by permission of the Pimlico Agency, Inc.

Volumes in the American Ghosts series:

Dixie Ghosts
Eastern Ghosts
Ghosts of the Heartland
More Dixie Ghosts
New England Ghosts
Western Ghosts

Into the Shadowy South

Step outside.

One glance at the night sky reveals the diamond points of the stars, the glowing nebulae that make up the Greater Magellanic Clouds and the Milky Way.

Some theorists have said that those twinklings are not stars, but the lights of London, Rome, Vienna . . . that we live on the inside of the earth, not the outside.

That theory is false, of course—a madman's dream, a fantasy. But such a notion makes you realize that we know very little about our universe and wonder, even if for only a split second, if there might not be something to it.

Could the universe contain other residents, non-human *things* that wink in and out of existence? The dead who return from someplace else, restless spirits, vengeful relatives, lost souls, unclaimed nightmares, childhood ghosts. . . .

The scary and entertaining stories in this volume are about just such beings—those that defy description—as they wreak their havoc in an equally unclassifiable setting: the American South, where mystery and majesty lurk behind the shadows of the beautiful and the bizarre. Running from the grassy plains of Texas, to the tangled swamps of Georgia, the rolling Virginia hills, the hot Mississippi night, and the stormy coastline of the Carolinas, Dixie is a land haunted by more than history.

Each story takes place in a state of the Old Confederacy, as in its companion volume, *Dixie Ghosts.* The authors are products of the South, by birth or by choice.

Manly Wade Wellman tells of the Civil War veteran-turned-preacher who clashes with an ebony-haired witchwoman in a land where men worshipped devils long before they worshipped God. Mississippian Elizabeth Spencer will have you doubting your eyesight, while Orson Scott Card crawls underneath a North Carolina house to discover strange boys at play. Plantation born and bred, Mary Elizabeth Counselman tells a tender and shivery tale of love and death in the Blue Ridge Mountains. Robert Bloch, the author of *Psycho,* takes you to exotic New Orleans, Louisiana, where a tourist gets caught between dreams and reality. And more.

Are there such things as ghosts? Is there a chance that you might one day walk into a house, round a corner, and step right through something made of meat and bones but no more solid than mist in the moonlight?

After you visit the curious world of these fourteen stories, chances are you'll suspect that something unfamiliar awaits. And if that's the case, we're all subject to the hauntings of this starry universe.

—Frank D. McSherry, Jr.
McAlester, Oklahoma

MORE DIXIE GHOSTS

Chances are, you never had imaginary playmates quite like these. . . .

ONE

Lost Boys

Orson Scott Card

I've worried for a long time about whether to tell this story as fiction or fact. Telling it with made-up names would make it easier for some people to take. Easier for me, too. But to hide my own lost boy behind some phony made-up name would be like erasing him. So I'll tell it the way it happened, and to hell with whether it's easy for either of us.

Kristine and the kids and I moved to Greensboro on the first of March, 1983. I was happy enough about my job—I just wasn't sure I wanted a job at all. But the recession had the publishers all panicky, and nobody was coming up with advances large enough for me to take a decent amount of time writing a novel. I suppose I could whip out 75,000 words of junk fiction every month and publish them under a half-dozen pseudonyms or something, but it seemed to Kristine and me that we'd do better in the long run if I got a job to ride out the recession. Besides, my Ph.D. was down the toilet. I'd been doing good work at Notre Dame, but when I had to take out a few weeks in the middle of a semester to finish *Hart's Hope*, the English department was about as understanding as you'd expect from people who prefer their authors dead or domesticated. Can't feed your family? So sorry. You're a writer? Ah, but not one that anyone's written a scholarly essay about. So long, boy-oh!

So sure, I was excited about my job, but moving to Greensboro also meant that I had failed. I had no way of knowing that my career as a fiction writer wasn't over. Maybe I'd be editing and writing books about computers for the rest of my life. Maybe fiction was just a phase I had to go through before I got a *real* job.

Greensboro was a beautiful town, especially to a family from the western desert. So many trees that even in winter you could hardly tell there was a town at all. Kristine and I fell in love with it at once. There were local problems, of course—people bragged about Greensboro's crime rate and talked about racial tension and what-not—but we'd just come from a depressed northern industrial town with race riots in the high schools, so to us this was Eden. There were rumors that several child disappearances were linked to some serial kidnapper, but this was the era when they started putting pictures of missing children on milk cartons—those stories were in every town.

It was hard to find decent housing for a price we could afford. I had to borrow from the company against my future earnings just to make the move. We ended up in the ugliest house on Chinqua Drive. You know the house—the one with cheap wood siding in a neighborhood of brick, the one-level rambler surrounded by split-levels and two-stories. Old enough to be shabby, not old enough to be quaint. But it had a big fenced yard and enough bedrooms for all the kids and for my office, too—because we hadn't given up on my writing career, not yet, not completely.

The little kids—Geoffrey and Emily—thought the whole thing was really exciting, but Scotty, the oldest, he had a little trouble with it. He'd already had kindergarten and half of first grade at a really wonderful private school down the block from our house in South Bend. Now he was starting over in mid-year, losing all his friends. He had to ride a school bus with strangers. He resented the move from the start, and it didn't get better.

Of course, *I* wasn't the one who saw this. *I* was at work—and I very quickly learned that success at Compute! Books meant giving up a few little things like seeing your children. I had expected to edit books written by people who couldn't write. What astonished me was that I was editing books about computers written by people who couldn't *program*. Not all of them, of course, but enough that I spent far more time rewriting programs so they made sense—so they even *ran*—than I did fixing up people's language. I'd get to work at 8:30 or 9:00, then work straight through till 9:30 or 10:30 at night. My meals were Three Musketeers bars and potato chips from the machine in the employee lounge. My exercise was typing. I met deadlines, but I was putting on a pound a week and my muscles were all atrophying and I saw my kids only in the mornings as I left for work.

Except Scotty. Because he left on the school bus at 6:45 and I rarely dragged out of bed until 7:30, during the week I never saw Scotty at all.

The whole burden of the family had fallen on Kristine. During my years as a freelancer from 1978 till 1983, we'd got used to a certain pattern of life, based on the fact that Daddy was *home.* She could duck out and run some errands, leaving the kids, because I was home. If one of the kids was having discipline problems, I was there. Now if she had her hands full and needed something from the store; if the toilet clogged; if the Xerox jammed, then she had to take care of it herself, somehow. She learned the joys of shopping with a cartful of kids. Add to this the fact that she was pregnant and sick half the time, and you can understand why sometimes I couldn't tell whether she was ready for sainthood or the funny farm.

The finer points of child-rearing just weren't within our reach at that time. She knew that Scotty wasn't adapting well at school, but what could she do? What could I do?

Scotty had never been the talker Geoffrey was—he spent a lot of time just keeping to himself. Now, though, it was getting extreme. He would answer in monosyllables, or not at all. Sullen. As if he were angry, and yet if he was, he didn't know it or wouldn't admit it. He'd get home, scribble out his homework (did they give homework when *I* was in first grade?), and then just mope around.

If he had done more reading, or even watched TV, then we wouldn't have worried so much. His little brother Geoffrey was already a compulsive reader at age five, and Scotty used to be. But now Scotty'd pick up a book and set it down again without reading it. He didn't even follow his mom around the house or anything. She'd see him sitting in the family room, go in and change the sheets on the beds, put away a load of clean clothes, and then come back in and find him sitting in the same place, his eyes open, staring at *nothing.*

I tried talking to him. Just the conversation you'd expect:

"Scotty, we know you didn't want to move. We had no choice."

"Sure. That's O.K."

"You'll make new friends in due time."

"I know."

"Aren't you ever happy here?"

"I'm O.K."

Yeah, right.

But we didn't have *time* to fix things up, don't you see? Maybe if we'd imagined this was the last year of Scotty's life, we'd have done more to right things, even if it meant losing the job. But you never know that sort of thing. You always find out when it's too late to change anything.

And when the school year ended, things *did* get better for a while.

For one thing, I saw Scotty in the mornings. For another thing, he didn't have to go to school with a bunch of kids who were either rotten to him or ignored him. And he didn't mope around the house all the time. Now he moped around outside.

At first Kristine thought he was playing with our other kids, the way he used to before school divided them. But gradually she began to realize that Geoffrey and Emily always played together, and Scotty almost never played with them. She'd see the younger kids with their squirtguns or running through the sprinklers or chasing the wild rabbit who lived in the neighborhood, but Scotty was never with them. Instead, he'd be poking a twig into the tent-fly webs on the trees, or digging around at the open skirting around the bottom of the house that kept animals out of the crawl space. Once or twice a week he'd come in so dirty that Kristine had to heave him into the tub, but it didn't reassure her that Scotty was acting normally.

On July 28th, Kristine went to the hospital and gave birth to our fourth child. Charlie Ben was born having a seizure and stayed in intensive care for the first weeks of his life as the doctors probed and poked and finally figured out that they didn't know what was wrong. It was several months later that somebody uttered the words "cerebral palsy," but our lives had already been transformed by then. Our whole focus was on the child in the greatest need—that's what you *do,* or so we thought. But how do you measure a child's need? How do you compare those needs and decide who deserves the most?

When we finally came up for air, we discovered that Scotty had made some friends. Kristine would be nursing Charlie Ben, and Scotty'd come in from outside and talk about how he'd been playing army with Nicky or how he and the guys had played pirate. At first she thought they were neighborhood kids, but then one day when he talked about building a fort in the grass (I didn't get many chances to mow), she happened to remember that she'd seen him building that fort all by himself. Then she got suspicious and started asking questions. Nicky who? I don't know, Mom. Just Nicky. Where does he live? Around. I don't know. Under the house.

In other words, imaginary friends.

How long had he known them? Nicky was the first, but now there were eight names—Nicky, Van, Roddy, Peter, Steve, Howard, Rusty, and David. Kristine and I had never heard of anybody having more than one imaginary friend.

"The kid's going to be more successful as a writer than I am," I said. "Coming up with eight fantasies in the same series."

Kristine didn't think it was funny. "He's so *lonely,* Scott," she said. "I'm worried that he might go over the edge."

It *was* scary. But if he was going crazy, what then? We even tried taking him to a clinic, though I had no faith at all in psychologists. Their fictional explanations of human behavior seemed pretty lame, and their cure rate was a joke—a plumber or barber who performed at the same level as a psychotherapist would be out of business in a month. I took time off work to drive Scotty to the clinic every week during August, but Scotty didn't like it and the therapist told us nothing more than what we already knew—that Scotty was lonely and morose and a little bit resentful and a little bit afraid. The only difference was that she had fancier names for it. We were getting a vocabulary lesson when we needed help. The only thing that seemed to be helping was the therapy we came up with ourselves that summer. So we didn't make another appointment.

Our homegrown therapy consisted of keeping him from going outside. It happened that our landlord's father, who had lived in our house right before us, was painting the house that week, so that gave us an excuse. And I brought home a bunch of videogames, ostensibly to review them for *Compute!,* but primarily to try to get Scotty involved in something that would turn his imagination away from these imaginary friends.

It worked. Sort of. He didn't complain about not going outside (but then, he never complained about anything), and he played the videogames for hours a day. Kristine wasn't sure she loved *that,* but it was an improvement—or so we thought.

Once again, we were distracted and didn't pay much attention to Scotty for a while. We were having insect problems. One night Kristine's screaming woke me up. Now, you've got to realize that when Kristine screams, that means everything's pretty much O.K. When something really terrible is going on, she gets cool and quiet and *handles* it. But when it's a little spider or a huge moth or a stain on a blouse, then she screams. I expected her to come back into the bedroom and tell me about this monstrous insect she had to hammer to death in the bathroom.

Only this time, she didn't stop screaming. So I got up to see what was going on. She heard me coming—I was up to 230 pounds by now, so I sounded like Custer's whole cavalry—and she called out, "Put your shoes on first!"

I turned on the light in the hall. It was hopping with crickets. I went back into my room and put on my shoes.

After enough crickets have bounced off your naked legs and squirmed around in your hands you stop wanting to puke—you just scoop them up and stuff them into a garbage bag. Later you can scrub yourself for six hours before you feel clean and have nightmares about little legs tickling you. But at the time your mind goes numb and you just do the job.

The infestation was coming out of the closet in the boys' room, where Scotty had the top bunk and Geoffrey slept on the bottom. There were a couple of crickets in Geoff's bed, but he didn't wake up even as we changed his top sheet and shook out his blanket. Nobody but us even saw the crickets. We found the crack in the back of the closet, sprayed Black Flag into it, and then stuffed it with an old sheet we were using for rags.

Then we showered, making jokes about how we could have used some seagulls to eat up our invasion of crickets, like the Mormon pioneers got in Salt Lake. Then we went back to sleep.

It wasn't just crickets, though. That morning in the kitchen Kristine called me again: There were dead June bugs about three inches deep in the window over the sink, all down at the bottom of the space between the regular glass and the storm window. I opened the window to vacuum them out, and the bug corpses spilled all over the kitchen counter. Each bug made a nasty little rattling sound as it went down the tube toward the vacuum filter.

The next day the window was three inches deep again, and the day after. Then it tapered off. Hot fun in the summertime.

We called the landlord to ask whether he'd help us pay for an exterminator. His answer was to send his father over with bug spray, which he pumped into the crawl space under the house with such gusto that we had to flee the house and drive around all that Saturday until a late afternoon thunderstorm blew away the stench or drowned it enough that we could stand to come back.

Anyway, what with that and Charlie's continuing problems, Kristine didn't notice what was happening with the videogames at all. It was on a Sunday afternoon that I happened to be in the kitchen, drinking a Diet Coke, and heard Scotty laughing out loud in the family room.

That was such a rare sound in our house that I went and stood in the door to the family room, watching him play. It was a great little videogame with terrific animation: Children in a sailing ship, battling pirates who kept trying to board, and shooting down giant birds that tried to nibble away the sail. It didn't look as mechanical as the usual videogame, and one feature I really liked was the fact that the player wasn't alone—there were other computer-controlled children helping the player's figure to defeat the enemy.

"Come on, Sandy!" Scotty said. "Come on!" Whereupon one of the children on the screen stabbed the pirate leader through the heart, and the pirates fled.

I couldn't wait to see what scenario this game would move to then, but at that point Kristine called me to come and help her with Charlie. When I got back, Scotty was gone, and Geoffrey and Emily had a different game in the Atari.

Maybe it was that day, maybe later, that I asked Scotty what was the name of that game about children on a pirate ship. "It was just a game, Dad," he said.

"It's got to have a name."

"I don't know."

"How do you find the disk to put it in the machine?"

"I don't know." And he sat there staring past me and I gave up.

Summer ended. Scotty went back to school. Geoffrey started kindergarten, so they rode the bus together. Most important, things settled down with the newborn, Charlie—there wasn't a cure for cerebral palsy, but at least we knew the bounds of his condition. He wouldn't get *worse,* for instance. He also wouldn't get well. Maybe he'd talk and walk someday, and maybe he wouldn't. Our job was just to stimulate him enough that if it turned out he wasn't retarded, his mind would develop even though his body was so drastically limited. It was do-able. The fear was gone, and we could breathe again.

Then, in mid-October, my agent called to tell me that she'd pitched my Alvin Maker series to Tom Doherty at TOR Books, and Tom was offering enough of an advance that we could live. That plus the new contract for *Ender's Game,* and I realized that for us, at least, the recession was over. For a couple of weeks I stayed on at Compute! Books, primarily because I had so many projects going that I couldn't just leave them in the lurch. But then I looked at what the job was doing to my family and to my body, and I realized the price was too high. I gave two weeks' notice, figuring to wrap up the projects that only I knew about. In true paranoid fashion, they refused to accept the two weeks—they had me clean my desk out that afternoon. It left a bitter taste, to have them act so churlishly, but what the heck. I was free. I was home.

You could almost feel the relief. Geoffrey and Emily went right back to normal; I actually got acquainted with Charlie Ben; Christmas was coming (I start playing Christmas music when the leaves turn) and all was right with the world. Except Scotty. Always except Scotty.

It was then that I discovered a few things that I simply hadn't known. Scotty never played any of the videogames I'd brought home from *Compute!* I knew that because when I gave the games back, Geoff and Em complained bitterly—but Scotty didn't even know what the missing games *were.* Most important, that game about kids in a pirate ship wasn't there. Not in the games I took back, and not in the games that belonged to us. Yet Scotty was still playing it.

He was playing one night before he went to bed. I'd been working on *Ender's Game* all day, trying to finish it before Christmas. I came out of my office about the third time I heard Kristine say, "Scotty, go to bed *now!*"

For some reason, without yelling at the kids or beating them or anything, I've always been able to get them to obey when

Kristine couldn't even get them to acknowledge her existence. Something about a fairly deep male voice—for instance, I could always sing insomniac Geoffrey to sleep as an infant when Kristine couldn't. So when I stood in the doorway and said, "Scotty, I think your mother asked you to go to bed," it was no surprise that he immediately reached up to turn off the computer.

"*I'll* turn it off," I said. "Go!"

He still reached for the switch.

"Go!" I said, using my deepest voice-of-God tones.

He got up and went, not looking at me.

I walked to the computer to turn it off, and saw the animated children, just like the ones I'd seen before. Only they weren't on a pirate ship, they were on an old steam locomotive that was speeding along a track. What a game, I thought. The single-sided Atari disks don't even hold a 100K, and here they've got two complete scenarios and all this animation and—

And there wasn't a disk in the disk drive.

That meant it was a game that you upload and then remove the disk, which meant it was completely RAM resident, which meant all this quality animation fit into a mere 48K. I knew enough about game programming to regard that as something of a miracle.

I looked around for the disk. There wasn't one. So Scotty had put it away, I thought. Only I looked and looked and couldn't find any disk that I didn't already know.

I sat down to play the game—but now the children were gone. It was just a train. Just speeding along. And the elaborate background was gone. It was the plain blue screen behind the train. No tracks, either. And then no train. It just went blank, back to the ordinary blue. I touched the keyboard. The letters I typed appeared on the screen. It took a few carriage returns to realize what was happening—the Atari was in memo-pad mode. At first I thought it was a pretty terrific copy-protection scheme, to end the game by putting you into a mode where you couldn't access memory, couldn't do anything without turning off the machine, thus erasing the program code from RAM. But then I realized that a company that could produce a game so good, with such tight code, would surely have some kind of sign-off when the game ended. And why did it end? Scotty hadn't touched the computer after I told him to stop. I didn't touch it, either. Why did the children leave the screen? Why did the train disappear? There was no way the computer could "know" that Scotty was through playing, especially since the game *had* gone on for a while after he walked away.

Still, I didn't mention it to Kristine, not till after everything was over. She didn't know anything about computers then except how to boot up and get WordStar on the Altos. It never occurred to her that there was anything weird about Scotty's game.

It was two weeks before Christmas when the insects came again. And they shouldn't have—it was too cold outside for them to be alive. The only thing we could figure was that the crawl space under our house stayed warmer or something. Anyway, we had another exciting night of cricket-bagging. The old sheet was still wadded up in the crack in the closet—they were coming from under the bathroom cabinet this time. And the next day it was daddy-longlegs spiders in the bathtub instead of June bugs in the kitchen window.

"Just don't tell the landlord," I told Kristine. "I couldn't stand another day of that pesticide."

"It's probably the landlord's father *causing* it," Kristine told me. "Remember he was here painting when it happened the first time? And today he came and put up the Christmas lights."

We just lay there in bed chuckling over the absurdity of that notion. We had thought it was silly but kind of sweet to have the landlord's father insist on putting up Christmas lights for us in the first place. Scotty went out and watched him the whole time. It was the first time he'd ever seen lights put up along the edge of the roof—I have enough of a case of acrophobia that you couldn't get me on a ladder high enough to do the job, so our house always went undecorated except the tree lights you could see through the window. Still, Kristine and I are both suckers for Christmas kitsch. Heck, we even play the Carpenters' Christmas album. So we thought it was great that the landlord's father wanted to do that for us. "It was my house for so many years," he said. "My wife and I always had them. I don't think this house'd look *right* without lights."

He was such a nice old coot anyway. Slow, but still strong, a good steady worker. The lights were up in a couple of hours.

Christmas shopping. Doing Christmas cards. All that stuff. We were busy.

Then one morning, only about a week before Christmas, I guess, Kristine was reading the morning paper and she suddenly got all icy and calm—the way she does when something *really* bad is happening. "Scott, read this," she said.

"Just *tell* me," I said.

"This is an article about missing children in Greensboro."

I glanced at the headline: CHILDREN WHO WON'T BE HOME FOR CHRISTMAS. "I don't want to hear about it," I said. I can't read stories about child abuse or kidnappings. They make me crazy. I can't sleep afterward. It's always been that way.

"You've got to," she said. "Here are the names of the little boys who've been reported missing in the last three years. Russell DeVerge, Nicholas Tyler—"

"What are you getting at?"

"Nicky. Rusty. David. Roddy. Peter. Are these names ringing a bell with you?"

I usually don't remember names very well. "No."

"Steve, Howard, Van. The only one that doesn't fit is the last one, Alexander Booth. He disappeared this summer."

For some reason the way Kristine was telling me this was making me very upset. *She* was so agitated about it, and she wouldn't get to the point. *"So what?"* I demanded.

"Scotty's imaginary friends," she said.

"Come on," I said. But she went over them with me—she had written down all the names of his imaginary friends in our journal, back when the therapist asked us to keep a record of his behavior. The names matched up, or seemed to.

"Scotty must have read an earlier article," I said. "It must have made an impression on him. He's always been an empathetic kid. Maybe he started identifying with them because he felt—I don't know, like maybe he'd been abducted from South Bend and carried off to Greensboro." It sounded really plausible for a moment there—the same moment of plausibility that psychologists live on.

Kristine wasn't impressed. "This article says that it's the first time anybody's put all the names together in one place."

"Hype. Yellow journalism."

"Scott, he got *all* the names right."

"Except one."

"I'm so relieved."

But I wasn't. Because right then I remembered how I'd heard him talking during the pirate videogame. Come on Sandy. I told Kristine. Alexander, Sandy. It was as good a fit as Russell and Rusty. He hadn't matched a mere eight out of nine. He'd matched them all.

You can't put a name to all the fears a parent feels, but I can tell you that I've never felt any terror for myself that compares to the feeling you have when you watch your two-year-old run toward the street, or see your baby go into a seizure, or realize that somehow there's a connection between kidnappings and your child. I've never been on a plane seized by terrorists or had a gun pointed to my head or fallen off a cliff, so maybe there are worse fears. But then, I've been in a spin on a snowy freeway, and I've clung to the handles of my airplane seat while the plane bounced up and down in midair, and still those weren't like what I felt then, reading the whole article. Kids who just disappeared. Nobody saw anybody pick up the kids. Nobody saw anybody lurking around their houses. The kids just didn't come home from school, or played outside and never came in when they were called. Gone. And Scotty knew all their names. Scotty had played with them in his imagination. How did he knew who they were? Why did he fixate on these lost boys?

We watched him, that last week before Christmas. We saw how distant he was. How he shied away, never let us touch him, never stayed with a conversation. He was aware of Christmas, but he never asked for anything, didn't seem excited, didn't want to go shopping. He didn't even seem to sleep. I'd come in when I was heading for bed—at one or two in the morning, long after he'd climbed up into his bunk—and he'd be lying there, all his covers off, his eyes wide open. His insomnia was even worse than Geoffrey's. And during the day, all Scotty wanted to do was play with the computer or hang around outside in the cold. Kristine and I didn't know what to do. Had we already lost him somehow?

We tried to involve him with the family. He wouldn't go Christmas shopping with us. We'd tell him to stay inside while we were gone, and then we'd find him outside anyway. I even unplugged the computer and hid all the disks and cartridges, but it was only Geoffrey and Emily who suffered—I still came into the room and found Scotty playing his impossible game.

He didn't ask for anything until Christmas Eve.

Kristine came into my office, where I was writing the scene where Ender finds his way out of the Giant's Drink problem. Maybe I was so fascinated with computer games for children in that book because of what Scotty was going through—maybe I was just trying to pretend that computer games made sense. Anyway, I still know the very sentence that was interrupted when she spoke to me from the door. So very calm. So very frightened.

"Scotty wants us to invite some of his friends in for Christmas Eve," she said.

"Do we have to set extra places for imaginary friends?" I asked.

"They aren't imaginary," she said. "They're in the back yard, waiting."

"You're kidding," I said. "It's *cold* out there. What kind of parents would let their kids go outside on Christmas Eve?"

She didn't say anything. I got up and we went to the back door together. I opened the door.

There were nine of them. Ranging in age, it looked like, from six to maybe ten. All boys. Some in shirt sleeves, some in coats, one in a swimsuit. I've got no memory for faces, but Kristine does. "They're the ones," she said softly, calmly, behind me. "That one's Van. I remembered him."

"Van?" I said.

He looked up at me. He took a timid step toward me.

I heard Scotty's voice behind me. "Can they come in, Dad? I told them you'd let them have Christmas Eve with us. That's what they miss the most."

I turned to him. "Scotty, these boys are all reported missing. Where have they been?"

"Under the house," he said.

I thought of the crawl space. I thought of how many times Scotty had come in covered with dirt last summer.

"How did they get there?" I asked.

"The old guy put them there," he said. "They said I shouldn't tell anybody or the old guy would get mad and they never wanted him to be mad at them again. Only I said it was O.K., I could tell you."

"That's right," I said.

"The landlord's father," whispered Kristine.

I nodded.

"Only how could he keep them under there all this time? When does he feed them? When—"

She already knew that the old guy didn't feed them. I don't want you to think Kristine didn't guess that immediately. But it's the sort of thing you deny as long as you can, and even longer.

"They can come in," I told Scotty. I looked at Kristine. She nodded. I knew she would. You don't turn away lost children on Christmas Eve. Not even when they're dead.

Scotty smiled. What that meant to us—Scotty smiling. It had been so long. I don't think I really saw a smile like that since we moved to Greensboro. Then he called out to the boys. "It's O.K.! You can come in!"

Kristine held the door open, and I backed out of the way. They filed in, some of them smiling, some of them too shy to smile. "Go on into the living room," I said. Scotty led the way. Ushering them in, for all the world like a proud host in a magnificent new mansion. They sat around on the floor. There weren't many presents, just the ones from the kids; we don't put out the presents from the parents till the kids are asleep. But the tree was there, lighted, with all our homemade decorations on it—even the old needlepoint decorations that Kristine made while lying in bed with desperate morning sickness when she was pregnant with Scotty, even the little puff-ball animals we glued together for that first Christmas tree in Scotty's life. Decorations older than he was. And not just the tree—the whole room was decorated with red and green tassels and little wooden villages and a stuffed Santa hippo beside a wicker sleigh and a large chimney-sweep nutcracker and anything else we hadn't been able to resist buying or making over the years.

We called in Geoffrey and Emily, and Kristine brought in Charlie Ben and held him on her lap while I told the stories of the birth of Christ—the shepherds and the wise men, and the one from the Book of Mormon about a day and a night and a day without darkness. And then I went on and told what Jesus lived for. About forgiveness for all the bad things we do.

"Everything?" asked one of the boys.

It was Scotty who answered. "No!" he said. "Not killing."

Kristine started to cry.

"That's right," I said. "In our church we believe that God

doesn't forgive people who kill on purpose. And in the New Testament Jesus said that if anybody ever hurt a child, it would be better for him to tie a huge rock around his neck and jump into the sea and drown."

"Well, it *did* hurt, Daddy," said Scotty. "They never told me about that."

"It was a secret," said one of the boys. Nicky, Kristine says, because she remembers names and faces.

"You should have told me," said Scotty. "I wouldn't have let him touch me."

That was when we knew, really knew, that it was too late to save him, that Scotty, too, was already dead.

"I'm sorry, Mommy," said Scotty. "You told me not to play with them anymore, but they were my friends, and I wanted to be with them." He looked down at his lap. "I can't even cry anymore. I used it all up."

It was more than he'd said to us since we moved to Greensboro in March. Amid all the turmoil of emotions I was feeling, there was this bitterness: All this year, all our worries, all our efforts to reach him, and yet nothing brought him to speak to us except death.

But I realized now it wasn't death. It was the fact that when he knocked, we opened the door; that when he asked, we let him and his friends come into our house that night. He had trusted us, despite all the distance between us during that year, and we didn't disappoint him. It was trust that brought us one last Christmas Eve with our boy.

But we didn't try to make sense of things that night. They were children, and needed what children long for on a night like that. Kristine and I told them Christmas stories and we told about Christmas traditions we'd heard of in other countries and other times, and gradually they warmed up until every one of the boys told all about his own family's Christmases. They were good memories. They laughed, they jabbered, they joked. Even though it was the most terrible of Christmases, it was also the best Christmas of our lives, the one in which every scrap of memory is still precious to us, the perfect Christmas in which being together was the only gift that mattered. Even though Kristine and I don't talk about it directly now, we both remember it. And Geoffrey and Emily remember it, too. They call it "the Christmas when Scotty brought his friends." I don't think they ever really understood, and I'll be content if they never do.

Finally, though, Geoffrey and Emily were both asleep. I carried each of them to bed as Kristine talked to the boys, asking them to help us. To wait in our living room until the police came, so they could help us stop the old guy who stole them away from their families and their futures. They did. Long enough for the investigating officers to get there and see them, long enough for them to hear the story Scotty told.

Long enough for them to notify the parents. They came at once, frightened because the police had dared not tell them more over the phone than this: that they were needed in a matter concerning their lost boy. They came: with eager, frightened eyes they stood on our doorstep, while a policeman tried to help them understand. Investigators were bringing ruined bodies out from under our house—there was no hope. And yet if they came inside, they would see that cruel Providence was also kind, and *this* time there would be what so many other parents had longed for but never had: a chance to say goodbye. I will tell you nothing of the scenes of joy and heartbreak inside our home that night—those belong to other families, not to us.

Once their families came, once the words were spoken and the tears were shed, once the muddy bodies were laid on canvas on our lawn and properly identified from the scraps of clothing, then they brought the old man in handcuffs. He had our landlord and a sleepy lawyer with him, but when he saw the bodies on the lawn he brokenly confessed, and they recorded his confession. None of the parents actually had to look at him; none of the boys had to face him again.

But they knew. They knew that it was over, that no more families would be torn apart as theirs—as ours—had been. And so the boys, one by one, disappeared. They were there, and then they weren't there. With that the other parents left us, quiet with grief and awe that such a thing was possible, that out of horror had come one last night of mercy and of justice, both at once.

Scotty was the last to go. We sat alone with him in our living room, though by the lights and talking we were aware of the police still doing their work outside. Kristine and I remember clearly all that was said, but what mattered most to us was at the very end.

"I'm sorry I was so mad all the time last summer," Scotty said. "I knew it wasn't really your fault about moving and it was bad for me to be so angry but I just was."

For him to ask *our* forgiveness was more than we could bear. We were full of far deeper and more terrible regrets, we thought, as we poured out our remorse for all that we did or failed to do that might have saved his life. When we were spent and silent at last, he put it all in proportion for us. "That's O.K. I'm just glad that you're not mad at me." And then he was gone.

We moved out that morning before daylight; good friends took us in, and Geoffrey and Emily got to open the presents they had been looking forward to for so long. Kristine's and my parents all flew out from Utah and the people in our church joined us for the funeral. We gave no interviews to the press; neither did any of the other families. The police told only of the finding of the bodies and the confession. We didn't agree to it; it's as if everybody who knew the whole story also knew that it would be wrong to have it in headlines in the supermarket.

Things quieted down very quickly. Life went on. Most people don't even know we had a child before Geoffrey. It wasn't a secret. It was just too hard to tell. Yet, after all these years, I thought it *should* be told, if it could be done with dignity, and to people who might understand. Others should know how it's possible to find light shining even in the darkest place. How even as we learned of the most terrible grief of our lives, Kristine and I were able to rejoice in our last night with our firstborn son, and how together we gave a good Christmas to those lost boys, and they gave as much to us.

Born on August 24, 1951, in Washington state, Orson Scott Card was educated at Brigham Young University and the University of Utah. After serving as a missionary in Brazil, Card turned to freelance writing. Success came with Ender's Game *in 1985, which won both the Nebula (1985) and the Hugo (1986); its sequel,* Speaker for the Dead *(1987), also won both awards—a unique occurrence. A current best-selling series is set in the American South. "Lost Boys" was first published in the October 1989 issue of* The Magazine of Fantasy and Science Fiction.

Revenge drives a young waitress over the edge. . . .

TWO

What Say the Frogs Now, Jenny?

Hugh B. Cave

Striding briskly along the road shoulder, the girl raised her left hand and turned her slender wrist to let the moonlight shine on her watch. Its hands stood at 2:19 A.M. and the road was empty of headlights as far as she could see in either direction. At any second now, though, she would be hearing the eighteen-wheeler, empty road or no. Heaven help her.

The road was a divided four-lane highway in central Florida, and since the accident to her car she had been forced to walk a mile of it every night after work. Her evening job was at the Lake Serena Café, a truck stop on the southern edge of town. Afternoons she worked as cashier in the prescription department of the Lake Serena Drugstore.

She was nineteen years old, pretty enough in face and figure to be justified in believing she might have been named Miss Florida had she been sponsored in the state's recent beauty contest. Her name was Jennifer Forrest and she was frightened. Not even the familiar croaking of frogs in the roadside ditches could diminish her terror as she waited for the tractor-trailer to come snarling up behind her. The rig she never saw, even when darting from the road to avoid becoming its victim.

Three weeks ago, when she had first heard it behind her, it had not been invisible as it was now. And she had not been on foot but proudly and happily driving her own car—the very first car she had ever owned.

It was not a new car, of course. It was a five-year-old Datsun that had already been driven more than fifty thousand miles when she bought it. But it was hers, and the good-looking young examiner who tested her for her driver's license had told her she was a first-class driver. (She hadn't told him how many guys had helped to teach her.) What she hadn't expected, on seeing the tractor-trailer come barreling up behind her at 2:15 in the morning, was that its driver would be stupid enough to play games.

She had known Willard Allison ever since getting the job as waitress at the café. He owned his own rig and thought he owned any girl he took a shine to, though he could still laugh his crazy, booming laugh on finding out he was mistaken. He was as big as a wrestler and had an enormous beard the color of the sandy soil in the citrus groves.

Half an hour before, while eating at the restaurant, he had grabbed her by a wrist and told her, with a grin, that she ought to quit slinging hash and marry him.

"Oh, sure, I'll do that."

"Hey, I'm serious, Jenny," he said, his grin making a liar out of him. And he pulled her down onto his knee and tried to kiss her.

Others had tried that, and she had learned how to handle them. You grabbed where it hurt. Not hard enough to make them really sore at you, of course, but enough to make them let go. Willard Allison had let go and laughed like a clap of thunder, then reached for her again so fast she fell down when leaping away from him. Then he jumped from his chair and lifted her to her feet, saying, "Jeez, Jenny, I'm sorry."

"Look at my knee!" It was scraped and bleeding, and she was furious. "It's a lucky thing for you I'm not wearing stockings, Willy Allison!"

He pulled a handful of paper napkins from the holder on his table and wiped the knee with them, all the time saying how sorry he was. "Jeez, girl, I was only horsing around. You know that. You know me."

"Well, you can horse around with Evelyn or Nadeen," she said, "because I'm not waitin' on you!"

"Aw, come on, Jenny. I never meant nothin'."

"Well"—it was hard to stay mad at the big ape sometimes—"I'm off now, anyway."

"I'll drive you home," he said. He had done that a few times when he was heading south and didn't have a buddy along. The house she lived in with her folks was right on the highway. In return, of course, he expected the right to do a little pawing . . . but didn't every man, these days?

Tonight was different, though. "I have a car now, Mr. Allison, thank you very much," she told him with a toss of her auburn hair.

"You have? Since when?"

"Since this morning."

"Well, whatta ya know! Where is it? Let's have a look at it."

She would have shown Jack the Ripper her car that night, she was so proud to be the owner of it. (So proud, too, of what the handsome young examiner had said about her driving.) Leading him out the back door, she unlocked the car and stood there with her arms folded over her breasts while he appraised it inside and out.

"Looks good if the price was right," was his verdict. "How much you pay for it?"

"None of your business." Just about every cent she'd had in the bank was what she had paid for it.

"Okay, kiddo," he said, grinning. "You leaving now?"

"When I've changed." She never wore her uniform home as some of the other girls did. How could you know who you might meet?

"This is for luck," he said, and kissed her.

She stepped back and slapped him, and his crazy laugh boomed through the almost empty parking lot. Again angry with him, she stormed back inside. When she drove out of the lot some ten minutes later, in a white pantsuit that showed off her figure, Allison was just stepping up into his cab. She had to pass within fifteen feet of him to reach the exit, and he waved to her. With what she hoped was obvious indifference she lifted an arm languidly in reply.

It was just under a mile from the café to her house. She had covered about half the distance, doing only thirty to thirty-five miles an hour in her brand-new (that morning) secondhand car, when she heard Allison's rig behind her. Just ahead the road sharply curved to the right in a blind bend hidden by a thick stand of pine trees. Allison sounded his horn as he swung out to pass her.

She pulled well over because she knew the size of the Goliath he was driving. As a new driver—even though pronounced first class by her good-looking young examiner—she was leery of anything that big, with that many wheels. He had plenty of room to zoom on by. Plenty. But did he? No.

He veered in at her, playing a game. Slowing to her speed, he swung the monster at her, then out again, like a cowboy making a skittish horse do tricks. Into the curve they went side by side, she clutching her wheel for dear life, he trying to frighten her while filling the night with his booming laughter.

Even before he gunned his rig and left her behind on the turn, she had lost control of her car and was headed for the deep, boggy ditch just off the pavement.

By the time she crawled out of her car, miraculously unhurt, he and his Goliath were long gone. Even the whine of the many tires had faded away to silence. Frogs croaked again in the ditch where her precious car lay on its side. Tears streamed down her face as she trudged homeward.

Bitter hatred for Willard Allison and his booming laugh filled her heart.

Again Jennifer raised her arm to catch the moonlight on her watch. The rig was a few minutes late tonight, or else her watch was slow. Most likely it was the watch—getting old now and only a cheapie to begin with. On leaving the café she hadn't stopped to set it by the electric wall clock as she usually did.

The highway was still empty. The only sound other than her own hurrying footsteps was the croaking of the frogs. What a fantastic mix of sounds frogs made, when you stopped to think about it. Anyone who thought they all croaked alike was plain crazy.

When, oh God, *when* would she get her car back? It was three weeks now, and she had been hearing the rig for two. Every night for two weeks! She should have spent the higher towing fee and had the work done by someone reliable, not given the job to Jarrett's just because they were closer. Jarrett's was probably the poorest garage in thirty miles.

But she hadn't known then that Willard Allison would be paying the bill, had she? How could she when the car had been in the garage for a week before he even showed up at the café again?

But, anyway, let them finish repairing it. Let them give it back to her before she got so scared of walking this road that she would have to give up her waitress job. She couldn't get by on the little she made by working part-time at the drugstore. Let them stop making excuses about waiting for parts, for God's sake. There were plenty of Datsuns on the road here. Parts must be available somewhere.

Maybe tonight—just this one night—the rig would not come. Or if it did come, maybe she would reach home ahead of it. Please God . . .

Evidently God was not tuned in to scared waitresses just then. The truck noise was in her ears already.

She stopped. Trembling all over, she turned swiftly to look down the road. She wouldn't see it, of course. She never saw it. But she always looked.

It made the same noise it had made when it came up behind her car and caused her to drive into the ditch. It always did, and because it did she knew it was always the same rig. His. Allison's. People thought all the big rigs made the same kind of noise, but they didn't. Not to her, anyway, and she'd been living within two hundred feet of this highway since she was born. They were as different as the frogs were different.

The noise that rushed toward her along the empty road now was a blend of many sounds, all terrifying. There was the high whine of all that rubber on the concrete. There was the snarl of a huge diesel engine being pushed to its limit. Even the invisible body of the trailer made a noise as it flung the sleeping air aside.

Now it set up a vibration in a stretch of metal guardrail that she had not yet put behind her. That told her how close it was and how little time she had.

Too scared to cry out, she leaped the rail like a hurdler and landed in a heap on the far side of it, in grass a foot high. As she struggled to her feet and continued running, she heard the unseen rig veer in her direction. Would it shatter the guardrail to pursue her? It could if it wanted to, she was certain. But it straightened—the sound of it did—and went on down the highway.

She had a feeling that if she could see it, it would be roaring along just an inch or so from the rail. With him at the wheel, of course, looking back to let her know there would be another time.

"Dear God," she sobbed as the silence returned, "let my car be finished tomorrow. I can't take this anymore!"

God didn't answer. The frogs began their serenade again.

The café had been crowded when Willard Allison parked his tractor-trailer and walked in, a week after causing her to wreck her car. "Leave him to me," Jennifer had told the other girls. "I've been waiting for this."

When she went to his table he had tried to talk to her, but she had silenced him with a curt, "We're busy, buster," and taken his order. He wasn't clowning as he usually did. He looked downright unhappy, in fact—probably afraid she would start yelling at him for what he had done, in front of all those customers.

She would have, too, if she hadn't already figured out a better way to get even.

He wanted coffee, of course. At every meal he drank three or four cups of coffee laced with so much sugar it must have tasted more like honey. Also he ordered the day's special, corned beef and cabbage, which was unlike him. He was usually in too big a hurry for that much food.

When he got it, he just picked at it until the place was almost empty. Then when she went to his table to fill his coffee cup for the umpteenth time, his hand closed over her wrist and he said with a sheepish kind of grin, "Sit down a minute, Jenny."

"With you?" she snapped. "Am I crazy?"

"Please. Sit down," he said, and there was no wild laugh to put a curse on it. "We were on a sharp curve there, remember? I never knew what I did to you till yesterday when Nick told me in Orlando." Nick DiAngelo was a regular at the café and a buddy of his. "I hadn't figured on coming down this way today," Allison went on, shaking his bushy face at her. "But here I am. How much is the car costing you?"

"What do you care?" she said.

"I care. It's why I'm here. How much?"

"Three-hundred sixty, Jarrett said. That's just the estimate. It'll be more, you can bet."

He reached into his hip pocket for his billfold and took a handful of hundred-dollar bills out of it. He counted out ten of them and pressed them into her hand. She was surprised not only by the amount but by his not having clapped the money down on the table with one of his crazy loud laughs.

He stood up, still holding on to her hand with the money in it. Reaching for her other hand he held both and stood there on wide apart legs solemnly looking down at her—a bearded bull moose gazing at a frightened fawn.

"I'm sorry," he said. "It was a stupid thing I did. I clean forgot you only just got your license to drive. Try not to be too sore, huh?"

For a second she thought he was going to try kissing her again, and she wasn't sure she could handle it. Not after what she had just done to him. But he didn't. He just grinned again—or almost did—and dropped her hands and walked out.

From the front window she watched him step up into his cab and wondered if she ought to tell him. But she was afraid to.

Her left hand, pressed hard against her stomach but shaking all the same, still clutched the thousand dollars he had given her.

She had been wrong about Jarrett. When he delivered her car to the café the evening after her crazy leap over the guardrail, he stuck to his estimate. Prepared for the worst, she had kept the whole thousand dollars in her handbag ever since Allison had given it to her two weeks before, and now most of it was pure profit. She could have kissed him. Not Allison. It was too late for that. She could have kissed old man Jarrett.

"Sorry it took so long, Miss Forrest," he said. "I really had a tough time finding some of the parts." He was a little dried-up man and his gaze roved happily over her bosom while he talked to her. Evidently he thought more of her looks than of her mind, though, for he didn't bother going into detail about what he had done to the car. Most of his customers had to hear it down to the last cotter pin, whether they wanted to or not.

Jenny was pleased with him, though. "Boy, will I be glad to be driving home tonight instead of walking!" she exclaimed as she paid him.

At her 2 A.M. quitting time she was so glad to have her brand-new once-wrecked secondhand car waiting for her in the parking lot, she sang all the time she was changing from her uniform into her white pantsuit. Then she sang some more as she slid in behind the wheel and started home.

She had almost forgotten Willard Allison when she heard the

sound of his rig behind her. With her car windows wide open she was even enjoying the chorus of frog calls from the roadside ditch. It was like an accompaniment to her own happy warbling, she had been thinking with a grin.

The roar of the rig destroyed her mood, of course. But completely. She sent a terrified glance into the rearview mirror and saw nothing but empty highway, but the sound became louder so rapidly that she knew she had to outrace it. Her sandaled right foot shoved the gas pedal flat onto the floor.

The little car leaped forward like a frightened deer, its speedometer streaking from thirty-five to over seventy before she knew what was happening. She had no idea how fast the car would go. After all, she hadn't owned it for even a day when the same rig that was now pursuing her had caused her to wreck it. Oh my God, she mentally wailed, I don't know how to drive this fast!

And even at seventy-five she was not outdistancing her pursuer. The tractor-trailer was roaring up beside her.

She saw it then for the first time since her nightly ordeal had begun. There was no moon tonight, and the God-awful thing was only a faint, misty outline—but it was his rig, all right. It was the same one that had carried him to his death when he fell asleep at the wheel after she laced his coffee with stuff from the drugstore. And he was at the wheel now, glaring accusingly across at her as the cab of his Goliath came abreast of her.

She saw him shaking his head as if to say, "You shouldn't have done that, Jenny. No, baby, you shouldn't have done that. After all, I more than paid for the repairs to your car."

"I know you did!" she shrieked at him as the monster veered over toward her. "Oh my God, Willy, I know you did. But I doped your first cup of coffee and you'd already drunk it. I wanted you to know what it was like to have an accident."

His roaring Goliath and her little car were tearing along the highway together, only inches apart, and he still shook his head at her. "You should have listened when I asked you to marry me, Jenny," he was saying. "A cute trick like you and a big lug like me—we'd have had fun. Killing me was the dumbest thing you ever did, baby."

Then he said "So long" and began laughing. And as the little car went off the road into the ditch, and through the ditch end over end into a bog full of frogs, she heard the bellow of his laughter long after the frogs were shocked into silence.

It was the last sound she ever heard.

Hugh B. Cave is one of the deans of modern horror. Brought to the United States from England at the age of five, Cave began selling fiction while still in his teens. Cave has published more than 1,100 stories and fifteen books. Many are feverish, nightmarish tales of terror, such as those Weird Tales *works collected in* Murgunstrumm and Others *(1977). Educated at Boston University, Cave served as a war correspondent in the Pacific, writing military histories (*Wings across the World, *1945). Born in 1910, he now lives in Washington state. "What Say the Frogs Now, Jenny?" was first published in* Whispers IV *(1983), an original anthology.*

As day turns to night, who can say what's real and what's imagined. . . .

THREE

First Dark

Elizabeth Spencer

When Tom Beavers started coming back to Richton, Mississippi, on weekends, after the war was over, everybody in town was surprised and pleased. They had never noticed him much before he paid them this compliment; now they could not say enough nice things. There was not much left in Richton for him to call family—just his aunt who had raised him, Miss Rita Beavers, old as God, ugly as sin, deaf as a post. So he must be fond of the town, they reasoned; certainly it was a pretty old place. Far too many young men had left it and never come back at all.

He would drive in every Friday night from Jackson, where he worked. All weekend, his Ford, dusty of flank, like a hard-ridden horse, would sit parked down the hill near Miss Rita's old wire front gate, which sagged from the top hinge and had worn a span in the ground. On Saturday morning, he would head for the drugstore, then the post office; then he would be observed walking here and there around the streets under the shade trees. It was as though he were looking for something.

He wore steel taps on his heels, and in the still the click of them on the sidewalks would sound across the big front lawns and all the way up to the porches of the houses, where two ladies might be sitting behind a row of ferns. They would identify him to one another, murmuring in their fine little voices, and say it was just too bad there was nothing here for young people. It was just a shame they didn't have one or two more old houses, here, for a Pilgrimage—look how Natchez had waked up.

One Saturday morning in early October, Tom Beavers sat at the counter in the drugstore and reminded Totsie Poteet, the drugstore clerk, of a ghost story. Did he remember the strange old man who used to appear to people who were coming into Richton along the Jackson road at twilight—what they called "first dark"?

"Sure I remember," said Totsie. "Old Cud'n Jimmy Wiltshire used to tell us about him every time we went 'possum hunting. I could see him plain as I can see you, the way he used to tell it. Tall, with a top hat on, yeah, and waiting in the weeds alongside the road ditch, so'n you couldn't tell if he wasn't taller than any mortal man could be, because you couldn't tell if he was standing down in the ditch or not. It would look like he just grew up out of the weeds. Then he'd signal to you."

"Them that stopped never saw anybody," said Tom Beavers, stirring his coffee. "There were lots of folks besides Mr. Jimmy that saw him."

"There was, let me see . . ." Totsie enumerated others—some men, some women, some known to drink, others who never touched a drop. There was no way to explain it. "There was that story the road gang told. Do you remember, or were you off at school? It was while they were straightening the road out to the highway—taking the curves out and building a new bridge. Anyway, they said that one night at quitting time, along in the winter and just about dark, this old guy signaled to some of 'em. They said they went over and he asked them to move a bulldozer they had left across the road, because he had a wagon back behind on a little dirt road, with a sick nigger girl in it. Had to get to the doctor and this was the only way. They claimed they knew didn't nobody lived back there on that little old road, but niggers can come from anywhere. So they moved the bulldozer and cleared back a whole lot of other stuff, and waited and waited. Not only didn't no wagon ever come, but the man that had stopped them, he was gone, too. They was right shook up over it. You never heard that one?"

"No, I never did." Tom Beavers said this with his eyes looking up over his coffee cup, as though he sat behind a hand of cards. His lashes and brows were heavier than was ordinary, and worked as a veil might, to keep you away from knowing exactly what he was thinking.

"They said he was tall and had a hat on." The screen door flapped to announce a customer, but Totsie kept on talking. "But whether he was a white man or a real light-colored nigger they couldn't say. Some said one and some said another. I figured they'd been pulling on the jug a little earlier than usual. You know why? I never heard of *our* ghost *saying* nothing. Did you, Tom?"

He moved away on the last words, the way a clerk will, talking back over his shoulder and ahead of him to his new customer at the same time, as though he had two voices and two heads. "And what'll it be today, Miss Frances?"

The young woman standing at the counter had a prescription already out of her bag. She stood with it poised between her fingers, but her attention was drawn toward Tom Beavers, his coffee cup, and the conversation she had interrupted. She was a girl whom no ordinary description would fit. One would have to know first of all who she was: Frances Harvey. After that, it was all right for her to be a little odd-looking, with her reddish hair that curled back from her brow, her light eyes, and her high, pale temples. This is not the material for being pretty, but in Frances Harvey it was what could sometimes be beauty. Her family home was laden with history that nobody but the Harveys could remember. It would have been on a Pilgrimage if Richton had had one. Frances still lived in it, looking after an invalid mother.

"What were you-all talking about?" she wanted to know.

"About that ghost they used to tell about," said Totsie, holding out his hand for the prescription. "The one people used to see just outside of town, on the Jackson road."

"But why?" she demanded. "Why were you talking about him?"

"Tom, here—" the clerk began, but Tom Beavers interrupted him.

"I was asking because I was curious," he said. He had been studying her from the corner of his eye. Her face was beginning to show the wear of her mother's long illness, but that couldn't be called change. Changing was something she didn't seem to have done, her own style being the only one natural to her.

"I was asking," he went on, "because I saw him." He turned away from her somewhat too direct gaze and said to Totsie Poteet, whose mouth had fallen open, "It was where the new road runs close to the old road, and as far as I could tell he was right on the part of the old road where people always used to see him."

"But when?" Frances Harvey demanded.

"Last night," he told her. "Just around first dark. Driving home."

A wealth of quick feeling came up in her face. "So did I! Driving home from Jackson! I saw him, too!"

For some people, a liking for the same phonograph record or for Mayan archaeology is enough of an excuse to get together. Possibly, seeing the same ghost was no more than that. Anyway, a week later, on Saturday at first dark, Frances Harvey and Tom Beavers were sitting together in a car parked just off the highway, near the spot where they agreed the ghost had appeared. The season was that long, peculiar one between summer and fall, and there were so many crickets and tree frogs going full tilt in their periphery that their voices could hardly be distinguished from the background noises, though they both would have heard a single footfall in the grass. An edge of autumn was in the air at night, and Frances had put on a tweed jacket at the last minute, so the smell of moth balls was in the car, brisk and most unghostlike.

But Tom Beavers was not going to forget the value of the ghost, whether it put in an appearance or not. His questions led Frances into reminiscence.

"No, I never saw him before the other night," she admitted. "The Negroes used to talk in the kitchen, and Regina and I—you know my sister Regina—would sit there listening, scared to go and scared to stay. Then finally going to bed upstairs was no relief, either, because sometimes Aunt Henrietta was visiting us, and *she'd* seen it. Or if she wasn't visiting us, the front room next to us, where she stayed, would be empty, which was worse. There was no way to lock ourselves in, and besides, what was there to lock out? We'd lie all night like two sticks in bed, and shiver. Papa finally had to take a hand. He called us in and sat us down and said that the whole thing was easy to explain—it was all automobiles. What their headlights did with the dust and shadows out on the Jackson road. 'Oh, but Sammie and Jerry!' we said, with great big eyes, sitting side by side on the sofa, with our tennis shoes flat on the floor."

"Who were Sammie and Jerry?" asked Tom Beavers.

"Sammie was our cook. Jerry was her son, or husband, or something. Anyway, they certainly didn't have cars. Papa called them in. They were standing side by side by the bookcase, and

Regina and I were on the sofa—four pairs of big eyes, and Papa pointing his finger. Papa said, 'Now, you made up these stories about ghosts, didn't you?' 'Yes, sir,' said Sammie. 'We made them up.' 'Yes, sir,' said Jerry. 'We sho did.' 'Well, then, you can just stop it,' Papa said. 'See how peaked these children look?' Sammie and Jerry were terribly polite to us for a week, and we got in the car and rode up and down the Jackson road at first dark to see if the headlights really did it. But we never saw anything. We didn't tell Papa, but headlights had nothing whatever to do with it."

"You had your own *car* then?" He couldn't believe it.

"Oh no!" She was emphatic. "We were too young for that. Too young to drive, really, but we did anyway."

She leaned over to let him give her cigarette a light and saw his hand tremble. Was he afraid of the ghost or of her? She would have to stay away from talking family.

Frances remembered Tommy Beavers from her childhood—a small boy going home from school down a muddy side road alone, walking right down the middle of the road. His old aunt's house was at the bottom of a hill. It was damp there, and the yard was always muddy, with big fat chicken tracks all over it, like Egyptian writing. How did Frances know? She could not remember going there, ever. Miss Rita Beavers was said to order cold ham, mustard, bread, and condensed milk from the grocery store. "I doubt if that child ever has anything hot," Frances's mother had said once. He was always neatly dressed in the same knee pants, high socks, and checked shirt, and sat several rows ahead of Frances in study hall, right in the middle of his seat. He was three grades behind her; in those days, that much younger seemed very young indeed. What had happened to his parents? There was some story, but it was not terribly interesting, and, his people being of no importance, she had forgotten.

"I think it's past time for our ghost," she said. "He's never out so late at night."

"He gets hungry, like me," said Tom Beavers. "Are you hungry, Frances?"

They agreed on a highway restaurant where an orchestra played on weekends. Everyone went there now.

From the moment they drew up on the graveled entrance, cheerful lights and a blare of music chased the spooks from their heads. Tom Beavers ordered well and danced well, as it turned out. Wasn't there something she had heard about his being "smart"? By "smart," southerners mean intellectual, and they say it in an almost condescending way, smart being what you are when you can't be anything else, but it is better, at least, than being nothing. Frances Harvey had been away enough not to look at things from a completely southern point of view, and she was encouraged to discover that she and Tom had other things in common besides a ghost, though all stemming, perhaps, from the imagination it took to see one.

They agreed about books and favorite movies and longing to see more plays. She sighed that life in Richton was so confining, but he assured her that Jackson could be just as bad; *it* was getting to be like any middle western city, he said, while Richton at least had a sense of the past. This was the main reason, he went on, gaining confidence in the jumble of commonplace noises—dishes, music, and a couple of drinkers chattering behind them—that he had started coming back to Richton so often. He wanted to keep a connection with the past. He lived in a modern apartment, worked in a soundproof office—he could be in any city. But Richton was where he had been born and raised, and nothing could be more old-fashioned. Too many people seemed to have their lives cut in two. He was earnest in desiring that this should not happen to him.

"You'd better be careful," Frances said lightly. Her mood did not incline her to profound conversation. "There's more than one ghost in Richton. You may turn into one yourself, like the rest of us."

"It's the last thing I'd think of you," he was quick to assure her.

Had Tommy Beavers really said such a thing, in such a natural, charming way? Was Frances Harvey really so pleased? Not only was she pleased but, feeling warmly alive amid the music and small lights, she agreed with him. She could not have agreed with him more.

"I hear that Thomas Beavers has gotten to be a very attractive man," Frances Harvey's mother said unexpectedly one afternoon.

Frances had been reading aloud—Jane Austen this time. Theirs was one house where the leather-bound sets were actually read. In Jane Austen, men and women seesawed back and forth for two or three hundred pages until they struck a point of balance; then they got married. She had just put aside the book, at the end of a chapter, and risen to lower the shade against the slant of afternoon sun. "Or so Cud'n Jennie and Mrs. Giles Antley and Miss Fannie Stapleton have been coming and telling you," she said.

"People talk, of course, but the consensus is favorable," Mrs. Harvey said. "Wonders never cease; his mother ran away with a brush salesman. But nobody can make out what he's up to, coming back to Richton."

"Does he have to be 'up to' anything?" Frances asked.

"Men are always up to something," said the old lady at once. She added, more slowly, "In Thomas's case, maybe it isn't anything it oughtn't to be. They say he reads a lot. He may just have taken up with some sort of idea."

Frances stole a long glance at her mother's face on the pillow. Age and illness had reduced the image of Mrs. Harvey to a kind of caricature, centered on a mouth that Frances could not help comparing to that of a fish. There was a tension around its rim, as though it were outlined in bone, and the underlip even stuck out a little. The mouth ate, it took medicine, it asked for things, it gasped when breath was short, it commented. But when it commented, it ceased to be just a mouth and became part of Mrs. Harvey, that witty tyrant with the infallible memory for the right detail, who was at her terrible best about men.

"And what could he be thinking of?" she was wont to inquire when some man had acted foolishly. No one could ever defend accurately the man in question, and the only conclusion was Mrs. Harvey's; namely, that he wasn't thinking, if, indeed, he could. Although she had never been a belle, never a flirt, her popularity with men was always formidable. She would be observed talking marathons with one in a corner, and could you ever be sure, when they both burst into laughter, that they had not just exchanged the most shocking stories? "Of course, *he*—" she would begin later, back with the family, and the masculinity that had just been encouraged to strut and preen a little was quickly shown up as idiotic. Perhaps Mrs. Harvey hoped by this method to train her daughters away from a lot of sentimental nonsense that was their birthright as pretty southern girls in a house with a lawn that moonlight fell on and that was often lit also by Japanese lanterns hung for parties. "Oh, he's not like that, Mama!" the little girls would cry. They were already alert for heroes who would ride up and cart them off. "Well, then, you watch," she would say. Sure enough, if you watched, she would be right.

Mrs. Harvey's younger daughter, Regina, was a credit to her mother's long campaign; she married well. The old lady, however, never tired of pointing out behind her son-in-law's back that his fondness for money was ill concealed, that he had the longest feet she'd ever seen, and that he sometimes made grammatical errors.

Her elder daughter, Frances, on a trip to Europe, fell in love, alas! The gentleman was of French extraction but Swiss citizenship, and Frances did not marry him, because he was already married—that much filtered back to Richton. In response to a cable, she had returned home one hot July in time to witness her father's wasted face and last weeks of life. That same September, the war began. When peace came, Richton wanted to know if Frances Harvey would go back to Europe. Certain subtly complicated European matters, little understood in Richton, seemed to be obstructing Romance; one of them was probably named Money. Meanwhile, Frances's mother took to bed, in what was generally known to be her last illness.

So no one crossed the ocean, but eventually Tom Beavers came up to Mrs. Harvey's room one afternoon, to tea.

Though almost all her other faculties were seriously impaired, in ear and tongue Mrs. Harvey was as sound as a young beagle, and she could still weave a more interesting conversation than most people who go about every day and look at the world. She was of the old school of southern lady talkers; she vexed you with no ideas, she tried to protect you from even a moment of silence. In the old days, when a bright company filled the downstairs rooms, she could keep the ball rolling amongst a crowd. Everyone—all the men especially—got their word in, but the flow of things came back to her. If one of those twenty-minutes-to-or-after silences fell—and even with her they did occur—people would turn and look at her daughter Frances. "And what do you think?" some kind-eyed gentleman would ask. Frances did not credit that she had the sort of face people would turn to, and so did not know how to take advantage of it. What did she think? Well, to answer that honestly took a moment of reflection—a fatal moment, it always turned out. Her mother would be up instructing the maid, offering someone an ashtray or another goody, or remarking outright, "Frances is so timid. She never says a word."

Tom Beavers stayed not only past teatime that day but for a drink as well. Mrs. Harvey was induced to take a glass of sherry, and now her bed became her enormous throne. Her keenest suffering as an invalid was occasioned by the absence of men. "What is a house without a man in it?" she would often cry. From her eagerness to be charming to Frances's guest that afternoon, it seemed that she would have married Tom Beavers herself if he had asked her. The amber liquid set in her small four-sided glass glowed like a jewel, and her diamond flashed; she had put on her best ring for the company. What a pity no longer to show her ankle, that delicious bone, so remarkably slender for so ample a frame.

Since the time had flown so, they all agreed enthusiastically that Tom should wait downstairs while Frances got ready to go out to dinner with him. He was hardly past the stair landing before the old lady was seized by such a fit of coughing that she could hardly speak. "It's been—it's been too much—too *much* for me!" she gasped out.

But after Frances had found the proper sedative for her, she was calmed, and insisted on having her say.

"Thomas Beavers has a good job with an insurance company in Jackson," she informed her daughter, as though Frances were incapable of finding out anything for herself. "He makes a good appearance. He is the kind of man"—she paused—"who would value a wife of good family." She stopped, panting for breath. It was this complimenting a man behind his back that was too much for her—as much out of character, and hence as much of a strain, as if she had got out of bed and tried to tap dance.

"Heavens, Mama," Frances said, and almost giggled.

At this, the old lady, thinking the girl had made light of her suitor, half screamed at her, "Don't be so critical, Frances! You can't be so critical of men!" and fell into an even more terrible spasm of coughing. Frances had to lift her from the pillow and hold her straight until the fit passed and her breath returned. Then Mrs. Harvey's old, dry, crooked, ineradicably feminine hand was laid on her daughter's arm, and when she spoke again she shook the arm to emphasize her words.

"When your father knew he didn't have long to live," she

whispered, "we discussed whether to send for you or not. You know you were his favorite, Frances. 'Suppose our girl is happy over there,' he said. 'I wouldn't want to bring her back on my account.' I said you had to have the right to choose whether to come back or not. You'd never forgive us, I said, if you didn't have the right to choose."

Frances could visualize this very conversation taking place between her parents; she could see them, decorous and serious, talking over the fact of his approaching death as though it were a piece of property for agreeable disposition in the family. She could never remember him without thinking, with a smile, how he used to come home on Sunday from church (he being the only one of them who went) and how, immediately after hanging his hat and cane in the hall, he would say, "Let all things proceed in orderly progression to their final confusion. How long before dinner?" No, she had had to come home. Some humor had always existed between them—her father and her—and humor, of all things, cannot be betrayed.

"I meant to go back," said Frances now. "But there was the war. At first I kept waiting for it to be over. I still wake up at night sometimes thinking, I wonder how much longer before the war will be over. And then—" She stopped short. For the fact was that her lover had been married to somebody else, and her mother was the very person capable of pointing that out to her. Even in the old lady's present silence she heard the unspoken thought, and got up nervously from the bed, loosing herself from the hand on her arm, smoothing her reddish hair where it was inclined to straggle. "And then he wrote me that he had gone back to his wife. Her family and his had always been close, and the war brought them back together. This was in Switzerland—naturally, he couldn't stay on in Paris during the war. There were the children, too—all of them were Catholic. Oh, I do understand how it happened."

Mrs. Harvey turned her head impatiently on the pillow. She dabbed at her moist upper lip with a crumpled linen handkerchief; her diamond flashed once in motion. "War, religion, wife, children—yes. But men do what they want to."

Could anyone make Frances as angry as her mother could? "Believe what you like then! You always know so much better than I do. *You* would have managed things somehow. Oh, you would have had your way!"

"Frances," said Mrs. Harvey, "I'm an old woman." The hand holding the handkerchief fell wearily, and her eyelids dropped shut. "If you should want to marry Thomas Beavers and bring him here, I will accept it. There will be no distinctions. Next, I suppose, we will be having his old deaf aunt for tea. I hope she has a hearing aid. I haven't got the strength to holler at her."

"I don't think any of these plans are necessary, Mama."

The eyelids slowly lifted. "None?"

"None."

Mrs. Harvey's breathing was as audible as a voice. She spoke, at last, without scorn, honestly. "I cannot bear the thought of leaving you alone. You, nor the house, nor your place in it—alone. I foresaw Tom Beavers here! What has he got that's better than you and this place? I knew he would come!"

Terrible as her mother's meanness was, it was not half so terrible as her love. Answering nothing, explaining nothing, Frances stood without giving in. She trembled, and tears ran down her cheeks. The two women looked at each other helplessly across the darkening room.

In the car, later that night, Tom Beavers asked, "Is your mother trying to get rid of me?" They had passed an unsatisfactory evening, and he was not going away without knowing why.

"No, it's just the other way around," said Frances, in her candid way. "She wants you so much she'd like to eat you up. She wants you in the house. Couldn't you tell?"

"She once chased me out of the yard," he recalled.

"Not really!"

They turned into Harvey Street (that was actually the name of it), and when he had drawn the car up before the dark front steps, he related the incident. He told her that Mrs. Harvey had been standing just there in the yard, talking to some visitor who was leaving by inches, the way ladies used to—ten minutes' more talk for every forward step. He, a boy not more than nine, had been crossing a corner of the lawn where a faint path had already been worn; he had had nothing to do with wearing the path and had taken it quite innocently and openly. "You, boy!" Mrs. Harvey's fan was an enormous painted thing. She had furled it with a clack so loud he could still hear it. "You don't cut through my yard again! Now, you stop where you are and you go all the way back around by the walk, and don't you ever do that again." He went back and all the way around. She was fanning comfortably as he passed. "Old Miss Rita Beavers's nephew," he heard her say, and though he did not speak of it now to Frances, Mrs. Harvey's rich tone had been as stuffed with wickedness as a fruitcake with goodies. In it you could have found so many things: that, of course, he didn't know any better, that he was poor, that she knew his first name but would not deign to mention it, that she meant him to understand all this and more. Her fan was probably still somewhere in the house, he reflected. If he ever opened the wrong door, it might fall from above and brain him. It seemed impossible that nowadays he could even have the chance to open the wrong door in the Harvey house. With its graceful rooms and big lawn, its camellias and magnolia trees, the house had been one of the enchanted castles of his childhood, and Frances and Regina Harvey had been two princesses running about the lawn one Saturday morning drying their hair with big white towels and not noticing when he passed.

There was a strong wind that evening. On the way home, Frances and Tom had noticed how the night was steaming, but whether with mist or dust or the smoke from some far-off fire in the dry winter woods they could not tell. As they stood on the sidewalk, the clouds raced over them, and moonlight now and again came through. A limb rubbed against a high cornice. Inside the screened area of the porch, the swing jangled in its iron chains. Frances's coat blew about her, and her hair blew. She felt herself to be no different from anything there that the wind was blowing on, her happiness of no relevance in the dark torrent of nature.

"I can't leave her, Tom. But I can't ask you to live with her, either. Of all the horrible ideas! She'd make demands, take all my time, laugh at you behind your back—she has to run everything. You'd hate me in a week."

He did not try to pretty up the picture, because he had a feeling that it was all too accurate. Now, obviously, was the time she should go on to say there was no good his waiting around through the years for her. But hearts are not noted for practicality, and Frances stood with her hair blowing, her hands stuck in her coat pockets, and did not go on to say anything. Tom pulled her close to him—in, as it were, out of the wind.

"I'll be coming by next weekend, just like I've been doing.

And the next one, too," he said. "We'll just leave it that way, if it's O.K. with you."

"Oh yes, it is, Tom!" Never so satisfied to be weak, she kissed him and ran inside.

He stood watching on the walk until her light flashed on. Well, he had got what he was looking for; a connection with the past, he had said. It was right upstairs, a splendid old mass of dictatorial female flesh, thinking about him. Well, they could go on, he and Frances, sitting on either side of a sickbed, drinking tea and sipping sherry with streaks of gray broadening on their brows, while the familiar seasons came and went. So he thought. Like Frances, he believed that the old lady had a stranglehold on life.

Suddenly, in March, Mrs. Harvey died.

A heavy spring funeral, with lots of roses and other scented flowers in the house, is the worst kind of all. There is something so recklessly fecund about a south Mississippi spring that death becomes just another word in the dictionary, along with swarms of others, and even so pure and white a thing as a gardenia has too heavy a scent and may suggest decay. Mrs. Harvey, amid such odors, sank to rest with a determined pomp, surrounded by admiring eyes.

While Tom Beavers did not "sit with the family" at this time, he was often observed with the Harveys, and there was whispered speculation among those who were at the church and the cemetery that the Harvey house might soon come into new hands, "after a decent interval." No one would undertake to judge for a Harvey how long an interval was decent.

Frances suffered from insomnia in the weeks that followed, and at night she wandered about the spring-swollen air of the old house, smelling now spring and now death. "Let all things proceed in orderly progression to their final confusion." She had always thought that the final confusion referred to death, but now she began to think that it could happen any time; that final confusion, having found the door ajar, could come into a house and show no inclination to leave. The worrisome thing, the thing it all came back to, was her mother's clothes. They were numerous, expensive, and famous, and Mrs. Harvey had never discarded any of them. If you opened a closet door, hatboxes as big as crates towered above your head. The shiny black trim of a great shawl stuck out of a wardrobe door just below the lock. Beneath the lid of a cedar chest, the bright eyes of a tippet were ready to twinkle at you. And the jewels! Frances's sister had restrained her from burying them all on their mother, and had even gone off with a wad of them tangled up like fishing tackle in an envelope, on the ground of promises made now and again in the course of the years.

("Regina," said Frances, "what else were you two talking about besides jewelry?" "I don't remember," said Regina, getting mad.

"Frances makes me so mad," said Regina to her husband as they were driving home. "I guess I can love Mama and jewelry, too. Mama certainly loved *us* and jewelry, too.")

One afternoon, Frances went out to the cemetery to take two wreaths sent by somebody who had "just heard." She drove out along the winding cemetery road, stopping the car a good distance before she reached the gate, in order to walk through the woods. The dogwood was beautiful that year. She saw a field where a house used to stand but had burned down; its cedar trees remained, and two bushes of bridal wreath marked where the front gate had swung. She stopped to admire the clusters of white bloom massing up through the young, feathery leaf and stronger now than the leaf itself. In the woods, the redbud was a smoke along shadowy ridges, and the dogwood drifted in layers, like snow suspended to give you all the time you needed to wonder at it. But why, she wondered, do they call it bridal *wreath?* It's not a wreath but a little bouquet. Wreaths are for funerals, anyway. As if to prove it, she looked down at the two she held, one in each hand. She walked on, and such complete desolation came over her that it was more of a wonder than anything in the woods—more, even, than death.

As she returned to the car from the two parallel graves, she met a thin, elderly, very light-skinned Negro man in the road. He inquired if she would mind moving her car so that he could pass. He said that there was a sick colored girl in his wagon, whom he was driving in to the doctor: He pointed out politely that she had left her car right in the middle of the road. "Oh, I'm terribly sorry," said Frances, and hurried off toward the car.

That night, reading late in bed, she thought, I could have given her a ride into town. No wonder they talk about us up

North. A mile into town in a wagon! She might have been having a baby. She became concience-stricken about it—foolishly so, she realized, but if you start worrying about something in a house like the one Frances Harvey lived in, in the dead of night, alone, you will go on worrying about it until dawn. She was out of sleeping pills.

She remembered having bought a fresh box of sedatives for her mother the day before she died. She got up and went into her mother's closed room, where the bed had been dismantled for airing, its wooden parts propped along the walls. On the closet shelf she found the shoe box into which she had packed away the familiar articles of the bedside table. Inside she found the small enameled-cardboard box, with the date and prescription inked on the cover in Totsie Poteet's somewhat prissy handwriting, but the box was empty. She was surprised, for she realized that her mother could have used only one or two of the pills. Frances was so determined to get some sleep that she searched the entire little store of things in the shoe box quite heartlessly, but there were no pills. She returned to her room and tried to read, but could not, and so smoked instead and stared out at the dawn-blackening sky. The house sighed. She could not take her mind off the Negro girl. If she died . . . When it was light, she dressed and got into the car.

In town, the postman was unlocking the post office to sort the early mail. "I declare," he said to the rural mail carrier who arrived a few minutes later, "Miss Frances Harvey is driving herself crazy. Going back out yonder to the cemetery, and it not seven o'clock in the morning."

"Aw," said the rural deliveryman skeptically, looking at the empty road.

"That's right. I was here and seen her. You wait there, you'll see her come back. She'll drive herself nuts. Them old maids like that, left in them old houses—crazy and sweet, or crazy and mean, or just plain crazy. They just ain't locked up like them that's down in the asylum. That's the only difference."

"Miss Frances Harvey ain't no more than thirty-two, -three years old."

"Then she's just got more time to get crazier in. You'll see."

That day was Friday, and Tom Beavers, back from Jackson, came up Frances Harvey's sidewalk, as usual, at exactly a quarter past seven in the evening. Frances was not "going out" yet, and Regina had telephoned her long distance to say that "in all probability" she should not be receiving gentlemen "in." "What would Mama say?" Regina asked. Frances said she didn't know, which was not true, and went right on cooking dinners for Tom every weekend.

In the dining room that night, she sat across one corner of the long table from Tom. The useless length of polished cherry stretched away from them into the shadows as sadly as a road. Her plate pushed back, her chin resting on one palm, Frances stirred her coffee and said, "I don't know what on earth to do with all of Mama's clothes. I can't give them away, I can't sell them, I can't burn them, and the attic is full already. What can I do?"

"You look better tonight," said Tom.

"I slept," said Frances. "I slept and slept. From early this morning until just 'while ago. I never slept so well."

Then she told him about the Negro near the cemetery the previous afternoon, and how she had driven back out there as soon as dawn came, and found him again. He had been walking across the open field near the remains of the house that had burned down. There was no path to him from her, and she had hurried across ground uneven from old plowing and covered with the kind of small, tender grass it takes a very skillful mule to crop. "Wait!" she had cried. "Please wait!" The Negro had stopped and waited for her to reach him. "Your daughter?" she asked, out of breath.

"Daughter?" he repeated.

"The colored girl that was in the wagon yesterday. She was sick, you said, so I wondered. I could have taken her to town in the car, but I just didn't think. I wanted to know, how is she? Is she very sick?"

He had removed his old felt nigger hat as she approached him. "She a whole lot better, Miss Frances. She going to be all right now." Then he smiled at her. He did not say thank you, or anything more. Frances turned and walked back to the road and the car. And exactly as though the recovery of the Negro girl in the wagon had been her own recovery, she felt the return of a quiet breath and a steady pulse, and sensed the blessed stirring of a morning breeze. Up in her room, she had barely time to draw an old quilt over her before she fell asleep.

"When I woke, I knew about Mama," she said now to Tom. By the deepened intensity of her voice and eyes, it was plain that this was the important part. "It isn't right to say I *knew,*" she went on, "because I had known all the time—ever since last night. I just realized it, that's all. I realized she had killed herself. It had to be that."

He listened soberly through the story about the box of sedatives. "But why?" he asked her. "It maybe looks that way, but what would be her reason for doing it?"

"Well, you see—" Frances said, and stopped.

Tom Beavers talked quietly on. "She didn't suffer. With what she had, she could have lived five, ten, who knows how many years. She was well cared for. Not hard up, I wouldn't say. Why?"

The pressure of his questioning could be insistent, and her trust in him, even if he was nobody but old Miss Rita Beavers's nephew, was well-nigh complete. "Because of you and me," she said, finally. "I'm certain of it, Tom. She didn't want to stand in our way. She never knew how to express love, you see." Frances controlled herself with an effort.

He did not reply, but sat industriously balancing a match folder on the tines of an unused serving fork. Anyone who has passed a lonely childhood in the company of an old deaf aunt is not inclined to doubt things hastily, and Tom Beavers would not have said he disbelieved anything Frances had told him. In fact, it seemed only too real to him. Almost before his eyes, that imperial, practical old hand went fumbling for the pills in the dark. But there had been much more to it than just love, he reflected. Bitterness, too, and pride, and control. And humor, perhaps, and the memory of a frightened little boy chased out of the yard by a twitch of her fan. Being invited to tea was one thing; suicide was quite another. Times had certainly changed, he thought.

But, of course, he could not say that he believed it, either. There was only Frances to go by. The match folder came to balance and rested on the tines. He glanced up at her, and a chill walked up his spine, for she was too serene. Cheek on palm, a lock of reddish hair fallen forward, she was staring at nothing with the absorbed silence of a child, or of a sweet, silver-haired old lady engaged in memory. Soon he might find that more and more of her was vanishing beneath this placid surface.

He himself did not know what he had seen that Friday evening so many months ago—what the figure had been that stood forward from the roadside at the tilt of the curve and urgently waved an arm to him. By the time he had braked and backed, the man had disappeared. Maybe it had been somebody drunk (for Richton had plenty of those to offer), walking it off in the cool of the woods at first dark. No such doubts had occurred to Frances. And what if he told her now the story Totsie had related of the road gang and the sick Negro girl in the wagon? Another labyrinth would open before her; she would never get out.

In Richton, the door to the past was always wide open, and what came in through it and went out of it had made people "different." But it scarcely ever happens, even in Richton, that one is able to see the precise moment when fact becomes faith, when life turns into legend, and people start to bend their finest loyalties to make themselves bemused custodians of the grave. Tom Beavers saw that moment now, in the profile of this dreaming girl, and he knew there was no time to lose.

He dropped the match folder into his coat pocket. "I think we should be leaving, Frances."

"Oh well, I don't know about going out yet," she said. "People criticize you so. Regina even had the nerve to telephone. Word had got all the way to her that you came here to have supper with me and we were alone in the house. When I tell the maid I want biscuits made up for two people, she looks like 'What would yo' mama say?' "

"I mean," he said, "I think it's time we left for good."

"And never came back?" It was exactly like Frances to balk at going to a movie but seriously consider an elopement.

"Well, never is a long time. I like to see about Aunt Rita every once in a great while. She can't remember from one time to the next whether it's two days or two years since I last came."

She glanced about the walls and at the furniture, the pictures, and the silver. "But I thought you would want to live here, Tom. It never occurred to me. I know it never occurred to Mama . . . This house . . . It can't be just left."

"It's a fine old house," he agreed. "But what would you do with all your mother's clothes?"

Her freckled hand remained beside the porcelain cup for what seemed a long time. He waited and made no move toward her; he felt her uncertainty keenly, but he believed that some people should not be startled out of a spell.

"It's just as you said," he went on, finally. "You can't give them away, you can't sell them, you can't burn them, and you can't put them in the attic, because the attic is full already. So what are you going to do?"

Between them, the single candle flame achieved a silent altitude. Then, politely, as on any other night, though shaking back her hair in a decided way, she said, "Just let me get my coat, Tom."

She locked the door when they left, and put the key under the mat—a last obsequy to the house. Their hearts were bounding ahead faster than they could walk down the sidewalk or drive off in the car, and, mindful, perhaps, of what happened to people who did, they did not look back.

Had they done so, they would have seen that the Harvey house was more beautiful than ever. All unconscious of its rejection by so mere a person as Tom Beavers, it seemed, instead, to have got rid of what did not suit it, to be free, at last, to enter with abandon the land of mourning and shadows and memory.

Born in Mississippi in 1921, Elizabeth Spencer won recognition for her first novel, The Voice at the Back Door *(1965), praised for its Southern atmosphere and its realistic depiction of race relations. After marrying a British businessman, she spent many years in Italy (setting of* The Light in the Piazza, *1960, filmed with Olivia de Havilland) and Canada. She has won several distinguished awards, including the Award of Merit from the Academy and Institute of Arts and Letters and grants from the Guggenheim Fellowship and the National Endowment for the Arts. "First Dark" was first published in the June 20, 1959, issue of* The New Yorker.

To some, it's a tree. But to Florella Dabney, it's a husband. . . .

FOUR

The Tree's Wife

Mary Elizabeth Counselman

I smiled at my companion, Hettie Morrison, county welfare investigator for the Bald Mountain district. When I dropped into her office that morning, mostly to dig up nostalgic old memories of our college days at the University of Virginia, I found her arguing over the telephone with a local mechanic. *"But I have to make a field trip this morning! . . . WHY can't you get the parts? Take them out of somebody else's car! . . . Oh, the devil with what you think wouldn't be right! This family may be starving. . . .!"*

Hettie had hung up, still sputtering, a gaunt severe-looking old maid with a heart as big as the Blue Ridge Mountains. She glanced up then to see me grinning at her, jingling the car keys of my new club coupe by way of an invitation. We were such close friends, no words were needed—Hettie merely jerked a nod, slammed on her hat, and started out the door with me in tow.

"You'll be sorry," she warned me. "The road I have to take is an old Indian trail—and if they had to get back and forth on *that,* no wonder they're called the Vanishing Americans! You'll break a spring."

I looked so dismayed, pausing to unlock my first new car in ten years, that she closed one eye in a crafty look I knew so well from days at college when she was about to ask the loan of my best hose.

"It's a dull trip, just routine field work. Of course you wouldn't be interested," she drawled casually, "in Florella Dabney—the girl who married a tree. We pass right by the Dabney place. No, no, dear; you're liable to scratch up that nice blue paint. And Holy Creek crosses the road four times; we'd have to drive through it, hub-deep. I always get stuck and have to—"

I scowled at my old friend, familiar with all her clever tricks of getting her way, but still unable to cope with them.

"*Tree?*" I demanded. "Did you say—? Married a—?"

"That's right," Hettie nodded with a smug grin. "It's a strange case—almost a legend up around Bald Mountain. Although," she added, blatantly climbing into my car, "it's not without precedent, in the old Greek legends. Zeus was forever turning some girl into a spring or a flower, or some inanimate object, so his wife, Hera, wouldn't find out about his goings-on. Even as late as the fifteenth century, there were proxy weddings, where some queen or other married her knight's sword because he was off at war. Then, there's an African tribe in which the men are married, at puberty, to some tree."

I grimaced impatiently, climbed into the coupe, and started it with a jerk. Hettie had aroused my interest, and well she knew it. She would get her ride over the wild, bushy crest of Bald Mountain—or I would never find out about that girl who married a tree.

An hour later, bouncing over a rocky trail pressed closely on both sides by scrub pine and mountain laurel, she began to tell me about Florella Dabney—and the bloody feud that, a trained psychiatrist might explain, had left her a mental case with a strange delusion.

The Dabneys (Hettie related) had built their cabin and begun to wrest a living out of the side of Bald Mountain about the time of Daniel Boone. Six generations of underfed, overworked mountaineers had lived therein, planting a little, hunting a little, and raising a batch of children as wild as the foxes that made inroads on their chicken supply. Florella was the youngest daughter, a shy, willowy child of fifteen, with flowing dark hair and big, luminous dark eyes like a fawn. Barefoot, clad in the simple gingham shift that all mountain girls wore, she could be seen running down the steep side of Old Baldy, as nimbly as a city child might run along a sidewalk. Her older brothers and sisters married and moved away, her mother died, and Florella lived with her father now on the sparse farm.

On the other side of the mountain lived another such family of "old settlers," the Jenningses. As far back as anyone could remember, there had been bad blood between the two, starting with a free-for-all over a load of cordwood, which had sent two Dabneys to the hospital and three Jenningses to jail. Both attended the little mountain church perched on the ridge that divided their farms, but no Jennings ever spoke to a Dabney, even at all-day singings, when everyone was pleasantly full of food and "home-brew." No Dabney would sit left of the aisle; and any baptizing that was done in Holy Creek, after a rousing revival meeting, had to be arranged with Jenningses and Dabneys immersed on alternate days. Reverend Posy Adkins, the lay preacher, recognized this as a regrettable but inevitable condition. And that was the law on Bald Mountain—up until the spring evening when Joe Ed Jennings and Florella Dabney "run off together."

When and how they had ever seen enough of each other to fall in love, neither family could imagine. Joe Ed was a stocky blond boy who could play a guitar and shoot the eye out of a 'possum at fifty yards—but not much else. What astonished everyone was Florella's regard for such a do-little, since she was halfway promised to a boy from Owl's Hollow. It was assumed, when a party of hunters saw them streaking through the woods one night, that Florella had been carried off by force, much against her will. She had gone out after one of the hogs, which had strayed. At midnight, when she had not returned, her pa, Lafe Dabney, went out to search for her, ran into the hunting party—and promptly stalked back to his cabin for his rifle.

He was starting out again, with murder in his close-set, mean little eyes, when a pair of frightened young people suddenly walked through the sagging front gate. With them was Preacher Adkins, dressed either for a buryin' or a marryin', with the Good Book clutched in a hand that trembled. But he spoke steadily.

"Lafe, these two young'nes has sinned. But the Lord's likely done forgave 'em already. Now they aim to marry, so don't try an' stop it!"

Without preamble, he motioned for Florella and Joe Ed to stand under a big white oak that grew in the front yard, towering over the rough cabin and silhouetted darkly against the moonlit sky. High up on the trunk, if Lafe had noticed, was cut a heart with the initials J. E. J. and F. D.

Solemnly, the old preacher began to intone the marriage ceremony, while Florella's pa stood there staring at them, his lean face growing darker with fury, his tight mouth working. Hardly had the immortal words, *"Do you take this man—?"*

been spoken, when he whipped the rifle to his shoulder and fired at Joe Ed, pointblank. The boy was dead as he crumpled up at his bride's small bare feet.

"I'll larn you to go sparkin' our girl behind my back!" Lafe roared. "You triflin' no-account!"

He never finished, for a second shot rang out in the quiet night. Lafe Dabney pitched forward on his face, crawled across the body of his prospective son-in-law, and fired twice toward the powder flash in the woods beyond the cabin. A moment later, all hell broke loose. It seems that Reverend Adkins had expected just such a blow-up. Someone had carried the news to Joe Ed's pa. Clem Jennings had also hastened to the spot, to stop the wedding. The old preacher, fearing this, had notified "the law." The sheriff, with a hastily gathered posse, had showed up at the moment when Lafe and Clem fired at each other, over the body of young Joe Ed and the prostrate, sobbing form of his near-bride.

In a matter of minutes, the posse had both fathers handcuffed and hauled off to jail. But, behind them, they left a tragic tableau—little Florella weeping over the body of her lost lover, with old Reverend Adkins standing dumbly in the background. Two of the posse had stayed behind to help with Joe Ed's body, which the weeping girl had begged the preacher to bury, then and there, "under our tree." It was there Joe Ed had first caught her and kissed her, holding his hand over her mouth and laughing, with Lafe not ten yards away. It was there, in the night, that she had first told him she loved him—and promised to slip away with him, into the deep, silent woods of Old Baldy, for a lover's tryst forbidden by both their families. It was there, months later, terrified and ashamed, that she had sobbed out to him that she was with child. She knew there was nothing left but to kill herself. Her lover was a Jennings, and she had expected no more from him than a few moments of wild secret ecstasy.

But Joe Ed had surprised her. Fiercely protective and loyal, he had announced that, the following night, he would stand with her under the tree in the Dabneys' yard, and have Preacher Adkins marry them—right in front of old Lafe. His child must bear his name, the boy said proudly and tenderly, and he hoped it would be a fawn-eyed little girl exactly like Florella.

All this old Preacher Adkins related to the two members of

the posse, while they took turns digging a grave for Joe Ed Jennings—at the foot of the big white oak under which he was to have been married. Florella stood numbly by, watching and no longer crying, like a trapped animal at last resigned to its bitter fate.

But, regarding her, the old lay preacher suddenly remembered a story from his school days, a myth, a legend. Walking over to the girl, he took her hand quietly and led her over to the tree, where the two pitying neighbors were just patting the last spadeful of dirt over Joe Ed's crude grave.

"Daughter," the old preacher said, "I've heard tell of queens in the old days marryin' a sword that belonged to some feller that'd been killt in battle. Now, Joe Ed, he'd want you should go ahead and take his name—so I'm goin' t' make out like this-here tree is Joe Ed, him bein' buried underneath it. I want you two men," he faced the gravediggers solemnly, "to witness this-here marryin'—of Joe Ed Jennings and Florella Dabney." He raised his eyes humbly. "If hit's a wrong thing I'm doin', punish me, Lord. If hit's right, bless this-here ceremony!"

There in the moonlit night, the old preacher proceeded with that strange proxy wedding of a girl to a tree. The two members of the posse stood by, wide-eyed and amazed, as they heard Reverend Adkins repeat the familiar words of the marriage ceremony, and heard Florella's sobbing replies. And then heard—was it only wind in the great tree towering above them? Or was it—? Both men later swore that what they heard sounded like a whispering voice. A man's voice, Joe Ed's, coming from the depths of those thick green branches. But (as Hettie remarked drily) it had been a hysterical night, and hysteria can play weird tricks on the human senses numerous times.

"Well? That isn't *all?*" I demanded, as my car lurched madly into Holy Creek's third crossing and plunged wetly out again. "What happened to the girl? With her father in prison, who looked after her while—? Was the child all right?"

"Slow down, you idiot!" Hettie snapped at me pleasantly, clinging to the car door on her side. "Yes, of course, the child was all right. A little girl. I had welfare send a doctor out there, when we got the message that Florella was in labor. She had been living on in her father's cabin, quite alone—for the simple reason that all her relatives and all of Joe Ed's were afraid to come near the place!"

I frowned, puzzled. "Why?"

"Because of the tree," Hettie said blandly. "Word got around that it was haunted. That Joe Ed had 'gone into that oak' and—well, that it was alive. Sentient, that is. That it—didn't behave like a tree any more. I must say—*look out for that rock, you goose! Want to wreck this thing?*—I must say some of the things that happened were—odd, to say the least!"

I slowed down obediently, picking my way over the rocky road. Anything to keep Hettie on the story that had so captured my imagination!

"What things?" I demanded. "Anybody can hear voices in the wind. Leaves rustling. Branches rubbing together."

"But," Hettie drawled, "just anybody can't see a tree catch a live rabbit, or a dove that has lit on a branch of it. Just anybody can't—"

"What?" I gaped at her. "I never heard of anything so ridiculous!" My attempted laugh sounded flat, however, even to my own ears. "How on earth could—?"

"Don't ask me," Hettie said cheerfully. "All I know is, the lower branch of that big white oak kept Florella supplied with meat. Rabbits, doves, once a possum. They—they got choked, someway. Got their necks caught in the twigs. She'd find them there, all ready to be cooked and eaten. The way any good mountaineer might trap to feed his family. So she got to believing—that *he* caught them. Joe Ed had quite a reputation as a hunter and trapper."

"Good Lord!" I tried to laugh again. "You're not hinting—? The poor kid," I broke off pityingly. "But an experience like that would naturally affect her mind. Living there all alone, too, with a baby!"

"Then," Hettie went on pleasantly, "there was the fall day, real cold, when a neighbor woman dropped in. Nosey old sister. Just wanted to say something spiteful to Florella about the baby. When she was leaving, though—well," Hettie chuckled, "it seems her coat got tangled in a tree branch that dipped down over the gate. It yanked the coat right off her back, the way she told it. She lit out of there, screaming bloody murder, and told everybody that Joe Ed took her coat for Florella! When the girl tried to return it to her, she wouldn't touch it. Said it wasn't her best coat, anyhow, and she wasn't going to argue with a tree!"

"Oh no!" I shook my head, laughing—but still trying to ignore a small shiver that kept running down my spine. "These mountain people are awfully superstitious, aren't they? Naturally, it was just the woman's fear that made her think—"

"Maybe," Hettie said drily, "but it wasn't fear that snatched my new hat off last spring, when I happened to walk under that tree. Checking up on Florella—she's a hardship case, of course. Yessir," she said in a queer tone. "Big limb swooped down and snatched that bonnet right off my head. I couldn't reach it, and Florella couldn't climb up and get it. Too soon after the baby's arrival; poor girl was still kind of weak. But the way she giggled, and started talking to that tree like it was a person! Honestly, it made my flesh crawl, she was so matter-of-fact about it! 'Joe Ed, you rascal,' she said, 'give Miss Hettie back her bonnet, now! I don't need no fancy clothes. Me and the baby's doin' just fine.' " Hettie peered at me, sheepishly. "Way she said it made me feel like—like a selfish old turkey gobbler! Besides, a hat like that was too pretty for an old hatchet-face like me. But it did give me a turn, I'll have to admit! When—" she gulped slightly, "when I told Florella she could have the hat, it—it immediately fell out of the tree. Plop! Right smack on that girl's head! I must say," she added crossly, "it was very becoming. Probably the first one she ever owned, poor little thing! Lafe was a stingy old coot; Florella's mother never had a rag she didn't weave herself!"

I turned the steering wheel sharply to avoid a raccoon ambling across the trail. Then I peered at Hettie.

"Go on," I said grimly. "Tell me how the tree shed its wood in stacks, so Florella wouldn't have to chop any!"

Hettie chuckled. "Oh, no. Mountain men take it for granted that their wives must work like mules. All they do is feed 'em, shelter 'em and protect 'em—with an occasional pretty thrown in when they feel in a generous mood. That's what Florella expected from her tree-husband, and that's what she got. Though I suppose a psychologist would say her delusion gave her a sense of security that merely made her able to fend for herself. Lots of people need a crutch for their self-confidence—if it's only a lucky coin they carry around. Coincidence and superstition, hm?

"Well," my friend smiled, "I *am* obliged to you for the lift. We had a message that Kirby Marsh, a farmer who lives near the Dabney place, got in a fight with somebody and crawled home, pretty banged up. His wife is bedridden, so they'll need help if he's seriously injured. You were a lifesaver to bring me. *This is the turn";* she broke off abruptly, grinning at me with a sly twinkle in her eye. "The Dabney farm is just around this bend."

I slowed down, feeling again that cold shiver run down my spine as we rounded the curve. An old cabin of square-hewn logs perched on the mountainside a few yards above the road, with the usual well in the yard and the usual small truck garden in back. A huge white oak towered over the gate of a sagging rail fence. Its sturdy trunk leaned a bit toward the house in a curiously protective manner, shading the worn front stoop with its thick, dark green foliage.

I braked the car outside the gate, and Hettie grinned at my expression.

"There it is," she announced drily. "There's where the girl lives who married a tree. And that's the tree. That's *him.*"

I got out of the coupe and walked warily up to the gate. Hettie climbed out stiffly, and called, in her pleasantly harsh voice:

"Hello? Hello the house?" in traditional mountain style.

There was no answer, but all at once I saw a quilt palet spread under the oak Hettie had indicated as "*him.*" A fair-haired baby girl was sprawled on the folded quilt, gurgling and cooing. She looked to be about two years old, with the sturdy good health of most mountain children, despite their skimpy diet and constant exposure to the elements.

I stood watching her for a moment, charmed by the picture she made. Then I frowned.

"She's too young to be left alone," I muttered. "Where's her mother?"

"Oh, out picking blackberries, I guess." Hettie shrugged. "Josie's all right, though. Her father's minding her," she added, with another impish grin at my expression. "Hello!" she called again. "Florella!"

At that moment a lovely slender girl came running around the house, her feet bare, her dark hair flying. There was a sprig of laurel over her ear, and blackberry stains on her brown fingers. I stared at her, thinking how like a dryad she looked—wild, free, and happily unafraid.

"Oh! Howdy, Miss Hettie!" she greeted my friend warmly. "Come in and set. Who's that with ye? Kinfolk?"

Hettie introduced me as a school chum, with no mention of the fact that I wrote stories of the supernatural for my bread and butter. We entered the gate, and Hettie stooped over to pat the baby, proffering a peppermint from the endless supply she always seems to carry around. I fidgeted beside her, at a loss for conversation with this pretty, normal-looking young mother who, from all Hettie had told me, was as crazy as a coot. Once, nervously, I started as a limb of the great tree under which we stood brushed my shoulder, plucking at my scarf. On impulse, I took it off and gave it to the girl, who beamed and thanked me shyly, then tied it proudly around her own neck. I caught Hettie's eye at that moment—and flushed as she grinned, winked, and glanced up at the giant tree.

Then she turned to Florella, lovelier than ever in my blue chiffon scarf—and with no more madness in her face than in mine.

"I got word that Kirby Marsh was hurt in a fight," my friend said conversationally. "Anybody over there looking after his wife and kids? Heard the doctor came, and took Kirby to the hospital with a concussion and a sprained shoulder. Must have been some fight, to have—"

Hettie broke off, noticing the girl's sudden expression of regret beyond the politeness expected of a neighbor. Florella ducked her head suddenly, with a rueful little smile.

"Yes, ma'am," she said simply. "He come over here to our place late last night, and went to pesterin' me. Oh, not that Kirby ain't a real nice feller," she apologized for her neighbor gently, "exceptin' when he's likkered up. I told him to leave go o' me," she added with wifely dignity. "Told him Joe Ed wouldn't like it. But he wouldn't listen. So I run out to Joe Ed, with it a-stormin' awful. He'd been a-bangin' on the roof, to warn Kirby, but he likely thought 'twas only the wind."

I gulped, wracked with pity, and threw a glance at my friend.

"Then—?" Hettie prompted softly, in an odd tone. "You ran out into the yard? Kirby ran after you, and—?"

"And Joe Ed, he whanged him over the head," the girl finished, half-apologetic, half-proud, as any other woman might speak of a husband who had stoutly defended her honor. "He like to busted Kirby's skull wide open. But he hadn't ought to've tried to kiss me," she defended primly. "Ought he, Miss Hettie? And me a married woman with a young'ne!"

"No, dear," Hettie answered, in the gentlest voice I have ever heard her use. "No—Joe Ed did the right thing. I don't think Kirby was badly injured, but somebody has to look after his folks while he's in the hospital. Did you go over and see his wife today?"

"Yes ma'am," the girl said quietly. "But they wouldn't let me in. I reckon, on account they was scared. I mean, of Joe Ed. But he wouldn't hurt nobody less'n they was botherin' me or the baby! He's real good-hearted."

"Yes," my friend said softly. "I understand. Well—don't worry about it, dear. Next time Kirby will know better! I rather imagine," she chuckled, "that this experience will keep him sober for some time!"

The girl nodded shyly and bent to pick up the child. But small Josie toddled away from her and ran around the great tree to where a low limb dipped almost to the ground.

"Pa!" she chirped suddenly, holding up her chubby arms to the giant oak. "Fing baby! Fing *high,* Pa!"

Florella laughed, shaking her head mildly and calling: "No! *No,* now, Joe Ed—you're liable to drop that young'un! Don't ye—"

But as I stared, that low limb dipped down as under unseen pressure. The child, Josie, seized it and, as I gasped at the spectacle, was tossed ten feet off the ground; as if a gust of wind had blown the branch skyward, it had scooped up the baby, swinging her high above us. Then, as gently, it set her down again, while the young mother shook her head again in laughing reproof. My scalp crawled at her matter-of-fact, unselfconscious manner.

"Joe Ed's always a-doin' that," she said pleasantly. "She loves it. Why, Miss Hettie!" she broke off, pouting as I sidled pointedly back toward the gate, "I thought you-all would stay for dinner! Joe Ed caught me a rabbit, and I was just fixin' to fry it real nice and brown. Cain't ye stay?"

But I was out the gate and climbing into my car by that time, shaking my head covertly and beckoning for Hettie to come away. For some reason—which I will always firmly deny—my teeth were clicking like castanets. And I kept glancing up nervously at that tall spreading oak tree, brooding over the little mountain cabin, and the woman and child who lived there alone.

Alone—?

"Pitiful case, isn't it?" Hettie murmured cheerfully, as she climbed into the car and waved goodbye to Florella Dabney—or "Mrs. Joseph Edward Jennings," as she was listed in the welfare files. "I mean," my friend expanded, "the way that poor girl lives, with her baby. From hand to mouth, and the prey of—well, men like Kirby. She'd be so lonely and frightened if it weren't for that pathetic delusion of hers. And she's got that child to believing it now! Guess you noticed her swinging on that tree—she called it *'Pa'!* Stout branch, to pick up a child that heavy, wasn't it?" she drawled carelessly. "Wind blew it, I guess—like the other night, when it whacked Kirby Marsh over the head. Awful windy up here on Old Baldy." She peeked at me slyly, lips twitching.

I glared at her and stepped on the gas, aware of the cold perspiration that had sprung out on my forehead. Because it was not windy. It was close and very still—and beside me, Hettie was chuckling softly as I glanced back at the barren little farm. Except for one low limb of that giant oak tree—again tossing that happy child playfully into the air while its mother looked on; lifting it gently, like a man's strong protective arms—not a leaf was stirring as far as we could see over the rugged mountainside.

Mary Elizabeth Counselman (now Vineyard) was raised on a plantation, a heritage often reflected in her stories. Her ghosts, she says, "are allies and not enemies of humankind," but they "are ruthless to the predatory." Born in Alabama in 1911, much of her best work is based on personal experiences and legends of haunted houses in the Old South, and are collected in Half in Shadow *(1978). "The Tree's Wife" was first published in the March 1950 issue of* Weird Tales, *and despite the fictitious place names used in the story, the author claims that the locales described do indeed exist in Alabama.*

Night beasts and headless figures were the least of Amos Malone's troubles. . . .

FIVE

The Chrome Comanche

Alan Dean Foster

Esau was checking the wagon's rear axle when the dog started barking. It was the middle of the day, and it made no sense. The dog ought to be asleep somewhere back of the barn, not out front barking in the sun. In any event, it stopped soon enough. The dog was as exhausted as the rest of them.

At first he didn't even bother to look up, so absorbed was he in his study of the wagon. It had to be loaded and ready to go by this evening, so they wouldn't have to spend another night in the cabin. It wasn't much of a house, but it was a home, a beginning. Rock and sod, mostly, braced with rough-cut cedar and mesquite. What milled lumber he'd been able to afford had gone into the barn. It wasn't finished, and the chicken house wasn't finished.

The only thing that was finished here on the south bank of the Red River was them, he thought.

He didn't raise his gaze until the dog came over and begin licking him.

"What the blazes ails you, hound?"

"He's scared, I think," said a deep voice. "I hope not of me."

Esau hesitated, then realized that the wagon offered little protection. Might as well crawl out and confront the speaker, whoever he might be. Were they now to have as little peace during the day as they'd found here at night?

No spirit gazed back at him, though the animal the speaker rode was unusual enough. Esau knew horses, but this particular mount appeared more jumbled than mixed. The rider was nearly as unclassifiable, though from what could be seen behind the flowing black beard, Esau was pretty sure he was white. Esau had to squint to make out individual features. The more he squinted, the more indefinable the details of that face seemed to become. Though it was as full of lines as a sloping field after a storm, it didn't hint of great age.

The man himself was immense. The pupils of his eyes were of a blackness extreme enough to spill over and stain the whites. He wore fringed boots and buckskin, his attire not so much dirty as eroded. Like the face, Esau thought. Had man put those lines there, or nature? Bandoliers of huge cartridges crisscrossed his chest, fuel for the Sharps buffalo rifle slung next to the saddle. The octagonal barrel was only slightly smaller than a telegraph pole.

"You're a long ways from the mountains, friend." Esau shielded his eyes as he spoke, while the dog began to sniff around the horse's hooves. The confused-breed piebald ignored the attention. "No beaver to trap around here. Not in north Texas."

"You'd be surprised what there is to trap in Texas." The mountain man considered the little cabin. "But you're right enough. I'm jest passin' through, out o' New Orleans on my way to Colorado." He nodded in the direction of the chimney. "Saw your smoke."

A vast growl arose from the vicinity of the giant's stomach, bellythunder heralding the approach of an expansive hunger. Esau smiled slightly, relaxing.

"You're welcome here, stranger. Come in and set a spell. Be right to have company for our last meal here."

Though the giant slipped off his mount, he seemed to lose nothing in stature as he stood on his own two feet. "I thank you for your hospitality. Your last meal, you say?"

Esau nodded gravely, indicated the wagon. "Just checking out the frame and the springs before loading her up. Never thought I'd have to do that again. We'd planned to live out our days here. This is a good place, mister. River's always running, and the grass is high. Best cattle country I ever saw." He shrugged fatalistically.

The mountain man addressed the uncomfortable silence. "Name's Malone. Amos Malone."

"Esau Weaver." The rancher's hand vanished inside the giant's gnarled grasp. "Sarah's inside fixin' dinner. You're welcome to stay for supper, too, if it suits you. We'll be out soon after. Have to be."

"It ain't in me to linger long in any one place, but I appreciate your offer, Weaver."

Esau led the visitor toward the home he was preparing to flee, unable to keep from glancing at his companion. "Didn't think there were any of you boys left. Thought the beaver had all been trapped out, and the market for 'em faded anyways."

"There's still places in the backcountry where a feller can make a livin' if he works hard and has half a mind for figures. Only real trouble's that the country's gettin' too citified. Even Colorado's fillin' up with folks tired of city life." He chuckled, an extraordinary sound. "So naturally, soon as they arrive, they all light out for Denver. Folks sure are a puzzlement sometimes."

"Wish all I had to deal with were country neighbors." Esau opened the door and called to alert his wife. Malone had to duck double to clear the low doorway.

Behind them the dog concluded its inspection and disdainfully peed on the horse's rear right leg, whereupon the mountain man's mount did a most unequine thing. It raised its leg and liked to drown that poor unsuspecting hound, sending it shaking and yapping around the back of the cabin. The horse, whose name was Useless, let out a soft snort of satisfaction and went hunting for fodder. Malone had not tied him. Would've been useless to try.

Sarah Weaver showed the lack of sleep the family had endured recently. She wore her hair pulled straight back and secured in a small bun, a simple long-sleeved dress, and an apron decorated with fine tatting. She hardly glanced at her husband and his guest. Her son, Jeremiah, was far less inhibited. He stared unbashedly at Malone, firing questions that the mountain man answered readily until the boy's mother warned him to mind his manners.

"Heck, ma'am, he don't bother me none," said Malone with a smile so ready and wide that the tense woman relaxed. "It's good to be around young'uns. Reminds a man what the future's for."

"I then take it that you're not married, sir?" She dipped stew from the black cast-iron kettle that hung in the fireplace. Once things got settled, Esau had promised her a real stove, but now. . . .

"Name's Malone, ma'am. As for lockin' up, I've had the urge

once or twice, but as I ain't the type to settle down, it wouldn't be fair to the woman."

"I hope you like this stew." She set the bowl in front of the visitor. "It's all we have. What's left of all I could salvage from my garden before *they* destroyed it."

Malone inhaled pointedly. "Ambrosia and nectar, ma'am. Though if you cleaned out your barn an' boiled the results, it'd be bound to be better than my own cookin'."

She smiled thinly and sat down opposite her husband. Jeremiah took the high seat opposite Malone.

An unnatural silence settled over the table. Any slight creak or groan caused both rancher and wife to look tensely at walls or windows before resuming their meal. There eventually came time when Malone could stand it no longer.

"Now, you folks tell me to shut my food hole if you want to, but I'm afflicted with a confusion I got to vent. Friend Esau, you told me what a fine place you had here, and havin' seen some of it, I don't find any reason to dispute. So maybe you'll sympathize with an ignorant bumpkin who sits here delightin' in your wife's fine cooking while wonderin' why you're in such an all-fired rush to leave?"

Esau Weaver glanced at his wife, who said nothing. He started to resume eating, then paused as though considering whether to speak. Clearly it burned within him to share this matter with someone else.

"Spirits, Mr. Malone." The rancher broke a chunk of bread from the round loaf in the middle of the table. "Ghosts. Devils. Indian devils."

"They come upon us in the middle of the night, Mr. Malone." Sarah Weaver had her hands on the table, the fingers twisting and twining. "Horrible sounds they make. They terrify Jeremiah. They terrify me."

"Got no heads." Weaver was chewing his bread unenthusiastically, but he needed something to do with his mouth and hands. "Thought it was just raiders at first, till I got a look at 'em during a full moon. No heads at all. That don't keep 'em from howling and yelling and tearing up the place. They want us off this land, and by God, they're going to have their way. I can't take any more of this, and neither can the woman." Love filled his eyes as he gazed across the table at his wife, love and despair. "White men or Indians I'd fight, but not things without heads."

"Esau went into town and spoke with one of the pacified Comanche medicine men," Sarah Weaver murmured. "He told Esau that this part of the country along the river was sacred to the tribe. But he couldn't say how much. He did say there could be spirits here."

"There are spirits all over this country," Malone said. "Some places don't matter so much to 'em. Others do." He sat back in his chair, and it creaked alarmingly. "But you were told straight, I think. This lands reeks of medicine, old medicine. But not," he added, his face twisting in puzzlement, "this place right here."

"You know about such things, do you, Mr. Malone?" Esau's tone was sardonic.

"A mite. I sensed the medicine when I was ridin' in. But not where we're sittin'. If there's spirits about, I wouldn't see them choosin' this place for a frolic. Upstream or down, maybe, but not right here. Besides which, it ain't like spirits to drive off cattle and tear up vegetables. If they're real and they wanted you off, they'd be a sight more direct in their intentions."

"They're real enough, Mr. Malone," said Sarah Weaver. "If you don't believe us, stay and see for yourself, if you dare."

"Well, now, ma'am, I jest might do that. Been awhile since I seen a gen-u-wine spirit. Oh, and that Comanche medicine man you talked to? He might've been right or he might've been wrong, but one thing's sure: he weren't pacified. You don't pacify the Comanche. They jest got plumb tuckered-out." He glanced at his host.

"Now, you say these here no-heads keep y'all awake a-yellin' and a-hollerin'. Do they sound somethin' like this?" Somewhere behind that wolf thicket of a beard, lips parted as Malone began to chant.

Jeremiah's jaw dropped as he stared in awe, while his parents sat stockstill, listening. Night not due for hours seemed to encroach on the little cabin, and a breeze probed curiously where moments earlier the air had been still as a bad man's eulogy.

"That about right?" Malone inquired.

Esau shook himself back to alertness. "Something like that, but deeper, long syllables."

Malone tried again. "Closer?"

Sarah Weaver found herself nodding unwillingly. "That's it, Mr. Malone. That's it exactly."

"Interestin'. First chant was Comanche. Second was Shoshone. Now, the Comanche and the Shoshones are related, but there ain't no love lost between the tribes, and there ain't no Shoshone in these parts. Too far east, too far south. Makes no sense."

"Neither do headless devils, Mr. Malone."

The mountain man nodded somberly at the rancher's wife. "That's a truth fine as frog hair, ma'am. The devils I know always keep their heads about them, if not their wits. A head's something man or spirit tends to get used to, and downright lonely without.

"You said they're about to run you off this land, but all they've done is make your lives more miserable than north Texas weather?"

"Maybe you're not afraid of devils, Mr. Malone, but I have a family to protect. I'll take no chances with something I do not understand."

"I comprehend your position, Esau. You're a good man in a bad spot. Now, a fool like myself loves to take chances with what he don't understand. Mrs. Weaver, I will take you up on your offer to stay and see for myself. But I don't fancy doin' so all by my lonesome. You've stuck it out this long. Could you see your way clear to stickin' around one more night? If my suspicions are wrong, I'll be the first to up an' confess my sins."

"Another night?" Sarah Weaver's exhaustion showed in her tone and expression. "I don't know. What would be the good in it?"

"Might not be any good in it, ma'am." Malone didn't mince words with her. "Might be only understanding, and that ain't always to the good. But I've got a hunch it ain't your place the spirits hereabouts are concerned with."

Esau Weaver leaned forward. "Then you believe there are spirits here?"

"Didn't I say that? This is old Comanche land. Lot of coups counted here, lot of warriors' bones interred along this river. What I said was, I don't see why they'd bear you folks any malice. You ain't even turnin' the soil."

"Why should you want to help us? You said you were just passing through."

"That's my life, Esau. Passin' through. The time to stop's when good people like yourselves are havin' trouble. It's what we do in the passin' that's remembered." He beamed at Sarah Weaver, and despite her exhaustion, she surprised herself by blushing. "Notwithstandin' that I owe you for the best meal I've had since leavin' New Orleans."

Weaver was wrestling with himself. His mind had been made up for days. He would not go so far as to allow himself to hope, but this towering stranger was so damned sure of things.

He glanced one last time at his wife, who acquiesced with her eyes. Then he turned back to Malone. "You mind sleepin' in the barn with the horses?"

"Not if the horses don't object. Uh, you got any mares in heat?"

Weaver made a face. "No. Why would you ask that?"

"Don't want to cause a ruckus." He jerked a thumb in the direction of the door. "Useless may not look like much, but he's able to do more than trot when his back's up."

"I'll find you some blankets, Mr. Malone." Sarah Weaver started to rise from the table.

"Now, never you mind me, missus. I've got my own blanket. Buffalo robe's good enough for me. Warmer than homespun, and strong enough to keep the mosquitoes away."

"Thick pile, is it?" Weaver inquired.

"Not especial. But it ain't been washed in a bit, and the smell's strong enough to mask my own."

Jeremiah gazed wide-eyed at the mountain man. "What if the headless spirits come for you, Mr. Malone? What if they come for you in the barn when you're asleep and all alone?"

That huge wrinkled face bent close. The boy could smell the plains and the mountains, the sea and suggestions of far-off places. For just an instant, those black eyes seemed to shine with a light of their own, and Jeremiah Weaver was sure he could see unnameable things reflected within them.

"Why, then, son, we'll have ourselves a set-to and gamble for souls or answers."

Malone guessed it was around two in the morning when Useless's cold, wet tongue slapped against his face. Grunting, the mountain man swatted at the persistent protuberance as he sat up in the darkness, hunting for his boots.

"Godforsaken miserable son-of-spavined mule, can't let a

man get a decent sleep." Useless snorted, turned toward his waiting saddle and blanket.

"No, you stay here." Malone hop-danced into one boot, then its mate. "Bright night like this, you'd stick out like Tom Sawyer's fence. I won't be too long. Meanwhile, you leave those two mares alone. They ain't interested in you, nohow."

As Malone traipsed out of the barn in the direction of the faint sounds, his mount stuck out his tongue at him. Then Useless turned to begin chewing at the rope that secured the paddock gate.

There was ample moon, though Malone didn't need it. He could track them by their movements. They were chanting already, but softly, as if practicing. Peculiar and peculiar. Spirits didn't need rehearsals, and it was hard to imagine any Indian, real or ghostly, crashing through the brush like a runaway mine cart.

But there were spirits here. That he knew. So he continued to tread silently.

Then he could see them. There were about a dozen, advancing slowly on the cabin, crouching as they walked. They wore painted vests and leggings and, just as the Weavers insisted, had no heads.

Maybe that explained why they were so clumsy, Malone thought. Spirits floated. Comanche floated, almost. These critters, whatever they were, bulled their way through the brush.

Only one of them was chanting louder than a whisper. Malone focused on him. There was something about the way he moved that was real. His feet caressed the earth instead of bludgeoning it, and he wore moccasins. His companion spirits wore boots. A few were equipped with spurs. Odd choice of footgear for a ghost.

The crackling anger of a thousand crickets made Malone look down and to his left. The snake was already tightly coiled. So intent had he been on observing the advancing "spirits" that he'd neglected to note the leathery one close by his feet.

The rattler's tongue flicked in Malone's direction. Malone's tongue jabbed right back. If it had any sense, the rattler would bluster a few seconds more, and then slither off among the grass. Snakes, however, were notoriously short on sense. This one struck, aiming for Malone's left leg.

The mountain man disliked killing anything without good

reason, and the snake's unwarranted attack was evidence enough it was already deranged. So, instead of drawing the bowie knife, Malone spat, faster and more accurately than was natural. His spit caught the snake in the eyes as its target leaped to one side.

Confused and queasy, the rattler lay silent a moment. Then it hurried off into the brush. It would not come back.

Unfortunately, it had been heard. Four headless figures surrounded Malone. All of them carried Colts, distinctly unethereal devices. The man in their midst regarded them thoughtfully.

"Didn't think you'd chance it forever on your singin' alone."

The one nearest Malone reached up and yanked at his chest. Painted fabric slid downward in his fingers, revealing a quite normal face. At the moment the expression on it was pained.

"You're a big one. Where'd you spring from?"

"The seed of an eagle and the loins of a cat—not that it's any of your business." Malone studied his captors thoughtfully as the speaker carefully removed bowie knife and LeMat pistol from the mountain man's person. Malone made no move to retain them. "What're you boys doin' out here in the middle o' the night in those getups? I didn't know the circus had made it this far west."

The speaker's expression turned sour. He was about to reply, when two other figures arrived. Those holding the Colts quickly made room for the newcomers. One of them was the real chanter. Malone studied his features intently. Shoshone, all right. Teetering the horizontal side of half-drunk, and by the look of him, not caring much about his condition.

His companion was bigger, older, and made up to look like what he wasn't. He was neither ghost nor spirit, though the scent of the devil was surely about him. He had about him the air of one with no time to waste, clearly a man poisoned by impatience.

"Who the hell are you?" he inquired belligerently of the mountain man.

"Malone's the name. Amos Malone. Mad Amos to some."

"That I can believe. Well, Mr. Malone, I don't know what you're doing out here, but I am told that the country on the north side of the river is more hospitable to strangers. I would suggest that you betake yourself there as soon as possible. Perhaps sooner."

"Your solicitude is touching, but I like it here, Mister. . . ?"

"Cleator. This is my associate, Mr. Little-Bear-Blind-in-One-Eye." He clasped the Shoshone possessively on the shoulder. It was enough to shake his none-too-stable equilibrium.

Malone murmured something in Shoshone to the chanter, who promptly and unexpectedly straightened. He blinked hard, as if fighting with his own eyes, trying to focus on the man who'd spoken to him. Meanwhile, the mountain man gestured at those surrounding him.

"Kind of an obscure locale for a theatrical performance, ain't it?"

"This is not theater, sir. This is seriously real."

"Might I inquire as to its purpose?"

Cleator gazed at him. "Why should I trouble myself to explain to a passing nonentity? Why should I not simply have you shot?"

"Because you don't want any shooting." Malone indicated the still-sleeping cabin. "If that's what you wanted, you'd have killed all three Weavers long ago instead of constructin' this elaborate masque."

"You are surprisingly perceptive. I am intrigued. You are, of course, quite right. I dislike killing because dead people cannot sign legal documents. It is much better for them to sign willingly, while they are still alive."

"This is all because you have a hankerin' for the Weavers' land?"

"Certainly. It lies between two of my holdings. But that is not the most important reason." He paused, studying Malone, and then shrugged. "I will show you. Understanding will make you dangerous to me. Then I will have no compunctions about having you shot if you refuse to depart."

They led him to the edge of the Red. Little Bear followed, but stayed as far away from Malone as possible. He was still fighting to focus his eyes.

Cleator pointed upstream, then down, and lastly at the far side of the river. "My land, Mr. Malone." He kicked dirt with his boots. "Weaver's land. Notice anything unique about it?"

Malone studied the river, the far bank and the near. "This is a narrows."

Cleator smiled, pleased. "Very good, sir. Very good, indeed. I may tell you that, in fact, this is the narrowest part of the Red

River for many miles in either direction. Can you suspect why it is of such interest to me?"

"You need a bridge."

"Running cattle across a bridge saves the need of fording them to reach the railhead north of here. Every extra mile a steer runs costs weight, and therefore money. I need this land to build my bridge."

"Why not simply lease the portion you need? I'm sure Weaver would be amenable to a fair offer. A bridge could be of benefit to his stock as well."

"Of course it would, but I don't want to benefit his stock, Mr. Malone. Nor do I wish the uncertainty of a lease. I want to own it all."

"You're goin' to all this trouble for that?"

"No trouble, Mr. Malone. I invent some mischievous spirits to frighten away the Weavers, and then I buy their land at auction."

"If you jest asked him, he might be glad to sell out direct."

"But in this fashion, I obtain a much better price."

Malone considered. "Mr. Cleator, you are an evil man."

Cleator shrugged. "I am ambitious. They are not the same."

"I find it hard to separate the two, much of the time. Joke's on you, though."

The rancher frowned. "What joke, sir?"

"You didn't have to invent no spirits to haunt this place. The spirits are here already. Have been for a thousand years or more." He turned sharply on Little Bear. "Ain't that right?" And he added something in Shoshone.

As wide as the chanter's eyes got, this time they had no difficulty in focusing. Little Bear began to gaze nervously around him. Ordinary rocks and bushes suddenly caused him to retreat, to stumble.

"What did you say to him?" asked Cleator curiously.

"Nothin' he don't know. The whiskey you give him kept his eyes from workin', if not his mouth. He's seein' now, takin' a good look around, and he don't much like what he sees. Always been bad blood between Shoshones and Comanche. He's feelin' dead Comanche around him now, and he don't care for it. I wouldn't neither, were I you, Mr. Cleator."

A couple of the hired gunmen were starting to glance around uneasily. Malone had started them thinking. North Texas is a bad place for a man to be thinking with the moon glaring down at him accusingly.

"Really? And why not? Am I supposed to fear a few dead Indians?"

"I'm jest sayin' that if I were you, I wouldn't try to put no bridge over these narrows."

Cleator was grinning now, enjoying himself. "Mr. Malone, you are a caution, sir. I defy the Weavers, I defy the Comanche, and I defy their dead or anything else that attempts to slow progress on this land. Do not try to frighten me with my own invention."

"Sometimes it's healthy to be a mite afeared o' progress, Mr. Cleator. It can jump up when you ain't lookin' an' bite you severe." He looked up suddenly at the opposite bank, his heavy brows drawing together like a small black version of the bridge Cleator proposed to build.

The gunmen jumped when Little Bear let out a cry and bolted. One of them raised his weapon, but Cleator stopped him from shooting.

"Let him go. We'll track him down later. He'll be in town, drunk."

"I wouldn't figure too near on that," Malone informed him. "I think our friend's seen the light. I reckon by tomorrow he'll be headed northwest, if he can find himself a horse. You see, he saw what was waitin' for him here, and did the sensible thing by lightin' out."

One of Cleator's men stepped forward. "We're losin' the night, boss." A very large knife gleamed in his right hand. "Let me stick him, and we'll dump him in the river and get on with this."

"Very well. Now that he knows, by his own wish, he is a threat, and as previously stated, I can have no compunction about terminating a threat. Therefore, you may. . . ."

He broke off, gazing across the river at the spot Malone was watching. One by one, the men wielding the Colts joined him in staring.

"Hell's bunghole," one of them stuttered, "what is *that?*"

It was larger than a bull buffalo, with teeth the size of an opium dream, and burning yellow eyes. Even at that distance, you could hear it growl as it raced toward them.

"Mr. Cleator, I wouldn't linger in this vicinity if I were you."

The rancher was shaken but otherwise unmoved. "I am not afraid of night beasts, Mr. Malone. That is no spirit. I don't know what it is, but if it is alive, it can be slain." He wrenched a rifle from the man next to him. "This will be my land, and I will build my bridge *here.* I will deal with any intruders." He glanced back and smiled. "You set this up, didn't you? You and the Weavers. Some kind of trick. It will not work. I am no gullible plainsman, sir. And you are dogmeat." He looked sharply at the man with the knife.

"Stick him or shoot him, as you please."

But the gunman was staring across the river, staring at the unbelievable thing that was coming toward them faster than a train could travel. As he stared, he kept backing up, until he prudently decided to turn and run. He was accompanied.

Cleator roared at them. "Come back! You cowards, idiots! Can't you see it's a trick! That damn farmer will be laughing at you tomorrow!"

A couple of the men slowed to turn, but what they saw made them tremble with fear and run faster still. The monster reached the far bank of the river. It did not stop, but kept coming, soaring through the night air as easily as the fabled roc of legend, as cleanly as a bad dream. They were not particularly brave, those men, and they were not being paid well enough to stay and tussle with hell.

The scream made Cleator turn. So fast had it traversed the river gorge that it was already almost upon him. It screamed again, a cross between a bleat and a howl. Malone whirled to flee, yelling at Cleator to do the same.

Perhaps he didn't have enough time, or chose to react instinctively. He raised his rifle and tried to aim.

The burning yellow eyes blinded him. He flung his gun aside and tried finally to dodge.

That was when Malone saw the Indian. He was riding the monster's muzzle.

It was solid and yet spirit, a brave clad in untraditional armor. Small but perfect, he thought as it turned toward the stumbling, half-paralyzed rancher and loosed a single shining arrow. It struck James Cleator squarely in the right eye, penetrating to the brain and killing him instantly.

Then the monster was upon him. Cleator was struck once and sent flying, his already-dead broken body landing ten yards away in a crumpled heap. Malone slowed. It had not come after him, but had vanished eastward, howling into the night.

Breathing hard, he waited until he was sure before returning to study the rancher's corpse. Nearby he found the monster's tracks. They were unlike any he'd ever seen. He knelt to examine them more closely.

A voice anxious from behind: "Mr. Malone! Are you all right, sir?"

The mountain man did not look up as Esau Weaver slowed to a halt beside him. The rancher was carrying a rifle, old and battered. There was nothing worn about his courage, however. He blanched when he espied Cleator's body.

"I know that man."

"Your antagonist, though you did not know it. Not spirits. Cold will buy a man much, but not truth, and not the spirits of the dead. Too easy by half to defile yesterday as well as tomorrow. I believe he were done in *by both.*" He put a comforting hand on the rancher's shoulder. "Nothin' more to be done here. Cleator was dead of heart before the rest of his body caught up with him. Let's go get some shut-eye. I'll have a go at explainin' it all to you and the missus tomorrow, while I'm helpin' y'all to unpack."

Weaver nodded wordlessly. Together they returned to the cabin, which would be no more disturbed. Around them the land and all it contained was once again at rest. Yesterday and tomorrow slept peacefully, flanking the present.

"Hell of a restoration job." The attendant looked on approvingly.

"Thanks." The owner was standing before the object of the other man's admiration, examining it minutely.

"Something happened; I can see that."

"Hit something coming over the bridge last night, just this side of Childress. Might've been a coyote. Might've been a small deer."

"Lot of damage?" The attendant was sympathetic. Out here you never knew what you might run into at night.

"Not as bad as it felt. Plenty of blood, though. That'll wash off O.K. Then there's this." He fingered the Packard's nose. "Bent halfway around. And there's a little arrow that went right here, see? Must've lost it in the collision." He straightened, shaking his head sadly.

"These cars from the thirties and forties, they built 'em tough, but it seems like something's always happening to the damn hood ornaments."

Born in 1946 in New York City, Alan Dean Foster received two degrees from the University of California at Los Angeles. He taught school and worked in public relations before becoming a professional writer, largely of science fiction. The author of more than forty-five books, he is best known for his novelizations of the films Alien *(1976) and* The Black Hole *(1980), which have sold more than a million copies, and his ten volumes of "Star Trek" stories,* Star Log One *to* Ten. *"The Chrome Comanche" was first published in the May 1990 issue of* The Magazine of Fantasy and Science Fiction.

Bible Jaeger needed more than religion to drive evil out of the Ozarks. . . .

SIX

Toad's Foot

Manly Wade Wellman

Bible Jaeger came to the Fearful Rock country among the Ozark Hills at the end of the war, sometime in May, just as the word was filtering in of the surrenders of Lee and Jo Johnston and Kirby Smith. He'd fought near Fearful Rock as a Yankee cavalry sergeant, but hardly anybody had known about that. People turned out to see him more in curiosity than in welcome.

The war in those parts hadn't been gentlemanly like the one in Virginia. Men who lived through it on either side came out with a sort of curse on their souls. Jaeger, the word flew round from somewhere, had skirmished with Quantrill's guerrillas thereabouts, had been mentioned in dispatches at Pea Ridge and Westport; he'd returned to be a preacher; he was stern and God-fearing. During the war, his men had called him Bible behind his back. So Fearful Rock people would call him that, too, even to his harsh, hairy face, and would wonder why he wanted to preach to them.

There was no preacher among those hills and hollows, though there were some interesting beliefs and rituals. A few folks thought that any kind of preacher would be better than none at all—even this squat, bench-legged Yankee, with the red thicket of beard and the rolling cavalry walk, dressed in leather-gallused jeans pants and scuffed knee boots and black umbrella hat, carrying a Bible he said weighed six pounds.

He rode in on a brown horse, stubby-built like himself, no show to it. Following him came some baggage and bits of furniture in a mule wagon driven by a grave, articulate black man named Scott. They had taken a little old house of big, rough-sawed planks out on a fairly empty road near Fearful Rock. That house had belonged to Jack Hunn, who'd gone in 1861 to join Bedford Forrest's first mounted rifle company and had never come home again. Jaeger and Scott moved their things in, while some folks ambled over to watch. Among those folks, it is still remembered, came Nessie Shipton.

It is also remembered what Nessie Shipton was like. Tall, proud-walking, with clouds of hair as dark as the storm, with a fine, full shape to her such as a queen should have and didn't often have. She lived among remote, shaggy trees in a hollow called Shipton's after whoever had once been her family, and some said she was a cunning woman, some a prophetess, some just a witch. She could conjure. She grew rich on conjuring. For those she liked she did things; to those she didn't like she did other things. She could tell you where to dig for a well of sweet water on your land, or she could mutter over your sick child and drive away a fever. If you vexed her, she could wither your crop in the field or make your sheep or pigs drop dead. Folks thought twice, and more than twice, before they came to her door. Standing there that day while Jaeger and Scott dragged in a table and chairs and bed springs, she was a pretty thing to look at. Yet nobody, not even Squire Carbrugh, with his eye for fine women, stood too close.

It was nearly sundown when Jaeger spoke his first word to the little gathering of watchers, saying who he was and why he'd come. "Let us pray," he said gruffly, holding his six-pound Bible to his deep chest.

Folks bowed their heads, all but Nessie Shipton. She turned her fine straight back and smoothed her dark hair. She looked to be laughing all the time Jaeger said something deep and solemn about bless this house and this work. At last he looked up.

"Tomorrow is a Sunday," he announced. "I will hold services in this yard at ten o'clock in the morning. I hope you will come and hear me."

Squire Carbrugh and several others said yes, sir, they'd be proud to be there, sure enough. Then they tramped away, this direction and that. All but Nessie Shipton. She walked into the yard to where Jaeger stood beside a skimpy willow tree. The down-dipping sun made a winking glory in her hair. Her eyes and teeth shone like stars. She was as tall as Jaeger, but not as wide, and another sight easier to look at.

"So," she said, "you're going to preach to the poor sinners tomorrow morning."

"And tomorrow afternoon," he said back. "Scott knows several families of black freedmen in this neighborhood. He says they'd be happy to hear the good word."

"What brings you here among us?" she asked. "Why come here where perhaps you're not wanted? I think that's what you did once before."

"I came here during the war because I was ordered to come," he replied. "I've been ordered to come here again, by the voice I always obey."

"Preacher man," said Nessie Shipton, "you don't act pleased to talk to me. That's not neighborly. After all, we have things somewhat in common. We represent the two oldest established firms, don't we? Only my firm's older than yours."

"True," he rumbled. "Men worshiped devils before they worshiped God."

"Here and there they still worship devils," she said, smiling radiantly. "People around here have done that, and profited."

"No profit in that worship," he said flatly. "And no health in it. Nessie Shipton, I heard someone name you. I doubt if there's room for your worship and mine too, here in the Fearful Rock country."

"I entertain the same doubt," she smiled. "Let's just see which of us has to go away."

"Let's just see," he agreed. And she walked away, a winnowing walk, and Jaeger went into the house to supper.

Scott served him with hoecakes and a bowl of cabbage soup, then went out in the early night to feed the horse and the mule. He came back fairly quickly. There was a grayness in the dark of his face. Jaeger got up from the table.

"What's the matter, Scott?"

"We have a kind of a visitor, Reverend." Scott's voice was tight.

"A mischief-maker?" growled Jaeger. "I wondered if any of those would come. I'll make a little mischief myself," and he reached to the wall for his shotgun, on pegs above his old Chicopee saber.

"No, sir, not any people," Scott made haste to say. "I'd never run out of my own barnyard for any man, black or white. This was something hunched down and hairy."

"A wildcat," said Jaeger, the shotgun in his hand.

"Not a wildcat, either. It had a sort of monkey look, Reverend. Only I don't reckon a monkey will say bad words when you meet it face to face."

Jaeger put the shotgun back on its pegs and stormed out at the rear door.

The moon was big and pale in the sky, showing him the little shed that did duty for a stable, and its fence of rough rails. As Jaeger came into the open, the mule neighed hoarsely, querulously. Jaeger hustled toward that noise. He saw the open stable door, and something that hunched darkly at its sill.

Whatever the something was, it saw Jaeger too. It swelled, it hiked its shaggy shoulders. It uttered a crooning growl, in which half-pronounced words seemed to be caught. Jaeger felt his red beard crawl on his jaw, like windblown brush on a hillside. He reached to his hip pocket and dragged out a little book bound in gray paper. He could not read from it in that dim light, and he quoted as best he could remember:

"Demon, I forbid thee my house and premises; I forbid thee my horse stable; I forbid thee my bedstead, until thou hast ascended every hill, until thou hast counted every fence post, and until thou hast crossed every water. And thus dear day may come again into my house; in the three holy names, Amen."

At once the shaggy shape was gone. Into the stable? Clutching his book, Jaeger tramped close to the door. Just inside, a lantern hung to a rusty nail on the jamb. Jaeger seized it, snapped a match into fire on his thumbnail, and kindled the wick. He held the lantern high as he walked in.

He saw nothing except the horse and the mule, still nervous in their stalls. Carrying the lantern, he peered at stacked away hay, a harness on pegs. As he looked, he kept saying the Lord's Prayer under his breath. Finally he went outside again. In the lighted back door of the house stood Scott, a watchful silhouette.

"All is well here," Jaeger called to him through the dark. "But I'll just camp in the stable tonight, in case of more visitors."

Scott vanished and closed the door. Jaeger returned to the stable. He blew out the lantern and lay down in the hay. Often he had made a harder bed. To the horse and the mule he spoke aloud another formula from the book of charms:

"Three false tongues have bound thee, three holy tongues

have spoken for thee. Heaven is above thee, the earth is beneath thee, and thou art between. Blessing be here and about us all. Amen."

Once during the night he wakened at a sudden rattle of sound. He wondered if a stone had been thrown upon the shingles above him. But silence closed in again, and he slept until sunrise.

People gathered in the front yard at midmorning. Jaeger came out to meet them. He wore his jeans and boots but had put on a white shirt with a stand-up collar, a flaring black cravat, and a black jimswinger coat. Donning square-lensed spectacles, he read a passage from his Bible. Then he asked his hearers to join in singing a hymn. Scott, in the house, raised a resonant bass with them. Jaeger announced his text, "I shall lift up mine eyes unto the hills," and preached with some stern emphasis about the true belief and certain false beliefs.

"When I was here in wartime, I found a curse of diabolism upon this unhappy place," he wound up. "I return, and hear another curse whispered. Moses, in his pronouncement of laws, told his people, 'Thou shalt not suffer a witch to live.' It is not for me to decree life or death, but I say unto you, 'Thou shalt not suffer a witch to prevail.' Let us pray."

He prayed, long and bleakly, for heavenly help in stamping out the power of black fear and malicious cunning.

Afterward, those who had heard came to thank him for his words. One housewife made a present of a crock of sausage meat; another brought a glass jar of watermelon pickles; a third proffered a tin pail of cane syrup and a bag of onions. And Squire Carbrugh stumped up on his gold-headed cane and put into Jaeger's hand a ten-dollar greenback.

"You took up no collection, but here's to help the work you hope to do," said the squire sonorously. He was lean, elegant, with a spike of gray-threaded beard. The gray frock coat he wore had been his when he was a major with Shelby's Iron Brigade. In contrast to the rumpled, squat Jaeger, he looked elegant, even aristocratic.

"Reverend, I glory in your coming here," he rolled out. "But if you'll hark to me as one friend to another, I advise you not to try too much at once. Make haste slowly, it says in the Latin."

"I don't know much Latin, sir," Jaeger said deeply, "and I

don't see how haste can be made slowly. I hope to make all the speed I can in my duty."

"These beliefs you aim to put down," said Carbrugh, "they've been here for long years, more than I can count back to. They'll take long years to root out."

Jaeger crumpled the greenback in his big hand. "It's human nature to believe in something," he offered weightily. "These people have sorely lacked preachers of the Bible. But now I am here. I cannot admit of aught hindering the right way and the right word."

"Bold words, Reverend."

"Fear got burnt out of me in the war, Squire."

"Out of me, too," declared Carbrugh. "Fear was a scarce article with the men of Shelby's command."

"I fought against Shelby at Westport," said Jaeger, "and I know how brave his men could be. But the war's over. You and I can be on the same side now."

"True," nodded Carbrugh, the gray in his beard gleaming like silver. "Let's stay on the same side. One thing interests me, a certain book you carry. No, not your Bible. Another book."

Jaeger gazed at him levelly. "*The Long Lost Friend,* sir. You seem well informed about my private affairs."

"Oh, neighbors tell me things," said Carbrugh. "Isn't that a book of black magic spells?"

"No," amended Jaeger, "white magic. For good against evil. John George Homan published it in 1820. When I was a boy in Pennsylvania, Homan was still alive near Reading. He was kind to all afflicted people. He lived and died in the true faith."

"Once again, I say I'm glad you've come to the Fearful Rock country," Squire Carbrugh changed the subject. "Why not let it be told around that you'll preach next Sunday at my big house? Perhaps the people will bring their dinners and eat together there on the lawn. You can be my guest. I promise you some yellow-legged chicken."

"Thank you, Squire. I'll come, if it's agreeable."

Carbrugh walked away, barely using the cane to favor his lame leg. Jaeger watched him go. A voice spoke at his elbow.

"Preacher man, you're eloquent," it said throatily. "I heard your sermon. You didn't see me, but I was here this morning."

He turned. Nessie Shipton was smiling at him. Her fine

shoulders rose naked above her blue blouse, and her hair shook down upon them.

"And you were here last night, I think," he said.

"You surmised that? You didn't see me then, either."

"I saw something," he nodded. "Not a pretty something. I spoke to it, and it went away. It didn't succeed in doing what you wanted."

"There will be other times," promised Nessie Shipton.

"I suppose that I saw what the old books call a witch's familiar," said Jaeger. "Those are unchancey things, but I don't feel they can be trusted, not even by their own witches."

She stopped smiling and drew her body up. "Nobody dares call me a witch to my face."

"Nobody?" he repeated, and his own smile was fierce in his beard.

"Preacher man," she said furiously, "you force me to dislike you."

"Good," he said, smiling.

"You and I might have been friends, done big things together."

"You mean evil things."

"You will find out," she assured him. "To your cost."

Away she went. Jaeger entered his house, where Scott was flattening wads of the sausage to fry for their dinner.

When the meal had been eaten and the dishes washed, they set out for the place where Jaeger had agreed to preach to the blacks. Jaeger rode his brown horse, Scott the patient mule. They came to a house, no more than a cabin of thin poles with clay chinking and a sagging porch. A dozen waited there, shabbily dressed, eager, courteous. Several black children were shy at first, but grew happy when Jaeger, sitting on the edge of the porch, told them a story of a boy lost from his parents and how he was found at last in the great temple where he astounded learned men with his questions and answers about religion and worship. After that, Jaeger announced his text, again from the Psalms, "All the workers of iniquity shall be scattered." Speaking as the trusted representative of a powerful deity, Jaeger assured his hearers that no harm could come to those of trusting and prayerful hearts. After that, he called on them to join him in singing a hymn, and tunefully, harmoniously, they did so. Then several diffidently asked for baptism. He led them to the brink of a nearby stream, dipped water in his great palm, spoke a blessing over it, and touched the heads of those who wanted it.

Home Jaeger and Scott rode, side by side.

"Your preaching did those people a world of good," observed Scott, in his careful, thoughtful way. "I've been thinking I might start a school for those little children. Teach them their letters and how to do sums, get along in the world."

"That would be a fine work for you, Scott. Tell me, is there any of this strange belief among them?"

"No more than with most of that range of folks," replied Scott. "I gathered somewhere that that lady—Miss Nessie Shipton—does her business with the white people. You see, sir, the whites are the only ones with money, even a little money. And she wants money for whatever she does."

"A practical woman," said Jaeger. "Though if she wants money from me, she'll be disappointed."

"She wants power." Scott studied the bobbing ears of the mule. "I keep remembering what was out at the stable last night. It looked all shagged over to me, like an animal. But such an animal I never saw or heard of."

"Let's hope it's a scarce one," said Jaeger honestly.

They rode into their own yard and dismounted. Scott gathered up the reins of the horse and mule, to lead them to the stable.

"Reverend," he said, his dark face thoughtful, "I've been turning over in my mind something that could help. Something in one of your books."

"The Long Lost Friend"?

"No, sir, a book you wrote in and drew in yourself. Once you showed it to me. It has pictures of crosses, flowers, stars, all like that. You drew them and colored them with crayons."

"Oh, my old notebook," nodded Jaeger. "Those were copied from houses and barns in Pennsylvania. *Haus-segen,* they're called. House-blessings would be the English of it."

"Yes, sir, I remember your telling me that. Now, then, I wonder in my mind, what if we put those pictures on our stable, to keep any more evil things away?"

Jaeger stared, then shot out his big red hand to grasp Scott's brown one.

"Scott, you may have the right of it," he fairly shouted. "Here, go and put the mule in his stall, but don't take the bridle off the horse. He can rest for a few minutes, but I'll be riding out again."

"Whatever you say, sir." Scott led the animals away, and Jaeger hurried into the house.

From its shelf he took his old notebook, a worn little ledger with black cloth covers and pages of lined paper. He turned to where there were rows and rows of figures drawn in pencil, with sketched-in colors in red, yellow, and green crayons. His blunt forefinger ran from one to another to another.

"Here we are," he said as Scott came back in. "*Gruttafoos*—the Toad's Foot."

"That sounds like voodoo," ventured Scott.

"Why?" demanded Jaeger. "The toad's a friend of man, a killer of bugs for him."

He tore a blank page from the book and sat down to copy the symbol. First he used a tin saucer to trace around for a circle, five inches across. Within the circle he carefully managed an outline like a three-spiked paw print, the points standing upward. He searched out a green crayon and filled in the symbol and shaded around it with the pencil. Above it he wrote the proper words he remembered: *Sanct Matheus, Sanct Markas, Sanct Lucas, Sanct Johanas.* At last he nodded, as though the work would pass.

Into the kitchen he went. From a battered wooden box he fished a handful of cutlery. He chose a dagger-like old knife with a cross hilt. This he stowed carefully in one tail pocket of his coat. Into the other he slid the folded diagram. He went outside, and Scott led his horse around.

"I hope not to be gone long," said Jaeger, swinging into the saddle and riding away.

He did not really know where he was going. After all, he had been here for little more than twenty-four hours; he was not acquainted as yet. But someone would tell him. The clay road ran between open fields with stake and rider fences, hills rising beyond. In the field toward the right, a farmer urged a double-shovel cultivator behind a swaybacked dun horse. He lifted a hand in the friendly southern way of greeting, and Jaeger waved back. He would get to know that neighbor, he would get to know all his neighbors, whenever he returned from his errand. If he returned from it.

Up ahead approached someone on a white horse. Nearer,

and he saw that the rider was a woman, a young girl really, sitting gracefully sideways on the horse. She came close and she, too, lifted a slim hand to him. Her hair was as red as Jaeger's beard. A red-haired girl on a white horse, people thereabouts said that meant good luck.

"Please, young miss," said Jaeger, doffing his hat, "can you tell me how to get to the home of Nessie Shipton?"

The girl reined to a halt. Her blue eyes gazed. "You truly want to see her, sir?"

"I have important business with her," said Jaeger.

The slim hand pointed back the way she had come. "Pass the first side-off road and take the second to the left. You'll need to look careful. It ain't much of a road, and there's woodsy trees thereabout."

"Thank you." Broad black hat in hand, Jaeger bowed from his saddle and rode on. He knew that she watched him in troubled wonder.

He found the road to the left, huddled between close-growing trees that joined their branches overhead, and turned his horse upon it. He fancied that the horse trembled, then told himself that that was only fancy. Horses didn't have imaginations, like their riders.

Things were immediately different on that narrow thread of a trail. It seemed to follow a stream, bend after bend, but the stream flowed out of sight among trees to the left—red and white oak, pine, hawthorn, and some less easy to identify. There was a thicket of tall, pale canes, like a phalanx of spears. Beyond that, trees with outflung branches and broad leaves that seemed to cock and listen like ears. A splash in the unseen waters there to the left, quite a big splash, as though from a heavy moving body. Grass grew at the sides of the trail with strange little flowers set here and there, flowers as pale and lean as fangs. Something rattled twigs in the thickets. Maybe a raccoon. Or maybe not.

Jaeger could understand why people hesitated to visit Nessie Shipton. He remembered telling Squire Carbrugh that he had outgrown the sensation of fear. That had been a vain boast, not a proper one for a preacher of the true faith. But he was going there, he wasn't turning back, though the horse trembled again. He hoped he had a pure heart against evil.

The stream shifted and flowed across the trail. His horse lifted its hoofs high to wade. Jaeger thought that the water looked reddish, as though it contained rust, and that it gave off a vapor, murky and dull. On the far side, he abruptly checked the horse. A snake ahead there, a big, wriggling snake . . . no. Only the shadow of a jutting branch that stirred, though there was no wind that he could feel.

More branches crowded above him from either side. He rode in a sort of gloomy tunnel. On beyond was light, a clearing.

Again he drew rein. If that was where Nessie Shipton was, better not ride in, better not be seen or heard until he was ready. He dismounted, turned the horse around, and fastened its halter rope to the thorny fork of an Osage orange. If he had to leave in a hurry, he could mount and ride straight back the way he had come. He reassured the beast with a hand on its neck, and then he headed for the light.

As he advanced, with the careful tread of an old army scout, he heard voices.

"I don't think you're in a position to ask anything of me, Squire, not even humbly," he heard Nessie Shipton saying. "You've prospered thus far by leaving me strictly alone."

"I don't more than suggest, Miss Nessie, and only in the interests of pleasantness in our neighborhood." That was Squire Carbrugh, being plaintive, being timid. "There would be room for both you and him, and I've already told him the same thing."

"Indeed?" A laugh in her rich voice. "And what did he say?"

"I still hope he can be persuaded."

"You hope he can, but you know he can't. Just leave him to me, Squire. I've dealt with one or two of his clumsy sort before this. And keep your own nose out of my business."

Jaeger had reached a point behind fronds of willow from which he could see into the clearing. It was a round space of bald, red clay, thickly enclosed among trees and brush. On the far side stood a cabin of squared logs, with dankly mossy shingles. Its door was faced with a great pelt of something, darkly shaggy, like the hide of a buffalo or a black bear. In front of the house stood Nessie Shipton, talking to Squire Carbrugh. The squire looked like somebody asking a favor, even asking mercy. One hand leaned on his cane, the other twisted the white hat it held. His shoulders sagged and trembled. Nessie Shipton stood straight and confident, a shawl of purple silk caught around her. She bracketed her hands on her hips and tilted her head back so that she could slant her fine eyes as though looking down at Carbrugh.

"You're wrong," she chuckled in her throat. "There isn't room for him and me here. And I was here first, as I pointed out to him. I'll stay and he'll go, if he's lucky enough to get away in time."

"When must he go?"

"By sundown," she replied, "if he has the wisdom to go. When the sun sinks, forces will be abroad, all around that place he thought to live in. Go warn him, tell him."

Carbrugh went unhappily to where his spotted horse waited, mounted, and rode away. Jaeger lurked in the willow scrub until the rider had passed him. Then he stepped out on the trail and tramped into the open where Nessie Shipton waited.

She looked at him as though she felt no surprise at his being there. "I didn't give you leave to call on me," she said.

"I came without leave," he told her. "I heard all you said to Squire Carbrugh."

"Then you were eavesdropping," she sneered at him. "It is like a brave man, to spy on a woman. But if you listened, you heard me say that it's time for you to leave."

"I heard," he nodded, "and it's you who must leave."

She laughed. He saw her pink tongue, her white, pointed teeth.

"Preacher man," she said at last, "you'd be funny if you weren't such a crashing bore. You don't understand anything. Listen, for once. This is my country. I do well here at what I like to do. We've gone on for years without preacher men. We'll go on for years more without one."

"I came here before, when nobody particularly wanted me here," said Jaeger. He had stopped, close to her. "That was during the war. I saw, when I had time to notice, that the word of truth was badly needed here."

"This is more or less a forgotten part of the world," she told him brightly, as though it were a social chat. "Once in a while in the old days, a traveling preacher rode through and preached a sermon. Then the war came and there weren't any more preachers. But I was here. My companions were here. People believe in us—even Squire Carbrugh, you heard him. Any sensible person ought to see that we don't want meddlers."

"I have returned to help," said Jaeger doggedly. "I'll stay to help. I have heard the call to help."

"Hear something else," bade Nessie Shipton. "Those whom I serve wouldn't have given me my work here without the power to do it. And you aren't staying. There are more things to fight than just myself. I've a legion of assistants, preacher man. I think you're coming to realize that."

"I ran something ugly out of my stable yard last night," Jaeger said.

"That was your ground—temporarily. This is mine, permanently. You're trespassing. You'd better leave while you can, and never come back."

Jaeger planted his booted feet and stroked his red beard.

"Not until I've had it out with you," he declared.

"It's already been had out. You don't see the danger for you." Her loftily searching gaze raked him from head to foot. "If I should make a certain sign with my hand, if I should speak a certain word in a certain tone, your hide would be hanging there on my house." She pointed. "Right next to that skin which you think you saw last night."

Jaeger studied the expanse of rank, black fur. "It was worn by one of the servants you boast about."

Again Nessie Shipton laughed, with menace in the mirth. "You keep saying, my servant wore it," she jeered at him. "How little you know, preacher man. You aren't gifted enough to realize what you're facing. I wore that skin. It's my usual dress after sundown. It rules my followers, it makes me fearful to those who may have lingering doubts of what I can do. I bought it years ago from an Indian medicine man. A man much appreciated by his tribe."

"You fled out of my yard wearing it," said Jaeger.

"Then profit by my example, and flee out of mine. We're not alone here, not by any means."

Nor were they alone. Without actually seeing, Jaeger was aware that things lurked in the deep shadows of the trees, among the bosky mats of undergrowth. He half-sensed eyes, greenly glittering, like the eyes of flesh-eating beasts. He heard a faint clash, as of dry talons, of tusks.

"Even by daylight, my friends are here," she said.

"Miss Shipton," and Jaeger was able to keep his voice steady, "isn't it awkward, all this host? I concede you have powers—"

"You compliment me, preacher man," she said, tossing her hair.

"If you help people in any way, can't they be grateful to you without being afraid?"

"I want them to be afraid," she replied, like a patient adult instructing a child. "Fear is the only power."

"I serve another power than fear," said Jaeger. "But without your comrades, I think you'd be nothing."

"I told you, a motion of my hand, a certain word spoken. That would finish you decisively."

His own hands hung at his sides. Suddenly he dived them into his tail pockets. One snatched out the folded paper on which he had made the diagram. The other came up with the cross-hilted knife. He made two long hurried strides past Nessie Shipton to the door of the house.

He opened the paper against the hewn log of the door's lintel. Into it he drove the point of the dagger, through and deep into the wood, with a sullen *chock*. The paper hung there, fluttering.

"Take that thing away!" screamed Nessie Shipton wildly.

Jaeger swung around to face her. His teeth gleamed in a bearded smile.

"Your shaggy dress of hide must be very old," he said, going himself into a tone of mockery. "Look, it's falling to pieces."

He spoke the truth. The hairy expanse seemed to quiver and crawl. It split into flakes that dropped away from the door like withered leaves in an autumn gale.

"Might the power be going out of it?" Jaeger inquired.

"I need that skin at night!" Nessie Shipton was chattering. "If I don't have it—"

"If you don't have it, you'll be at a disadvantage, you can't command," Jaeger finished for her, his smile bright and hard. "This design," and he pointed, "is the Pennsylvania-Dutch *Gruttafoos*. The Toad's Foot. In that state it drives all evil from a house, and I think it works as well here. What is a blessing to the godly is a curse to the wicked."

She ran past him and clawed at the paper, but jumped back as though her hand had been burnt. She moaned and retreated half a dozen steps, cherishing her fingers.

"And there's the added protection of the cross in the hilt of that knife," went on Jaeger. "Evil has been banished from your house, Nessie Shipton. You are evil. You can't cross your own threshold."

"It's my house," she stammered. "My house—"

"Now it's for you to leave this country and find another place," Jaeger said, almost gently. "I apprehend that your companions, yonder in the woods, won't have any great mercy on failures."

As he spoke, sound rose among the trees and undergrowth, like a stealthy, unhappy sigh of wind. She shivered and cowered.

"Oh, please," she tried to say, her hands to her face.

"Now," announced Jaeger, "I'll go, as you asked me."

He went walking away, toward where the trail led out of the clearing. As he entered among the trees, he heard Nessie Shipton scream shrilly, in pain or terror, or both. That windy murmur had risen to a roar. Sternly he lectured himself that no man, especially a man of God, should run from the place where he had been victorious. But in spite of himself he walked more swiftly to where his horse strained and nickered. He wrenched the halter loose from its knot and vaulted into the saddle. The horse had no hesitation about running, running like the wind, as though something pursued it. Galloping away, Jaeger heard another scream, broken off suddenly into silence.

The sun fell toward the horizon as he rode into his own yard and dismounted in front of the stable. Scott was there, a burnt stick in his hand, carefully tracing designs on the door.

"I had another look into your sketchbook, Reverend," said Scott. "I had it in mind, that Toad's Foot picture and maybe some of the others might do all right for us here."

"I don't think the charm is needed any more, but your idea was good," said Jaeger.

Leading the horse into its stall, he stripped off the saddle and bridle. He swabbed away sweat with a wisp of straw and flung a cloth over the brown back. Scott fetched a bucket of water. Finally the two men walked back into the open.

"It's sunset," observed Scott, gazing westward.

A flaming light hung at the horizon, touching wisps of cloud to rose and pink.

"That's beautiful," said Scott. "Peaceful."

"Peaceful," Jaeger echoed him. "Yes."

Born in 1903 in Portugese West Africa (now Angola), Manly Wade Wellman was brought to the United States at the age of six. He wrote more than seventy-five books and 200 short stories, perhaps the best known being his ghostly stories for Weird Tales, *many of which were collected in* Worse Things Waiting *(1973) and* Lonely Vigils *(1981). Also noteworthy is* Who Fears the Devil? *(1963). Wellman won the 1946 Ellery Queen's Awards contest and his nonfiction book of murder cases,* Dead and Gone *(1954), won the Mystery Writers of America's Edgar Award in 1955. He also received the North Carolina Literary Award and the World Fantasy Award for Lifetime Achievement. He died in 1986. "Toad's Foot" was first published in the April 1979 issue of* The Magazine of Fantasy and Science Fiction.

In the Blue Ridge Mountains, a man loses his son, while others gain salvation. . . .

SEVEN

The Ghost Whistle

Eugene K. Jones

Uncle Bob Holman, habitat the Blue Ridge Mountains of Virginia, feared neither God nor the devil. His profession was moonshining, his chief recreation taking potshots at his feudal enemies, and his age seventy-two. He also had a hobby—David, his only son.

Now David, having been educated in the district school, followed his own inclinations instead of his father's lawless footsteps and became an engineer on the Richmond, Fredericksburg, and Western Railroad, which passed close to Uncle Bob's cabin in the Blue Ridge. When, after some years of faithful service, the young man was assigned to drive the Limited, Uncle Bob merely grunted; but deep down in his wicked old heart he was tickled to death.

And so it came to pass that every day the mountaineer would cross the field between his cabin and the railroad upon hearing the Limited whistle at the top of the bend. David blew for the grade the customary two long and two short blasts, but he always allowed the last toot to die away in a peculiar manner, thus informing his parent that he himself was at the throttle. Invariably Uncle Bob reached the track before the locomotive had rounded the bend, where he would wait for the brief view of his son leaning from the cab window. He never waved or changed the expression of his face, yet no rainstorm or blizzard could prevent that daily trip across the fields.

One day the crack train struck a boulder that had rolled down from the mountain fifty feet ahead of the locomotive. Uncle Bob, standing near, saw the engine rear up like a frightened horse and topple sideways into the ditch; he saw Pullman after Pullman crumple into a mass of twisted scrap iron. But the shrieks of the imprisoned passengers did not touch his heart. All that he thought of was his son. With his own hands he dragged forth David's crushed body, and with his own hands carried it to his cabin.

Next morning he buried David in a grave he had dug on the hill, even as he had buried his wife many years before. A group of neighbors peered over the fence during the interment, Uncle Bob allowing them no nearer. Nor would he tolerate the presence of a minister. After he had thrown in the last shovelful of earth, he returned to his cabin and picked up his rifle, upon the stock of which he cut a new notch. The old notches had been varnished over, signifying the cancellation of certain debts. But this last notch was very white, very fresh, like a new wound.

A week later the railroad sent an emissary to interview Holman. The visit, however, did not concern the wreck. After a few tactful remarks on the part of the emissary, who was young and hopeful, Uncle Bob gleaned that the RF&W wanted his property—the very spot, in fact, upon which his cabin stood. Witnesses still awesomely discuss the speed developed by a certain party on leaving those premises, but Uncle Bob really deserved the credit for that. Although had he happened to pick up his rifle instead of his shotgun, the railroad would undoubtedly have lost another employee.

Now, one man in the mountains who did not fear Uncle Bob Holman was the redheaded missionary, Timothy Brockwell. Yet in spite of his temper, which was as fiery as his hair, he had never openly resented Uncle Bob's belligerent attitude toward the church. Always in the back of his mind had lain the hope that the taciturn old moonshiner would someday, and of his own volition, see the light. He was certain nobody could teach him, because in the past the people who had attempted to teach a Holman anything had found themselves violently removed to the next world.

Although the road had been rough, Brockwell had won a following in his illiterate parish. During his years of struggle he had fought and laughed and prayed his way into the hearts of the people. His Irish wit and sympathy had helped him over many dangerous spots. Once he had stood off a gang of revenue men with a rifle while illicit whiskey was being hastily poured onto the unappreciative earth, and the next day extracted a promise from the grateful still owner to manufacture only enough of the "white lightning" for "family use." When a mountaineer was ill he turned to Timothy Brockwell for aid; when a farmer lost his crop he found the missionary ready to share his last dollar with him. Brockwell did not look down from his superior position on the souls to whom God had given so little, but straight across, and wherever he looked he smiled.

Of course, he occasionally met failure—witness the case of Uncle Bob Holman. For that old and professional sinner fought the church and every one who stood for law and decency with his colors nailed to the mast. But when his son David met his death, the missionary felt his time had come. Now, if ever, the redoubtable Holman would turn toward religion for comfort. And so the same day that the railroad sent its agent to interview the mountaineer, Brockwell contrived to intercept Uncle Bob as he was returning from the general store. Halting in front of the towering figure, he said, "Holman, we want you to know our hearts are bleedin' for ye. David was a fine boy."

"What business ought that be o' yourn?" growled Uncle Bob.

"None," admitted Brockwell, smiling. "Sure it isn't business at all. It's sympathy and friendliness we're offerin'."

The mountaineer scowled.

"I hain't wantin' none of yer slobberin'. Take hit back thar to them that's a-payin' yeh for hit!"

"Are ye tryin' to insult Timothy Brockwell?" asked the missionary.

"No," replied Uncle Bob. "Hit cain't be done. Thar hain't enough man in yeh for that."

Suddenly Brockwell doubled one fist and shook it under Holman's nose—quite a way under, due to his lack of height.

"Don't ye go to sassin' me, you spalpeen! If you weren't so old that you make Methuselah look like a little bye in short pants, I'd teach ye with me bare hands to respect God. I stopped to ask you to come to meetin'—so the Lord would forgive the shriveled soul in ye. Now I dare you to come!"

The mountaineer's answer was indicative of his character.

"I hain't never took a dar!" he snarled, and strode down the road.

Although nobody but Brockwell knew that Uncle Bob Holman's entrance into the meetinghouse the following Sunday was in answer to a challenge, his appearance there might have been likened to the advent of a bombshell. Had the devil suddenly materialized in the center aisle, the ensuing consternation could have been no more profound.

Previous to his arrival, the meeting had been progressing with all the funereal solemnity that characterizes the mountaineers at worship. The little frame structure with bare floors, unpainted walls, and hard benches was crowded. Through the cobwebbed windows came the strong light of midmorning, revealing the congregation in all its pathetically incongruous Sunday attire—old, wizened faces under gay bonnets conceived in the eighties; bright young faces framed in gray shawls. Some of the women wore pinched waists, and others obviously lacked a waistline. Some of the men had crowded their broad shoulders into narrow and moth-eaten dress coats, while the less pretentious paraded their belief that God preferred simple raiment.

Every pair of lips was close pressed, every pair of brows drawn together, because to the poor whites of the Virginia mountains religion was a serious business.

The Reverend Timothy Brockwell was just beginning his sermon when the interruption occurred. The main door opened, revealing Uncle Bob Holman. It seemed that his towering figure must hit the top of the jamb. He ignored the faces turned wonderingly toward him. His grizzled hair stood on end; his heavy brows met in a bushy ridge. Ferocity and contempt flashed from his gray eyes. His nose was beaked, his chin thrust upward because of an almost total absence of teeth. As he paused in the doorway, one clawlike hand still gripping the knob, his face suggested the vindictive countenance of an eagle.

Every man and woman in the meetinghouse knew that figure in the doorway. They knew he was the last of the "fighting Holmans"; they knew he had killed his feudal enemies and successfully defied the law. They knew that, no matter how drunk he might be, he was a dead shot with a rifle. All of them feared him; none of them loved him. The majority of the men had followed him into battle against the revenue officers for two reasons. First, because he was a natural strategist, a born leader, and a relentless foe. And second, because they recognized the truth of the mountain slogan: "If ye hain't *with* Uncle Bob ye're agin him; and if ye're agin him ye'd better be dade!"

Mindful only of the short, red-haired person behind the wooden rostrum, the mountaineer strode up the aisle. As he passed bench after bench, every eye followed. Upon reaching the clear space before the platform he stopped. His voice held the booming quality of a big gun.

"Yeh dar'd me ter meetin', and I hain't never took a dar. Now, what the hell do yer want?"

The silence that followed chilled the congregation. It was like the calm before a terrific battle. Suddenly Uncle Bob aimed a gnarled forefinger at the missionary.

"Ye're a fool," he bellowed, "if yeh reckon yeh kin git me ter swaller this yere pap ye're a-handin' aout. Why in hell dontcher bring back that son o' mine? Why dontcher git him back whar I mought talk to him? Because yeh cain't! Because thar hain't no Gawd nor no heaven. Yeh stand thar and tells us critters ter be thankful—fer what? Hain't the railroad took my boy? Hain't they tryin' ter take my home? Hain't the revenoos a-chasin' and a-harryin' me? And what aire you doin' about hit?" He struck his fist into the palm of his left hand. "You and yer followin' o' milk-drinkin', soft-brained swine kin go to hell! Show me that son o' mine hain't jest whar I laid him. Show me *that,* will yeh?"

Brockwell came slowly from behind the rostrum. His eyes were dangerous.

"If it's me answer ye want, ye shall have it," said he. "Brother Holman, the Lord took yer son just as the devil will take you some day. I can't give him back to ye; but mark me words, man! He may *come* back if you don't mend your ways. He's watchin' you now and hopin' he didn't die in vain; and when he finds he did, you'll hear from him! Yes; I know about the railroad wantin' your land, and 'tis wicked man ye are to refuse. For all you know, David's spirit may be ridin' on the Limited—when he isn't hauntin' ye.

"The names you called the people here haven't hurt them. We hold no grudge for that, because we daren't judge lest we be judged. But when you say there isn't a God and that David's soul still lies in the grave ye dug, it's up to the Lord to call ye to account. Go home to your cabin, Brother Holman, and wait for the ghost of your son—and no need to bar the door or put up the shutters, because he'll come through 'em. When convinced you are, when God has had his way, come back here and you'll find us ready to receive ye."

Uncle Bob turned, his eyes blazing, but he made no reply. Perhaps something in the missionary's words had stirred into life a secret fear in his heart, for Brockwell had cunningly played upon the mountaineer's one weakness. Like most of his race, Holman feared the supernatural. Looking neither to right nor to left, he strode down the aisle and out of the meetinghouse.

Now, in spite of the cavalier fashion in which he had rid himself of the railroad envoy, Holman went to town on his mule Monday morning to see Forbes Lathrop, attorney for the RF&W. Not that he had changed his mind. Oh, no! A Holman had never been known to do that. But he realized the advisability of learning whether or not the railroad considered his action a declaration of war. For the code of the towns differed from that of the mountains, where a fight might occur without a previous disagreement but a disagreement never occurred without a fight.

Hitching his mount in front of the local offices of the RF&W, Holman stalked into the presence of one Miss Gladys Van Horn, who chewed gum and stood guard over the sanctums beyond. Miss Van Horn surveyed him with raised brows, then, scratching her head with her pencil, returned her languid attention to the telephone switchboard. All of which failed to impress the mountaineer.

"I'm a-searchin' fer a man named Lathrop," he said. "Whar's he at?"

Miss Van Horn yawned and plugged in for a number. After a moment she gurgled, "That you, Gertie? Say—"

But Uncle Bob was not to be so summarily disposed of. Approaching the switchboard, he deliberately prodded her with a horny and not overclean finger.

"I aim ter see Lathrop. Hain't yer better tell me whar he's at?"

Miss Van Horn contracted violently, as if she had found herself in close proximity to something loathsome. Then, turning scornful eyes upon the caller, "Keep your hands to yourself, you big rube! Can't you see I'm busy? As I was saying, Gertie—"

Now the leader of the Holman faction recognized no barriers other than those defended by rifle. He had sought Miss Van Horn's assistance merely because it was the easiest way, and not because of the propriety of the proceeding. With a snort of disgust he flung open the glass-paneled door leading into the offices and stepped through.

It so happened the first office he came upon was tenanted.

Behind a flat-topped desk sat an elderly man with gray hair and a pleasant face.

"I'm a-huntin' Lathrop," explained Uncle Bob from the threshold.

"My name is Lathrop," admitted the person, rising. "And you are Bob Holman, father of the engineer who was killed on the big bend."

Uncle Bob entered and sat down.

"I don't aim to talk none about that. What I aims ter talk about is this yere land business. T'other day I run off a feller yeh sent to buy my farm. Next feller yer send won't git run off; I'll plant 'im jest whar he draps!"

Forbes Lathrop, local counsel of the road, knew something of the mountaineer's character. Lighting a cigar, he lay back in his desk chair.

"So," he said, "you will shoot any man we send to your land? Very well, Holman, we have a way of handling that. But what interests me is *why*, if you won't sell, you took the trouble to ride down here."

Uncle Bob, sitting awkwardly on the stiff office chair, crossed his legs and dug his hands into his trousers pockets.

"I wanted ter warn yeh. I don't aim ter do no killin' if I don't have to. The place my pap was born in is good enough fer me!"

"Do you know why your son lost his life on the bend?" asked Lathrop abruptly.

"I aims not to talk about that."

"He lost it," continued the lawyer, "because the bend is too close under the mountain. We intend to widen the curve. When our new bend is laid, it will be far enough away from the slope to prevent the possibility of landslides. Which means we must use the ground your cabin stands on. It is not a matter of profit to us—the job will cost hundreds of thousands of dollars. It's a matter of making safe our right of way, so that what happened to your son cannot occur again."

"I don't kere nothin' fer yer plans. I won't sell!" growled Uncle Bob.

The lawyer drew on his cigar.

"You will have to, Holman."

Suddenly the mountaineer was towering over the desk. His big fist came down with a crash, rattling the inkwell and calendar.

"Yer damn railroad killed my son. Yeh hain't goin' ter git

nothin' more o' mine. The fust man yer sends up thar won't never know what hits him. I got a repeatin' rifle, and I kin set in my cabin and pick off a whole army! Hit's my land, and I don't aim ter sell. Hain't yeh never heered a Holman pays his debts? Wall, I got a debt agin the road—hit's marked on my gun—and I'll pay part of hit by holdin' on to my property."

The lawyer deliberately knocked the ash off his cigar. His expression was more compassionate than angry.

"No, Holman; you see, the law is on our side. Your refusal of our fair offer simply means that we must appeal to the state. The land will be condemned and a referee appointed to place a valuation on it. You can't hope to whip the state of Virginia single-handedly, you know. And if you give in now it may save lives. Why, man, if your own son was living, he would be the first one to urge you to sell."

"David's underground!" roared Uncle Bob. "Don't yeh go ter speakin' fer him; he won't never speak no more."

Lathrop pressed a button on his desk.

"I'm sorry," he said. "We will give you one week to decide. If we don't hear from you, we must appeal to the authorities. Good day, sir."

Uncle Bob turned to find Miss Van Horn at the door. As he slouched past she drew away her skirts, and when he had left the building she murmured, as she moved her pencil soothingly over her scalp, "The big rube!"

Snow! Nothing but snow everywhere. For three days the white flakes had been drifting out of a leaden sky, hiding the dump heaps round Uncle Bob's cabin, burying deeper the body of the son he had loved. For three days the mountaineers of the section had waded stoically back and forth between the general store and their homes.

Then came the blizzard. The wind swept out of the north with a howl; the clouds huddled earthward, as if to escape its fury, and the snowflakes grew smaller. No longer did they flutter down like butterflies, but, close-packed and driven by a sixty-mile gale, they flew horizontally.

Uncle Bob, in his cabin, kept himself warm—externally with a light-wood blaze, internally with moonshine. But his bloodshot eyes and unsteady hand told of sleepless nights. When darkness crowded the single window, he sat very close to the fire, his loaded rifle within reach and his door barred, for he was secretly afraid of the noise of the wind. Also, he cursed ardently the man who had suggested his son's possible return.

On the afternoon of the third day Uncle Bob heard a knock at the door. In spite of the ghost-dispelling daylight, he answered cautiously, "What do yeh want? Speak up!"

Came a quavering voice, "Hit's me, Bobby—Soldier. I'm mighty nigh froze solid."

The mountaineer opened the door far enough to allow the bent figure of an old man to stumble in. Although wrapped in Union uniform, his hair was gray, and his age-dimmed eyes sunken in a wrinkled face. Shuffling to the fire, he held his hands to the blaze.

"Hit's a turruble stomm, Bobby! Ol' Soldier 'twas powerful close ter givin' up the ghost—yes sir, powerful close!"

During the latter part of the Civil War, Soldier helped seven-year-old Holman and his father fight off renegades who were trying to loot their house. And Holman, with the gratitude of a mountaineer, had been Soldier's friend ever since. Pouring a stiff drink of 'shine, Holman gave it to the octogenarian, who swallowed it at a gulp. After a moment Soldier squatted down, hands still extended. His eyes swept the cabin until they rested on the rifle.

"What're yeh skeered of, Bobby?"

"Revenoos," muttered Uncle Bob. "Yeh cain't tell when they mought happen 'long."

"Hain't skeered o' nothin' else?"

The mountaineer removed his corncob.

"Hit takes a Holman to scare a Holman, and thar hain't no more Holmans!"

After a moment Soldier began to rub his left foot. "Powerful bad doins on this yere mountain tonight, Bobby—powerful bad! The railroad track's a-hid by a pile o' rock—yes sir; hit must 'a' slid with the snow."

Uncle Bob started. "Be yer certain, Soldier?"

"As thar's a Lawd God above!"

"Yer say the track's got enough rock on hit ter wreck a train?"

"Enough ter wreck forty trains—yes sir."

Uncle Bob strode to the other end of the cabin, halting before the window. The gray light of late afternoon revealed the right-of-way of the RF&W—a long embankment following the mountain base. A short distance southward a dark heap, not yet covered with snow, marked the spot where tons of rock and earth had slid down from the slope, completely burying the rails. At present it offered no particular menace because of its visibility, but by nightfall the blizzard would effectually disguise it. The next train came through at eleven o'clock, and small chance was there for her engineer to recognize the death trap in time.

Uncle Bob remained peering forth until the storm spread a whirling curtain between him and the right-of-way. Then he returned to the fire.

"Soldier," he said, "thar's a few of them fotched-on railroaders goin' ter hell tonight."

The old man shivered convulsively.

"Dontcher aim ter stop the Limited, Bobby? Ye're the only man nigh enough that kin."

Into Uncle Bob's eyes came a gleam so vindictive that even Soldier's ancient orbs could not fail to note it.

"They killed my David," said he. "Tonight I'm a-goin' ter watch 'em pay!"

"Hallelujah, Lord!" whispered the frightened man. "I wouldn't be in yere boots, Bobby. Not with all them ghosts 'twill be a-floatin' an' a-wailin' round yere shack! No sir!"

"Shut up!" snarled Holman. "Thar hain't no sech thing as ghosts."

The old soldier began to rock backward and forward, his hands clasped about his knees and only the whites of his eyes showing.

"Yes thar is, Bobby; yes thar is. After Gettysburg, I saw 'em fust. And those Virginia men I shot still ha'nt me. Right now 'tis certain thar's ghosts an' ha'nts an' debils a-roostin' on that rock pile, just a-waitin' fer them mortals to jine 'em. I know what I know! So don't yeh harry me about ghosts."

Uncle Bob took another pull at the corn whiskey. Then, getting some bread and meat from the shelf, he shared it with his friend. Outside, darkness came swiftly; inside, the blazing pine knots illuminated the cabin and sent strange shadows chasing over the walls. The wind tore at the roof, whistled round the eaves, and rushed on. The noise of the storm dissolved into individual and terrifying sounds—groans, sighs, shrieks.

For several hours Soldier crouched by the fire, muttering to himself now and then, while Uncle Bob, pipe in mouth, sat in his dilapidated chair and watched the blaze consume the logs. He would have liked to heap on fuel until the last shadow had been driven from the cabin, but his stock of firewood was too scanty to brook such extravagance.

It must have been nearly nine o'clock when the old man suddenly straightened, his eyes bulging.

"Oh, Lordy!" he screamed. "I seen it! It's o'er thar—in the corner!"

With surprising speed Uncle Bob reached for his rifle.

"Shet up, yer fool!" he ordered. "Thar hain't nothin' thar!" But the muzzle of his weapon swung in a half-circle about the room.

"Yes sir, Bobby, I seen it! Oh, hallelujah! Them ghosts is a-comin'—they's a-comin'!" Backward and forward he rocked in mental anguish. "I kin feel 'em, and I kin hyeah 'em, an' my left foot itches jest like it done when I got hit at Gettysburg!"

Uncle Bob grabbed Soldier by the shoulder.

"I aims ter lam' yer hade open with this yere shootin'-iron if yeh don't keep hit shet," he growled.

The old man subsided with reluctance, continuing at intervals to groan dismally. But he had succeeded in directing the mountaineer's thoughts into disastrous channels.

Holman saw in his mind the place where he had buried David. Was the grave as he had left it? Could there be any truth in what Brockwell had said? The screech of the wind more and more resembled voices crying out in agony. The log structure shook and shuddered, while an old coat hanging in the corner suddenly began to swing on its peg. Possibly a draft from under the door . . . yes, possibly. . . . All the eerie stories Uncle Bob had ever heard came creeping through his harassed brain. But very clear was the image of his son David. Whenever he stared at a particular spot, the figure took up a position to right or left of it. It never quite encountered his direct gaze, or entirely disappeared from his field of vision.

Now Soldier was rocking backward and forward again, his eyes rolled up exposing their whites.

"I'm a-listenin', young Dave. I hyeah yeh hollerin'. But yere pap he don' hyeah yeh. Glory be! For the Lawd's sake, spirit, don' yeh shout any louder."

Uncle Bob leaned forward. "Who says I don't hyeah David?"

Soldier increased his pendulatory movements, seeming to build upon the younger man's interest.

"You, young Dave, keep offen that train a-comin'. I'm warnin' you, 'cause yer pap's goin' to let it smash kerplunk into them rocks. Hallelujah! Hallelujah! Amen!"

The mountaineer drew his hand across his eyes. "Shet'up!" he muttered. "Fust thing hit'll be me that's a-seein' ghosts." He was trembling, and as he got out of his chair his legs shook. Pacing the length of the cabin, he returned to stand over the crouching veteran. "I tells yeh David's in his grave. That preacher lied ter me. Thar hain't nothin' goin' ter mess round hyeah. Nobody kin come back—not from the grave."

The wind shook the log structure as a dog shakes a rat, and brought with it other more terrifying sounds.

"Fer Lawd's sake, Bobby, hain't you fixin' to stop that train?" Soldier's tone held entreaty.

"I aims," answered Uncle Bob, "ter pay up them railroad fellers."

Soldier went back to his swaying, with a groan.

"Yer better quit," advised the mountaineer. "Hit won't help none—you goin' on so. And I cain't hyeah—"

Suddenly, grabbing up his rifle, he flung open the door.

"Come in!" he bellowed. "Hit's yer dad, David!" But only the storm entered. The snow swirled about his head and shoulders; great puffs of smoke belched from the fireplace, and Soldier held up his hands as if begging for mercy.

"Don't yer hyeah me?" pleaded Holman. "Hain't yer a-comin'?"

The blizzard's answer was a shriek of wind that nearly tore the door from his fingers. But the shapes dancing in the snow, the creatures just beyond the light from the fire, only shrank further away.

Stumbling back to his chair, he shook his fist at the shadows on the walls.

"Git inter the open! Thar's a Holman hyeah!"

"Hallelujah!" screamed Soldier in an ecstasy of fear.

The mountaineer let his arms fall. His beaked face was gray, and into his voice crept the monotonous intonation of a hypnotized man.

"Soldier's right, David. Don't yeh go ter ridin' on the Limited.

Thar's a rock-pile in front of her, and hit hain't a fit place ter come up on. Go back ter the hill, David, whar yer pap put yeh—"

His words died away, leaving him staring fixedly into the fire. A half-hour passed, a half-hour of cold and of horror, for the cabin had been chilled by the opening of the door. Then out of the night came a sound that again brought Uncle Bob to his feet. Long-drawn, wailing, it contrived to pierce the noise of the gale. Soldier heard it also, and his face worked convulsively.

"The Limited!" muttered Holman.

Once more the locomotive whistle screamed, but this time the blast died away in a peculiar manner. It was as if someone had struck Uncle Bob a terrific blow. He reeled across the cabin drunkenly.

"Hit hain't him! Damn the wind! You, Soldier, did yer hyeah David a-blowin' that whistle? Did yeh, I say?" Reaching the opposite wall, he groped along it like a blind man, only to halt the next moment and swing about, his eagle face working. "Hain't yeh got a tongue? Cain't yeh answer?"

"Yes sir, Bobby; I heered it!" screamed the veteran.

" 'Twas David."

"Yes sir! Hallelujah! Amen!"

Gone was the self-contained leader of the Holman faction, and in his place cowered an old man. Uncle Bob was shaking all o'er. He put his hands before his face as if to shut out some terrible picture.

"Ye're up on th' hill, David! I'm a-hearin' things. Hit's the wind. Ye cain't be a-signalin' yeh pap." He was pleading now, his voice a whine. "Keep offen that train, son! Don't yeh go to meddlin'. Git back to yeh grave whar I left yeh. Hit won't come agin. Hit was a trick of the storm—"

But it did! Like the call of a banshee, the sound penetrated the mud-chinked logs, ending with the wail Uncle Bob knew so well. Only one man had ever blown for the bend like that, and that man was dead. No; he couldn't be dead . . . if he were dead, his spirit had jerked the whistle cord . . . David's spirit on the Limited. . . .

Brockwell's warning flashed before Uncle Bob: "Wait for the ghost of your son." He saw the train five miles above the bend, rushing downward to where the landslide lay waiting, hidden under its white coat. He saw the long line of Pullmans, the sleeping passengers; but what appeared most vivid was the engine cab with David at the throttle. The whistle could mean but one thing: his boy was calling him! His boy who, he'd thought, could never call again.

And now a change came over Holman. The old light crept back into his eyes. He ceased trembling. It took but a moment for him to jerk on his coat and pick up his rifle. Some irresistible force suddenly commanded his body and brain. To reach the track in the short ten minutes required by the Limited to run the length of the bend—that was all that counted.

As he flung open the door Soldier stopped his rocking.

"Yeh cain't run off, Bobby! They'll get you . . . them ghosts!"

"I'm a-stoppin' the train!" shouted Uncle Bob. "David's a-ridin' on hit. Hain't yeh heered th' whistle?"

Shutting the door with a crash, he stumbled through the loose snow. The wind cut his face; the flying swirl blinded him, but he was unconscious of his own discomfort. He had received the one call he dared not disregard. His conviction that there was no hereafter crumbled, for had he not been presented with irrefutable proof to the contrary?

Battling every step, he struggled on. The night was black. Holman traveled entirely by the wonderful sense of direction that is a gift of the mountaineers. Already his hands were numb, and he found breathing difficult. Somewhere ahead lay the railroad and the rock pile; and somewhere ahead the Limited was racing to destruction. Even now the horror of what might happen to the passengers and crew did not affect him. What drove him on, heedless of the cold, of the snow, was the conviction that David had spoken from another world through the medium of that whistle.

Time and again Uncle Bob fell, and time and again he was forced to beat his hands against his body so he might continue to grip his rifle. Those vague shadows that had lurked outside the cabin did not bother him now. Perhaps they were pleased with him. Perhaps they, too, had been in league with David!

Ah! What was that? His foot had hit something hard. Bending swiftly, he managed to uncover a section of rail. He had reached the right-of-way in time! With a yell, which was instantly stifled by the storm, Holman began to follow the track northward. Here the going was comparatively easy, from a lack of drifts. Before leaving his cabin he had conceived a simple plan for stopping the train, and all that was necessary for its execution was to put as much distance as possible between himself and the rock pile, thus giving the engineer a chance to apply the brake.

Suddenly a headlight flashed round the bend and bore down upon him. He cocked his rifle and waited. Nearer, nearer drew the ball of fire, reflecting itself in the snow. When the locomotive was hardly a hundred yards away, Uncle Bob raised his gun. With the sharp report came absolute blackness. There was the crash of falling glass, followed by the shriek of the whistle. He stumbled clear of the track in time to watch the cars flash past, wheels striking sparks.

Five minutes later found Holman the center of a little group standing beside the panting locomotive. The engineer, fireman, and train and Pullman conductors were there, but those passengers who had suffered rude awakening by the abrupt application of the brakes did not venture forth into the storm to investigate the trouble.

An oil-torch on the tender platform was carrying on its own battle with the blizzard, while, far behind, the Limited had set off a fusee. The brilliant fire painted the snow in its immediate vicinity, attempted to reach flaming fingers through the night, and failed. From the engine the fusee looked like a pink moon perched between the rails.

"You sure can shoot," remarked the engineer for the third time, as he peered at the lanky figure of the mountaineer. "How'd you happen to see the slide on such a night?"

"I saw hit this evenin' afore dark," returned Uncle Bob.

There was a brief silence.

"Then," put in a conductor, "why the devil didn't you warn the nearest tower? What's the idea of smashing our headlight?"

"I reckon yeh wouldn't understand if I told yeh. My son David kept a-callin'. . . ."

The fireman leaped forward.

"Not Dave Holman?"

"That was his name."

"Look here, my friend," said the fireman; "quit kiddin' us. Dave Holman is dead. Don't I know! I fired for Holman for years—up to a couple of weeks before his train got smashed on this bend. If I hadn't happened to be laid off with a fever, I'd have been in that wreck, too. This is the first time I've ridden the Limited since he cashed in."

The train conductor spoke. "Whoever you are, you better come across with some facts. How do we know but what you're lying to us? Maybe this is a hold-up game?"

Uncle Bob stepped close to the man in uniform. "Don't yeh go to accusin' no Holman of that! I mought let daylight through yeh. Thar hain't another feller ever blew a whistle like David. He did it special fer me . . . so's I could see the train pass. Tonight hit come . . . hit's the fust time since he died."

"I'll be eternally damned!" ejaculated the fireman. "So *that* was it! You're Dave's father, eh? And when you heard me blow for the bend—"

"You—"

"Sure! The fireman generally pulls the whistle—not the engineer. Your son used to get me to blow what he called his 'private signal.' What made me do it tonight I don't know. Habit, I guess."

There was a huskiness in Uncle Bob's voice.

"It weren't habit, young feller. Don't yeh go to belittlin' the dead! Hit was David a-savin' his train. Yeh didn't see him, but my son was a-ridin' on that 'ere enjine jest now. No; yeh needn't look"—as incredulous eyes were turned toward the cab—"he hain't thar no more."

Abruptly the mountaineer shouldered his way clear of the group and plunged into the blizzard.

The following day the Reverend Timothy Brockwell, returning from the general store, discovered a visitor waiting for him in his little cabin. Uncle Bob Holman had entered unbidden, according to mountain custom. The missionary at once recognized the angular figure standing by the stove, but there was something unfamiliar in Holman's carriage. His shoulders seemed stooped; he looked older, less vindictive.

"Howdy!" greeted Brockwell, stamping the snow from his boots.

"Howdy," returned Uncle Bob.

"It's surprised and pleased I am to see ye," went on the missionary cheerfully. "Me conscience has been pesterin' me o'er what I said to you in meetin'. After all, a man has a right to his own opinion."

The mountaineer ignored the apology, his face stony.

"When a Holman finds he's wrong he comes aout with hit. I was wrong about David. He hain't up thar on the hill no more; he's a-takin' kere of the Limited. I'm a-goin' ter help him by sellin' my land to the railroad."

Brockwell showed his amazement, but he managed a smile.

"That's fine, Brother Holman! 'Tis a man ye are to say it. Of course, you know you are welcome at meetin'. . . ."

Uncle Bob drew himself up.

"Don't yeh go ter misunderstandin'. I hain't got no use fer you or yer fotched-on idees. You was right about David—which makes me hate the worse. I'm on one side, Brockwell, and you're on t'other. A Holman don't never change sides. But yeh hain't nothin' agin David; have yeh?"

The missionary controlled his rising anger.

"No," he replied.

"Then," said Uncle Bob, his voice quivering, "yeh mought pray fer his soul. 'Twouldn't do no hurt."

As he went out of the door he stumbled a little, and his step was none too steady in the snow.

Born in Virginia in 1885, Eugene Kinckle Jones became one of the most prominent black Americans of the twentieth century. He earned an A.B. from Virginia Union University, an M.A. from Cornell, and an honorary LL.D. from Virginia Union. He began his career in Kentucky as a teacher, and placed about a dozen stories in the 1920s and 1930s. His busy professional life forced him to quit writing. His efforts increased the size of the National Urban League from one full-time employee and a $2,500 annual budget to 399 full-time employees and a $1,500,000 annual budget. He died in 1954. "The Ghost Whistle" first appeared in Everybody's Magazine *in October 1923. This is the first time it has been reprinted.*

Richard claims his father was a crocodile. . . .

EIGHT

The Crocodile

Gouverneur Morris

The first locality of which I have any recollection was my father's library—a tall, melancholy room devoted to books and illusions. Three sides were of books, somberly bound, reaching from the floor to within three feet of the ceiling. Along the shelf, which was erroneously supposed to protect the tops of the top row of books from the dust with which our house abounded, were stationed, at precise intervals, busts done in plaster after the antique and death masks. Beginning on the left was the fury-haunted face of Orestes; next to him the lachrymose features of Niobe; following her Medusa, crowned with serpents. The rest were death masks— Napoleon, Washington, Voltaire, and my father's father. The prevailing dust, settled thick upon the heads of these grim images, lent them the venerable illusion of gray hair. The three walls of books were each pierced by a long, narrow window, for the room was an extension from the main block of the house, but over two of these the shutters were opaquely closed in winter and summer. The third window, however, was allowed to extend whatever beneficence of light it could to the dismal and musty interior. A person of sharp sight, sitting at the black oak table in the middle of the room, might, on a fine day, have seen clearly enough to write on very white paper with very black ink, or to read out of a large-typed book. Through the fourth wall a door, nearly always closed, led into the main hall, which, like the library itself, was a tall and melancholy place of twilight and illusions. When my poor mother died, in giving me birth, she was laid out in the library and buried from the hall. Consequently, according to old-fashioned custom, these apartments were held sacred to her memory rather than other portions of the house in which she had enjoyed the more fortunate phases of life and happiness. The room in which my mother had actually died was never entered by any one save my father. Its door was double locked, like that of our family vault in the damp hollow among the sycamores.

The first thing that I remember was that I had had a mother who had died and been buried. The second, that I had a father with a white face and black clothes and noiseless feet, whose duty in life was to shut doors, pull down window shades, and mourn for my mother. The third was a carved wooden box, situated in the exact center of the oak table in the library, which contained a scroll of stained paper covered with curious characters, and a small but miraculously preserved crocodile. I was never allowed to touch the scroll or the crocodile, but in his lenient moods, which were few and touched with heartrending melancholy, my father would set the box open upon a convenient chair and allow me to peer my heart out at its mysterious contents. The crocodile, my father sometimes told me, was an Egyptian charm which was supposed to bring misfortune upon its possessor. "But I let it stay on my table," he would say, "because in the first place I am without superstition, and in the second because I am far distant from the longest and wildest reach of misfortune. When I lost your mother I lost all. Ay! but she was bonny, my boy—bonny!" It was very sad to hear him run on about the bonniness of my mother, and old Ann, my quondam nurse, has told me how at the funeral he stood for a long time by the casket, saying over and over, "Wasn't she bonny? Wasn't she bonny?" and followed her to the vault among the sycamores with the same iteration upon his lips.

It was not until I was near eight years old that my father could bear the sight of me, so much had we been divided by the innocent share which I had had in my mother's death. But I was not allowed to pass those eight years in ignorance of the results of my being, or of the constant mourning to which my father had devoted the balance of his days. I was brought up, so to speak, on my mother's death and burial. Another child might have been nurtured thus into a vivid contrast, but I ran fluidly into the mold sober, and came very near to solidifying. Death and its ancientry have a horrible fascination for children. And for me, wherever I turned, there was a plenitude of morbid suggestion. Indeed, our plantation—held by the family from the earliest colonization of Georgia, spread along the low shore of a turbid river tributary to the Savannah, and dwindled, partly by mismanagement and partly by the nonsuccess of the rebellion, into a sad fulfillment of its bright colonial promise—was itself moribund. In the swamps, still showing traces of the dikes, which had once divided it into quadrilaterals, the rice which had been our chief source of income no longer flourished. The slave quarters, a long double row of diminutive brick cubes, each with one chimney, one door, and one window at the side of the door—such dwellings as children draw painfully on slates—still standing, for the most part, damp and silent, showed that the labor which had made the rice profitable was also a thing of other days. The house itself, a vastly tall block of burned bricks, laid side by side instead of end to end, as in modern building, stood on a slight rise of ground with its back to the river, among lofty and rugged red oaks, rotten throughout their tops with mistletoe. An avenue, roughened by disuse into a going worse than that of a lumber road, nearly a mile long, straight as justice, shaded by a double row of enormous live oaks, choked and strangled with plumes and beards of gray moss, led from the county road through the scant cotton fields and strawberry fields to the circle in front of the house. I used to fancy, and I think Bluebeard's closet lent me the notion, that the moss in the live oaks was the hair of unfortunate princesses turned gray by suffering and hung among the trees in wanton and cruel ostentation by their enemies.

Nothing but a happy and cheerful woman, a good housewife, ready-tongued and loving, could have lent a touch of home to our melancholy disestablishment. Women we had in the house, two black and ancient Negresses, rheumatic and complaining, one to cook and one to make the beds, and old Ann, my mother's Scots nurse, a hard, rickety female, whose mind, voice, and memory were pitched in the minor key. We had a horse, no mean animal, for my father had known and loved horses before his misfortune, but ugly and unkempt, and it was the duty of an old Negro named Ecclesiastes, the one lively influence about the place, to look after the interests of this little-used creature. My father and myself completed the disquieting group of living things. Concerning things inanimate, we had enough to eat, enough to wear, and enough to read. And the clothes of all of us were black. Until I was twelve years old I believed fervently that to mourn all his life long for dead wives and mothers was the whole end and destiny of man. In my twelfth year, however, my Uncle Richard, a florid, affectionate, and testy sportsman, paid us a visit on matters connected with the mismanagement of the estate. He stayed three days. On the first he shot duck, on the second quail; on the morning of the third he talked with my father in the library; in the afternoon he took me for a walk. In the evening he went away and I never saw him again.

"Richard," he had said, for I had been given his name, "I want to see the vault before I go. I haven't seen it since your mother was buried."

It was a warm, bright, still December day, the day before Christmas, and my uncle seated himself nonchalantly on the low wall which surrounded the vault, his knees crossed, his mouth closed on a big cigar, and his eyes fixed on the "legended door."

"People who go into that place in boxes," he said, "never come out. Has that ever occurred to you, Richard?"

I said that it had.

"You never saw your mother, my boy," he went on, "but you wear mourning for her."

"It seems to me almost as if I had known her," I said, "because—"

"Yes," cut in my uncle, "your father has kept her memory alive. He has neglected everything else in order to do that. Now tell—what was your mother like?"

I hesitated, and said finally, "She was very tall and beautiful."

My uncle smiled grimly.

"You would know her then," he said, "if you saw her? Answer me truthfully, and remember that other women are sometimes tall and beautiful."

I admitted a little ruefully, that I should not know my mother if I saw her.

"No, you wouldn't," said my uncle, "and for this reason, too: your mother had an amusing little face, but she was neither beautiful nor tall."

"But—" I began.

"Your father," my uncle interrupted, "has come to believe that his wife was tall and beautiful because he thinks that the idea of lifelong devotion to a memory is tall and beautiful. He is a little hipped about himself, my boy, and it makes me rather sick. I will tell you an anecdote. Once there was a man. He met a girl. For three weeks they talked foolishly about foolish things.

Then they were married. Nine months later a son was born to them, and the girl died. The man mourned for her. At first he mourned because he missed her. Then because he respected her memory. Then because he liked to pose as one everlastingly unhappy and faithful till death. He made everybody about him mourn, including the little child, his son, and finally he died and was put in the vault with the girl, and no one in the world was the better by one jot for any act of the man's life . . . Let me hear you laugh. . . ."

I looked up at him, much puzzled.

"Not at the anecdote," he said, "which isn't funny—but just laugh."

I delivered myself of a soulless and conventional ha-ha. My uncle put back his head and roared. At first I thought he must be sick, for until that moment I had never heard anyone laugh. I had read of it in books. And as a dog must have a first lesson in digging, so a child must have a first lesson in laughing. My uncle never stopped. He roared harder and louder. Tears ran down his cheeks. Something shook me, I did not know what. I heard a sound like that which my uncle was making, but nearer me and more shrill. I felt pain in my sides. My eyes became blurred and stinging wet. With these new sounds and symptoms came strange mental changes—a sudden knowledge that blue was the best color for the sky, heat the best attribute of the sun, and the act of living delightful. We roared with laughter, my uncle and I, and the legended door of the tomb gave us back hearty echoes. In the desert of my childhood I look back upon that oasis of laughter as the only spot in which I really lived. When my uncle went away he said: "For God's sake, Dickie, try to be cheerful from now on. I wish I could take you with me. But your father says no. Remember that the business of living is with Life. And let Death mind his own business."

The door closed behind that ruddy, cheerful man, and left us mourners facing each other across the supper table.

"Papa," said I presently, "haven't we a picture of Mama?"

"I had them all destroyed," said my father. "They were not like her. The last picture of her—" here he tapped his forehead—"will perish when I am gone. Ay, but laddie," he said, "she is vivid to me."

"Tell me about her, please, Papa," I said.

"She was a tall, stately woman, laddie," he said, "and

bonny—ay, bonny. Life without her has neither breadth nor thickness—only length."

"What color was her hair?" I asked.

"Boy," he said, "you will choke me with your questions. Her hair was black like the wing of a raven. Her eyes were black. She moved in beauty like the night."

Here my father buried his white face in his white hands, and remained so, his supper untasted, for a long time. Presently he looked up and said with pitiful effort:

"And what did you with your Uncle Richard?"

"We sat on the wall of the vault," I answered, "and laughed."

It was a part of my father's melancholy pose to renounce anger together with all the other passions, but at the close of my thoughtless words he sprang to his feet, livid.

"For that word," he cried, "ye shall suffer hellish."

And he dragged me, more dead than alive, to the library. But what form of punishment he would have inflicted me with I do not know. For a circumstance met with in the library—a circumstance trivial in itself and, to my mind, sufficiently explicable—shook my father into a new mood. The circumstance was this: that one of the servants (doubtless) had opened the carved box in the center of the table, taken out the crocodile, probably to gratify curiosity by a close inspection, and forgotten to put it back. But I must admit that at first sight it looked as if the inanimate and horrible little creature had of its own locomotion thrust open the box and crawled to the edge of the table. To instant and searching inquiry the servants denied all knowledge of the matter, and it remained a mystery. My father dismissed the servants from the library, returned the crocodile to its box, and remained for some moments in thought. Then he said, very gravely and earnestly:

"The possession of this dead reptile is supposed to bring misfortune upon a man. For me that is impossible, for I am beyond its longest and wildest reach. But with you it is different. Life has in store for you the possibility of many misfortunes. Take care that you do not bring them upon yourself. Pray that you have not already done so by giving vent to ghoulish laughter in the presence of your dead mother. Now take yourself off—and leave me with my memories."

That night there was an avenue of moss-shrouded live oaks in dreamland, down which I fled before the onrush of a mighty and ominous crocodile.

The next day was Christmas, and we resumed the monotony of our stolid and gloomy lives.

At eighteen I was a very serious and colorless youth. It may be that I contained the seeds of a rational outlook upon life, but so far they had not sprouted. My father's pervading melancholy was more strong in me than red blood and ambition. With him I looked forward to an indefinite extension of the past, enlivened, if I may use the paradox, by two demises, his and my own. I had much sober literature at my tongue tips, a condescending fondness for the great poets, a normal appetite, two suits of black, and a mouth stiff from never having learned to smile. I stood in stark ignorance of life, and had but the vaguest notion as to how babies are made. My father, preserved in melancholy as a bitter pickle in vinegar, had not aged or changed an iota from my earliest memory of him—a very white man dressed in very black cloth.

One morning my father sent from the library for me, and when I had presented myself said shortly:

"Your Uncle Richard is dead. He has left nothing. He was guardian, as you may know, of Virginia Richmond, the daughter of his intimate friend. She is coming to live with us. Let us hope that she is sedate and reasonable. You have never seen anything of women. It may be that you will fall in love with her. You may consult with me if you do, though I am no longer in touch with youth. She is to have the south spare room. You may tell Ann. She will be here this evening (my father always spoke of the afternoon as the evening). You may tell her our ways, and our hatred of noise and frivolity. If she is a lady that will be sufficient. I think that is all."

My father sighed and turned away his face.

"To a large extent," he said, "she has been educated abroad. I hope that she will not bore you. But even if she should, try to be kind to her. I know you will be civil."

"Shall you be here to welcome her?" I asked.

"I shall hope to be," said my father. "But I have proposed to myself to gather some of the early jasmine to—If I am urgently needed for anything I shall be in the immediate vicinity of the vault."

Virginia Richmond arrived in an express wagon, together

with her three trunks and two portmanteaus. She sat by the driver, a young Negro, with whom she had evidently established the most talkative terms, and did not wait for me to help her deferentially to the ground, but put a slender a foot on the wheel, and jumped.

"It's good to get here," she said. "Are you Richard?"

"Yes, Virginia," I said, and felt that I was smiling.

"Where's Uncle John?" she said. "I call him Uncle John because his brother was my adopted Uncle Richard always. And you're my Cousin Richard. And I'm your Cousin Virginia, going on seventeen, very talkative, affectionate, and hungry. How old are you?"

"I shall be nineteen in April," I said, "and my father is somewhere about the grounds"—I did not like to say *vault*—"and I will try to find you something edible. Are you tired?"

"Do I look tired?"

"No," I said.

"How do I look?"

"Why," I said, "I think you look very well. I—I like your look."

A better judge than I might have liked it. She had a rosy face of curves and dimples, unruly hair of many browns, eyes that were deep wonders of blue, a mouth of pearl and pomegranate.

"You," she said, "look very grave—and—yes, hungry. But you have nice eyes and a good skin, though it ought to be browner in this climate, and if you don't smile this minute I shall scream."

So I smiled, and we went into the house.

"My God! Cousin," she cried, to my mind most irreverently, "can't you open something and let in the light?"

"My father," I said, "prefers the house dark."

"Then let it be dark when he's in it," she cried, "and bright when he's out of it." And she ran to a window and struggled with the shutter. When she had flung that open she braced herself for an attack upon the next; but I bowed to the inevitable and saved her from the trouble of consummating it. The floods of light let thus into the hall and dining room seemed to my mind, sophisticated only in dark things, a kind of orgy. But Virginia was the more cheered.

"Now a body can eat," she said. "Ham—hoe-cake—Sally Lunn—is that Sally Lunn? Oh, Richard, I have heard of these things—and now—" wherewith she assaulted the viands.

"Don't you have ham in Europe, Virginia?" I asked.

"Ham!" she cried. "No, Richard, we have quarters of pig cut in thick slices—but meat like this was never grown on a pig. This," and she rapped the ham with her fork, and laughed to hear the solid thump, "was once part of an angel—a very fat angel."

"And you are a cannibal," I said. It was my first gallantry.

She gave me a grateful look.

"I had not hoped for it," she said. And for twenty minutes she ate like a hungry man and talked like a running brook.

"And now," she said, "for the house. First the library. Uncle Richard told me about all the death heads with dusty brows."

"Did he tell you about the crocodile?" I asked.

"Which crocodile?" said Virginia gravely.

"We have one only," I answered. "And I'm afraid it won't interest you very much. This is the library."

She was for having the shutters open.

"My father wouldn't like it," I said.

"This once," said she, and I served the whim.

"Yes," she said, after examination, "it *is* dreadful. Show me the crocodile, and then let's go."

But she was more interested in the scroll.

"It's Arabic," she said. "I can read it."

"You can read Arabic?"

"Indeed, yes. When Papa's lungs went bad we lived in Cairo. He died in Egypt, you know. Listen . . . It says: *'That man who holds me* (it's the crocodile talking) *in both hands, and cries thrice the name of Allah, shall see the face of his beloved though she were dead.'* "

"That's not our version," I said. "We believe that the possession of that beast invites misfortune."

"But you don't read Arabic," said Virginia. "Quick, Richard, take this thing in your two hands and call 'Allah' three times—loud, because it's a long way to Egypt—why, the man doesn't want to play—"

I had taken the crocodile in my hands, but balked, and I believe blushed, at the idea of raising my voice above the conversational pitch to further so absurd an experiment.

"Don't you want to see the face of your beloved?"

"I have none," said I.

"Then I'd cry 'Allah' till I had," said she. "Please—only three times."

So I held the crocodile, looking very foolish, and called three times upon the prophet. Then I turned to Virginia and met her eyes. The same thought occurred to us both, for we looked away. It was then that my father entered.

"Richard," he said, "the shutters—"

I made haste to close them, for I was blushing.

"This is Virginia!" said my father. "Welcome to our sad and lonely house. I thought just now that I heard some one calling aloud."

"It was Richard," said Virginia. "This scroll—" and she translated to my father.

"Oh, for faith to believe," said he. He took the crocodile in his hands and examined it with sad interest. "I have just come from her tomb, Virginia," he said. "I have been laying jasmine about it."

"Oh, the dear jasmine!" cried Virginia. "It's splendidly out, and tomorrow I shall fill the house with it."

"The house—" said my father hazily.

"Don't you like flowers, Uncle John?"

"I neither like nor dislike them," said my father.

"Then why, for heaven's sake—" but she stopped herself. "And you, Richard, don't *you* like them?"

"I have grown to think of them," said I, "if at all, as something odorous and sad, vaguely connected with funerals."

"Oh, no!" cried Virginia. "They are beautiful and gay, and they are connected with weddings—"

"Don't," said my father quickly. He was still holding the crocodile. "But I do not blame you, child. You will soon learn our ways. Since our great loss we have kept very quiet. . . . Ay, my dear, but you should have seen Richard's mother—was she not bonny, Richard?"

I bowed.

"I could fain look upon her again," he said. "And the scroll—does it not say *'even though she were dead?'* . . . Who was it called 'Allah'? . . . You Richard? . . . And what face did you see? . . ."

"Tell him," said Virginia.

"Ay, tell me," said my father.

"I saw Virginia's face," said I.

Then we left him. But in the hall Virginia laid her hand on my shoulder.

"Haven't you noticed?" said she.

"What?" said I.

"Your father," said she.

"No," said I. "What ails him?"

Virginia tapped her forehead.

"Mildewed here," said she.

"I don't understand," said I.

"Never mind then, Richard," said she. "I'll take care of you."

That night I dreamed that I heard my father calling the name of Allah. But in the morning I rose early, and, going to the woods, gathered an armful of jasmine for Virginia.

She received it cheerfully.

"Is this—er—in *memory* of any one?" she asked.

"Yes," I said boldly, "it's in memory of me."

"Then I will keep it, Richard," she said. "Flowers are for the living."

"Yes," I said.

"And crocodiles," said she, "are for the dead."

For a long time I looked upon the innocent gayness and frivolity of Virginia with blinking eyes, as a person blinks at the sudden match lighted in the middle of the night. I had been pledged to darkness from my eariest years, and now, while my character, still happily plastic, was receiving its definite stamps, I blinked hankeringly at the light that I might have loved, and at the same time steeled myself to go through with the prearranged marriage. As in the Yankee states children are brought up to believe that it is wicked to be joyous on Sunday so I had been taught to believe of every twenty-four hours in the week.

I cannot think peacefully of that unhappy period in Virginia's life forced on her by us two moribunds. She was the sun, soaring in bright, beneficent career, brought suddenly to impotence by a London fog. And I take it that to be bright and happy, and to fail in making others so, is the most grievous chapter in life. But Virginia's glowing nature had its effect on mine, and in the end she set my spirits dancing. With my father, however, the effect of a madcap sunbeam in the house was altogether different. For it served only to plunge him deeper into gloom and regret. If we came to dinner with him fresh from the joyous morning and in love with laughter, the misery into which he was too palpably thrown reacted so that for all three of us the afternoon became clouded. Sometimes his sorrow would take the form of mocking at all things peaceful and pleasant. In particular the institution of marriage aroused in him hostility.

"Ay, marry," he would say, "Richard, and beget death. It may be hereditary in our family. Exchange your wife, who is your soul, for a red and puling inconsequence, that shall serve down the tiresome years to remind you day and night of the sunshine which has been extinguished for you."

And I remember once retorting on him sharply to the effect that if he threw me so constantly in my own face I would leave his roof, and in the intemperance of the moment I fully purposed to do so. "I will do no worse among strangers," I said, "or in hell, for that matter."

My father fairly shriveled before the unfilial words and retreated so pathetically from his foolish position that my attack melted clean away.

"But why," I said afterward to Virginia, "wouldn't he let me go? Why did he say that he could not live without me? And why, in God's name, when it was all over, did he cry?"

And Virginia thought for a few moments, which was unusual with her, and said presently: "Richard, either your father is the greatest lover that ever lived, or else he is a tiresome egomaniac. Frankly, I believe the latter. You are an accessory, a dismal carving on the moldy frame in which he pictures himself. When I first came I used to tell him how terribly sorry I was that he had lost his wife. But I've given that up. Between you and me, it made him a little peevish. Now I say to him, 'Uncle Richard, you're the unhappiest man I ever saw,' and that comforts him tremendously. Sometimes he asks me if I really think so, and when I say that I do he almost smiles. And I have caught him, immediately after a scene like that, looking at himself in the mirror and pulling his face even longer than usual. . . . There, I've shocked you."

"No, Virginia," I said, "but I should hate to believe of any man what you believe of my father. His grief must be sincere."

"It may be," said Virginia, "or it may have been once. I believe it isn't now. I believe that if your mother came to life your father would—"

Virginia did not finish. We were seated in the cool hall, for the porch was piping hot, and our conversation was interrupted by a loud cry emanating from the library.

"Allah—Allah—Allah!"

"If I weren't charitable, which I am," said Virginia, "I would say that that was done for effect. He knows we're here. Bet you, he's looking at himself in the glass."

"Virginia," I began angrily, and I was for telling her that she was ill-natured, when the library door opened and my father came out.

"Oh!" said he, with a fine start, "I did not know you were there. . . ."

Virginia gave me one look, at once hurt and amused. Then she turned to my father and said gravely: "Did anything happen, Uncle Richard, when you called? Did you see the—the face—of—"

"No, child," said my father sadly. "I was so foolish, I may say undignified, as to try a childish and foolish experiment. It is unnecessary to say that the tall and stately form and classic face of Richard's dear mother did not appear to me. But I caught a glimpse of another face, Virginia—a face white and broken by sorrow and regret, a face that it was not pleasant to see . . . How it all comes back to me," he went on. "Here I stood by her casket, ignorant of time and place—ignorant of all earthly things but loss—and for the last time looked upon her beauty. No, not for the last time,

For all my daily trances
 And all my nightly dreams
Are where thy bright eye glances
 And where thy footstep gleams.

"Ay, child, but she was bonny! Was she not bonny, Richard?"

I do not know what prompted Virginia to ask the sudden question which turned my father's face for a moment into a painful blank and placed him in a position from which he extricated himself, I am forced to believe, only by a real and searching act of memory.

"What was her name?" said Virginia quickly.

It was a full half minute before my father managed to stammer my mother's name. But during the ensuing days it was constantly on his lips, as if he wished to make up to it for the oblivion into which it had been allowed to drop.

That afternoon it rained violently, and Virginia persuaded me to explore with her the mysteries of the ancient and cobwebby attic that occupied the whole upper floor of our house. It was a place in whose slatted window blinds sparrows built their nests, and in which a period, that of my mother's brief mistress-ship, had been perfectly preserved. It was the most cheerful part of the house.

Among other things we found in a trunk of old fashion my mother's wedding regalia. A dress of apple-green silk embroidered about the neck and wrists with tiny forget-me-nots, faded to the palest shade of lilac; a pair of tiny shoes of the same apple-green silk, with square toes and dark jade buttons; a veil of venetian point, from which a large square had been cut, and the brittle remnants of a wreath—my mother's wedding wreath, which old Ann had often told me was combined of apple and orange flowers. When Virginia stood up and held the neck of my mother's dress level with the neck of her own, it did not reach to her ankles, and she smiled at me.

"Richard," she said, "I could not get into this dress. Your tall and stately mother was no bigger than I."

"And no sweeter, I fancy," said I. For the being together with Virginia over my mother's things had suddenly opened my heart to her.

"Oh, Virginia," I went on, "it makes me sick to think of your living on in this dead house. I want you to be happy. I want to make you happy. You are the only good thing that was ever in my life. I know it now. And I—I want to be happy, too. . . ."

We explored the attic no more that day, and after supper we told my father.

From the very announcement to him of our engagement a marked change came over my father. Hitherto his influence had been for darkness, but of a silent and quiet character, like that which clouds spread through a wood at noon; but now he had become baleful and pointed in his efforts to make us unhappy.

To set in motion any machinery of escape was too impracticable and tedious to be thought of. Had I been for myself alone, I would have left him at this period and endeavored to support myself. But with Virginia to care for—and I could not leave her while I made my own way—the impulse was empty. He made attacks on our happiness with tongue and contrivance. He descended to raillery and sneers, even to coarseness. Yet when the confines of endurance had been approached too closely, and I threatened to cross them, he clung to me with such a seeming of feeling and patheticalness that I was forced to hold back. Through these harsh times Virginia was all sweetness and patience, but her cheeks lost their color and her body the delicious fullness of its lines.

My father was at times so eccentric in his behavior that I had it often in mind to ask the investigations of a physician. But as often the horror of a son prying after madness in his father withheld me. As always, his actions centered around the observance of his private grief. And to that great mental structure which he had made of my mother's beauties and virtues, he added incessantly wings and superstructures, until we had portrayed for us a woman in no way human or possible. To draw odious comparisons between Virginia and my mother, between his capacity for loving and my own, were his constant and indelicate exercises.

"Do you think you love, Richard?" he would say. "If she were to die this night, where would your love be at the end of the year? Is she bonny enough to hold a man's heart till death shall seek him out too? She's well enough in her way, your Virginia, I'll not deny that. But does a man remember what was only well enough? Does a man remember the first peach he ate? Nay, he will not remember that. But will he forget the first time that he heard Beethoven? Your mother, she was that—rich, strong music, she was—the bonny one—the unforgettable. Ah, the majesty of her, Richard, that was only for me to approach!"

And such like, till the heart sickened in you. Often he made us go with him to the vault and listen to his speeches, and kneel with him in the wet. Finally he played on us a trick that had in it something of the truly devilish, and was the beginning of the end. He began by insisting that we should be married and appointing a day. There was to be a minister, ourselves, and the servants. We were glad enough to be married, even on such scanty terms, and I well remember with what eagerness I arose on the glad morning, and slipped into my better suit of black, for I had no gayer clothes. Virginia did not come down to breakfast, but toward the close of that meal, at which my father was the nearest he ever came to being cheerful, I heard her calling to me from the upper story. When I knocked at her door she opened it a little and showed me a teary face. "Richard," she said, "they've taken away my clothes and left only a black dress. I *won't* be married in black."

"Does it matter, dear?" I said. "Put it on and we will ransack the attic for something gayer."

But we found the attic locked. My father had provided against resistance.

"Does it matter, dear?" I said. "It's not your clothes I'm marrying—it's my darling herself."

So she smiled bravely and we went downstairs. The ceremony was appointed for eleven in the morning. But at that hour neither the minister, nor my father, nor the servants were to be found. We waited until twelve. Then I went out to look for my father. I went first to the vault and there found him. He was kneeling in the wet, facing the door, and holding in his hands the stuffed crocodile. He had, I suppose, been calling the name of Allah in the wild hope of seeing my mother's face.

"Have you forgotten that we are to be married today?" I said.

He rose, hiding the crocodile beneath his coat.

"No," he said. "I had not forgotten that. Why should I be forgetting that? But the minister, he could not come—at the last minute he could not come."

"Then you should have told us," I said sternly.

"Would you be angry with me, Richard, my son?" he answered gently.

"Why couldn't the minister come?" I said, giving no heed to his question.

The gentleness, which must have been play-acting, went out of my father's voice.

"The minister," he said sneeringly, "faith, the minister, he had a more important funeral to attend."

My gorge rose and fell.

"What have you done with Virginia's trunk?" I said.

"It will be back in her room by now," said my father.

"Thank you," said I, "and good-day to you."

"Good-day, Richard? Good-day?"

"Yes," said I. "I am going to take her away."

"You'll not go far without money," said he.

"With heart," said I, "we shall go to the ends of the earth."

My father turned to the vault and addressed the shade of my mother. "Hear him," cried he, "hear him that took you from me. He's going to the ends of the earth. He turns his back upon your hallowed bones . . ." His words became unintelligible.

During the packing of my trunk I left off again and again to go to Virginia's door to ask if all were well with her. For there had been a look in my father's face which haunted me like a hint of coming evil. And although nothing but good came of that afternoon, still its events were so strange as to make me believe that men are often forewarned of the unusual. It was about three o'clock that suddenly I heard my father shrieking aloud in his library. Thinking that sickness must have seized him, I bounded down the stairs to offer assistance or search for it if necessary. But except for a pallor unusual even with him, he was not apparently sick. The crocodile lay belly up on the table, as if it had been hastily laid down.

"What's the matter?" I asked.

"Richard," said my father, in great excitement, "the door of the vault is open. But now I heard it creaking upon its hinges—"

Virginia, who had heard the shrieks, now joined us, her face white with alarm.

"What is it?" she cried.

"The resurrection of the dead!" cried my father, and, thrusting my detaining arm suddenly aside, he literally burst out of the house. I followed at my best speed, and Virginia brought up the rear. In this order we raced through the woods, brightly mottled with sunshine and shadows, in the direction of the vault. Run as I would, I could not gain on my father, who seemed to possess the speed of a pestilence. As he ran he kept crying: "God is merciful! I shall see the face of my beloved."

I cannot account for what happened. A little lady, dressed in apple-green silk, with a wreath of flowers upon her head, appeared suddenly in the path, ahead of and facing my father. She held out her arms as if to detain him. But he bore down upon her at full speed, and I cried out to warn her. Then they met. But there was no visible or audible sign of collision. My father literally seemed to pass through her. He ran on, always at top speed, and the little lady in the apple-green silk was no longer to be seen in any direction. Yet she seemed to have left an influence in the bright forest, gentle and serene, and I could swear that there lingered in the air a faint smell of apple blossoms and orange blossoms. And it may be the echo of a cry of pain—the ghost of a cry.

When I came to the vault, its door was wide open, and I found my father within, breaking with his thin hands the lid from my mother's coffin. I was not in time to prevent him from completing his mad outrage. The lid came clean away with a ripping noise, and my father gazed eagerly at the face thus rudely revealed to the light of day. But what horrible alchemy of the grave had brought into shape the face upon which my father looked so eagerly is not for mortal man to know. For the face was not my mother's, but his own.

Gently he laid his hand on the forehead, and gently he said: "Was she not bonny, Richard? . . . Was she not bonny?"

Our honeymoon was nearly a week old, when one morning Virginia and I were taking breakfast in the glass dining room of the old Hygeia Hotel. The waiters, the other guests, the cups, saucers, knives, and spoons all made eyes at us, but we were wonderfully happy. An old gentleman approached our table with a kind of a sad tiptoe gait. Tears were in his eyes.

"My dear boy," he said, "I have not the heart to congratulate you on your happiness, for I cannot help remembering what a good father you have so recently lost. I was present at his wedding, and I have not seen him since. But as you see—" and the old gentleman drew attention to the tears in his eyes.

"Aren't you mistaken, sir?" said I. "Aren't you thinking of somebody else's father?"

"Why, no," said he, "your father was ________________. Don't tell me that he wasn't."

"I shall have to," I said, "for he wasn't. My father was a crocodile."

*Gouverneur Morris, a banker and a writer, was born to a wealthy New York family in 1876. He received his B.A. from Yale. Morris produced more short stories than O. Henry but is virtually forgotten now. Sprinkled throughout his works are several striking examples of fantasy and horror such as "Back There in the Grass," in which island natives live on the beach because of their terror for what lies back there in the grass (*It and Other Stories*, 1912). Morris died in 1953. "The Crocodile" was first published in the November 25, 1905, issue of* Collier's. *A droll satire of Poe's obsessive plotlines, it is anthologized here for the first time.*

Valentine's Day on the bayou brings more than red roses. . . .

NINE

The Jabberwock Valentine

Talmage Powell

Out of New York, the Memphis-bound jetliner slanted its nose below the horizon and knifed into the cumulus. The clouds, so pristinely white and inviting moments ago, swallowed the aircraft in a slithery gray ooze. In my present mood it was no strain on the imagination to feel that the descent was into a repulsive nether region, primeval, roiling with unknown forces.

I looked at her lovely profile hovering in the seat beside me, looked away, forced my head to rest against the seat, and drew a long, careful breath.

I was not experiencing a reaction to flying. I flew as naturally and exuberantly as I sang off-key in an invigorating morning shower.

I was ridden with this certainty: she was going down into the presence of death.

Since the spiritualist and shrink can't explain it, I can go no further than the experts, the specialists. I can only make a statement about that which transpires.

The first transpiration in my memory was of myself as a young boy out racing about on his first bicycle. From nothingness came a sudden sensation. It burst over me with the force of a silent scream. Colors spun through my head; they froze, in an image of a boy, myself, tangled and bleeding in the ruin of the bicycle at the next intersection.

I had stopped the bike somehow, left foot extended and touching the pavement, and now I looked wildly about, as if trying to find out what I should see.

The intersection was empty, peaceful. The image slipped away, leaving an unpleasant patina on the skin and a shortness of breath in its wake.

The sound of an engine broke the quietude, rising from snarling whisper to thunder. A car careened through the intersection, a man lolling drunkenly behind the steering wheel.

And I, having stopped my bike in the place and time that I did, missed my appointment. I saw the drunken face in profile, rather than gazing straight ahead at the loose, slavering features swaying behind an onrushing windshield.

I pedaled quietly home, said nothing to anyone, and the moment slipped into the maw of the memory of an active, growing boy.

I became a senior in high school, took a job as counselor at a summer camp. And I snapped awake one warm, soft night swathed in the peculiar sweat. I punched the pillow to go back to sleep, telling myself I'd dreamed, had a nightmare. I lay back, closed my eyes. And the scene flashed against my lids: boys mindless with terror, milling and screaming while tongues of hungry flames curled over them.

Muttering scorn for my own stupidity, I rose from my sweaty cot. Wearing the shorts in which I slept, I padded from the counselor's quarters across the moon-kissed quadrangle to cabin B: it was dark, serene, steeped in sleep. But having already behaved like a fool, I went on inside.

I smelled the first acrid taint of smoke, saw the fireflylike flickering in the corner. I turned on the lights, rousted eight confused, blinking boys from their bunks, and put out the small fire before it made its way out of the waste can. It had moldered and finally found life in a wadding of shoeshine rags. Some boy, experimenting with cigarettes after lights-out, had left a spark in a butt tossed in the waste can. We turned up the identity of the culprit, notified his parents, and put him on garbage detail for a week. He departed camp, thumbing his nose and lighting a cigarette.

I was eighteen, and the Vietnam War was winding down, but the draft board had no precognition that America would cut and get out within eighteen months. So I came to manhood in walks through steaming jungles, firefights, and temporary forgetfulness in Saigon whorehouses.

The patrol that day was a piece of cake—to take up station in a friendly village. But the colors burst in my head and I halted my men. I scattered them to cover, enfilading the trail. On their bellies, like bugs, vermin, they sweated in the heat, scratched insect bites, and muttered about the sergeant's guts and sanity. ComPost crackled the radio. Where the hell is Sergeant Barnard? And I made no reply, no move, except to threaten to shoot a skinny private who finally said to hell with this, ain't it a friendly?

And as the sun was sinking, Vietcong came creeping from the village to wonder why the intended victims hadn't come. The Cong were killed; the fire sweeping the trail was too deadly for it to be otherwise. One was a thin-faced boy who had no excuse to own a razor. I wept inwardly and wished the sun would not show itself over the jungle tomorrow morning.

Back in the alien world of home, I enrolled in the University of North Carolina at Chapel Hill. Lacking the sophistication of a 'Nam education, my peers seemed childish, callow, and naive, and I formed no lasting relationships.

One day during my senior year one of those fractured moments of nontime came from nowhere, and I got in the VW and drove home to Asheville. I was not empowered to alter this future moment, but I was with my father at my dying mother's bedside.

Upon graduation, I landed a junior exec post in marketing in a corporation that made mufflers for cars, trucks, tractors, lawn mowers, boats. Lucky me. Enviable start from which I could one day achieve the privilege of lunching in the penthouse dining room.

I saved some money, got miserably seasick on a freighter wallowing its way to ports in Europe, and backpacked and bummed my way through Spain and Italy.

I thought a lot about going to India, land of gurus. But I already knew the lingo: channeling, trans-spatial existence, the Akhasic Records, trance-states, astral projection. I had done my reading and research; I had sampled cult experiences. I was way ahead of most of the field and had discovered no guru, medium, or reincarnate worth emulating. They were either charlatans—or touched reality even more tenuously than I.

I went to work in the State Department as an assistant to an assistant secretary. As the years ticked off I became an assistant secretary, liaison to the White House, director of research, ambassadorial courier. Very nice life. Good pay, expense money, movement among the powerful, consorting with intellectual equals, lots of travel first class, in and out of American embassies in Europe. Female relationships of course, but never the satisfying of the quiet hunger within me.

Then in Paris I met her. The mellifluous voice of the ambassador at a party for a bigwig from Algiers: "Cody, I want you to meet Valentina Marlowe. Val, Cody Barnard, one of the unsung who mop up spills of politicians."

Of course I had heard her name, seen her picture. What model has been more photographed than Valentina Marlowe? I turned, and our eyes met, and I don't know how long the ambassador lingered. I can't say what she was wearing or what was said in those first moments, or how we escaped the cloying boredom of the chitchat, clink of glasses, muted strains of a string quartet. By unspoken mutual agreement we sought out quiet in the lights of Paris. We had known each other always. We talked as if picking up a conversation begun and suspended perhaps a week ago.

We had four days that time. Simple pleasures. Communion. Lovers. But more—also friends.

"I'll be leaving tomorrow, Cody. I always spend Valentine's Day with the home folks. My birthday, you know. Reason my mother tagged me with the given name."

Home was Wickens, Louisiana.

"How long will you be in Wickens, Val?"

"I'll leave the day after Valentine's Day."

"To Washington," I said.

The oblique look from the expressive violet eyes in the wonderfully devised face. A toss of the mane of black, a wisp immediately returning to nuzzle her cheek. "You rat, I might have known you were behind the invitation."

"Made a suggestion in the right ears, that's all." I laughed. "Doing my duty for my country. A symposium on women's rights wouldn't be complete without the presence of the world's most beautiful model."

"Then write my speech! I need ten minutes, and it's been driving me up a wall."

Now it was another February, month of the odd day every fourth year to reset the calendar, month of the day given to Saint Valentine . . . Which? There were two saints of the name, you know.

And the clouds outside the descending aircraft were as filthy as the darkness in which I'd awakened three nights ago. The colors in frozen frame . . . her face in death, partly obscured by a swirling of water . . . the sounds of bullfrogs *harrumping,* the smell of swampy Louisiana bayou earth . . . then only the smothering darkness.

Luminous dial of the bedside clock: 3:00 A.M. I'd got dressed, gone out, and walked the quiet streets of Georgetown until the eastern sky showed gray.

From a phone booth I had called my secretary. No apology for rousting her out of bed. "I won't be in today, nor for the next several days."

Her voice cleared the cobwebs of sleep. "I don't understand, Mr. Barnard."

"It isn't necessary for you to do so."

"But your appointments, correspondence, the report—"

"Make excuses, Miss Clowerson! You're very good at that sort of thing. Parcel out my chores, take up the slack, use your Washington logic."

"Well, I can always say that someone very close to you suddenly died."

I slammed the phone in its hook. Damn bitch! Damn unwitting, cruel, cruddy bitch!

A shuttle flight. A taxicab. Val surprised, her face lighting happily, heartbreakingly, when she saw me standing with a packed overnight and garment bag.

A kiss. Hug. A herding into the apartment with its view of Central Park.

"You're going to Wickens this year with me!"

"Isn't it time I met your mother, and this George you're always talking about, and Keith, Lissa, and Reba who runs the house like a Captain Bligh, and the others?"

"Oh, Cody . . . I'm so glad you could arrange it. God, this will be the best Wickens year ever!"

Now her elbow nudged me. "Hey, Cody . . . Memphis below. Then a short commuter flight and you'll experience Wickens, no less."

My sham yawn was convincing enough. She'd turned her attention from my closed eyes to look out the window as the jet broke cloud level, and Memphis and the Mississippi River spread like a far-flung relief map.

She laughed. "He was a great songwriter, but he was wrong on one point."

"Who is that?"

"Ira Gershwin . . . the lyricist. Look down there at the city, the farms, fields, docks, river craft just rolling along. I ask you. Is that an Old Man River? Male chauvinism, that's what. Old Man River indeed! Any dummy from this part of the world knows the Mississippi is female."

Our shoulders pressed as we both looked down before the plane wheeled for approach and the wing cut the river out of sight.

"Pure female," I agreed. "Giver of life. Mercurial in mood from her icy beginnings in the north to her turgid joining with the gulf. Comforter. Angry mistress, when she spews over her banks, scorning the levees trying to hem her in."

"Don't forget her mysteries." Val smiled. "Beneath the warm, peaceful invitation of her surface are snags to rip the stoutest boat to pieces."

"Oh, her mysteries fascinate me most."

"I'm glad you understand, Cody." She tweaked my nose. "How could I respect a man who didn't see a truth so clearly?"

"Hell, it's obvious. If the Mississippi is an old man, then the Statue of Liberty is a transvestite."

She laughed, but I had a shriveling coldness inside.

For the *n*th time I thought to myself: Keep her away from Wickens, Louisiana, this Valentine year. If you can't think of a logical reason, let her think you've lost your mind. Coerce, plead. Do it physically. Lock her in a room someplace and stand guard at the door until the Valentine hour is past.

But somehow I knew that this was not the alternative future that would work. Neither Wickens nor the forces would vanish at my whim. Wickens would be there all the years of her life. The issue had to be settled. There was no escape or normal safety until the issue was put to rest.

Val and I were among a trickle of passengers exiting the commuter plane in Wickens. We were hardly down the ramp steps when a man and woman gathered us in, beaming joy, smothering Val, pumping my hand.

"Mom, George, this is the man!"

"Wow! Toss you for this one, Val. Hi, Cody. I'm Elva."

"I know," I said, smiling. "Would have known you anywhere." And it was true. She was the gracefully aging pattern from which Val had been cut.

"And this is George," Elva said.

"Glad to know you, George."

"Likewise." His handshake was good—firm, but not bone crushing. He was a man who didn't have to display, to prove anything. Mentally I agreed with what Val had said about George Crandall. He was a presence. You either liked him immediately or shied away. I liked the little echo of gentleness in the boom of his voice. I liked the intelligence of the perceptive brown eyes in the face that might have been carved from oak with a trench knife.

This retired army officer, this Colonel George R. Crandall, was second father to Valentina. He was hardly the stereotype southern colonel. No fine-boned aristocrat, no white Vandyke, no broad-brimmed, floppy panama hat or string necktie. He was a tanned, fit light heavyweight in sandals, poplin slacks, and a knitted shirt on which the corners of the collar curled slightly. A man who sweated easily but wouldn't particularly mind heat or cold.

"Would you like a drink?" he was asking.

"You kidding?" Val said. "We won't have to wait for the luggage. I want a drink—at home."

Elva drove. Her car was a modest Chevy. The day was lovely, February cool but touched with that southern Louisiana sense of semitropic in the breath from the gulf, the river, the bayous and swamps. George pointed out landmarks of possible interest and asked about my work. It was the usual, expected small conversation, but his interest was real, quick, lively.

My impression of Wickens was of modern hustle and a scorn for the passage of time. Taking sustenance from its busy waterfront and natural gas industry, Wickens was state-of-the-moment shopping centers, half a dozen high-rise buildings over a downtown where revitalization had preserved the more historic sites. Wickens was also previous-century on streets where time had been barred, where there was still a corner grocery, a drugstore in an ancient building . . . it surely had a marble-counter soda fountain. A statue of a Confederate soldier stood guard over a park where old men played checkers beneath hoary live oaks and aged palm trees and pines bearded with Spanish moss. A few young mothers chatted on benches, rocking baby carriages and watching older children at play near an iron-railed fountain. Tract homes and condos hadn't conquered Wickens. There were broad, tree-shaded streets of impeccable old gingerbread houses from which maidens in crinoline might burst forth at any moment to prepare for a lawn party.

George saw my interest in passing details. "Get to you, if you're not careful," he laughed. "Best damn spot on earth—except during hurricane season. Phobia of mine."

He didn't strike me as a man of any phobias, which just goes to show.

"Last year, by God, when Charlie was taking on such a load coming up through the gulf, twisting a drilling platform like it was wet spaghetti, Elva loaded me onto a plane and we shopped and saw the sights in Montgomery, Charlie having aimed straight for Wickens. You were in 'Nam, I understand. Jesus . . . in those parts I was once in a typhoon . . . left me without a nail on a single finger. You strike me as a tolerable sportsman, Cody. Golf? Fish? Maybe one night you'd like to break out a watersled and try your hand at frog gigging? Nobody cooks fresh frog legs quite like Elva."

"I've eaten them in Paris." I grinned.

"Paris? Where the hell is that? For good food you got to go to New Orleans, or Elva's kitchen."

We had reached the eastern suburbs, not quite in the country. The houses dotted a landscape of sweeping lawns, small pastures, hedges, fences of wood, iron, chain link, split rail; lines of trees suggested boundaries between acreages of sizes to be called estates.

Elva turned onto a white-graveled driveway that wended between rows of sheltering willows. I saw a farmhouse that was comfortably old southern, white frame, two stories, tall windows, a porch rambling across the front, a towering fieldstone chimney snugged against the eastern end.

George led me upstairs to a spacious front corner bedroom. Beneath the tall ceiling was a solid, old poster bed, chest, bureau, huge oval mirror, writing desk, a Tiffany lamp on a table beside the invitation of a lounging chair.

"Your bath is right there." George nodded at a door in the rear wall. "The wardrobe filling the corner should do. No closet

. . . House was built by Valentina's great-grandpa, and houses were taxed by rooms in those days. Bureaucrats of course counted a closet as a room, and a hell of a lot of people decided to make the wardrobe industry what it was for a while."

He paused in the doorway. "Just follow your druthers while you're with us, Cody. We don't live on ceremony. Shoot any food allergies, or preferences, up front. We'll do our best."

"Thanks, George. Not picky in the mess hall. If it's creeping, just kill it before you serve."

"Stow your gear, freshen up if you like, and come on down as it suits your mood."

Half an hour later, I heard the pleasant rise and fall of voices as I went down the oaken-banistered stairway into the spacious lower hallway.

They were in the living room, the forepart of the house off the hall, and Val saw me instantly when I appeared in the broad doorway.

She came and took my hand, ran the fingers of her other hand lightly along my temple. "Your hair is curling a little from the shower damp." She smiled. "Come let me display you. People, this is Cody. Cody, meet Lissa Aubunelli, with whom I've had some pigtail pullings, and Keith Vereen. Careful with State Department classified in Keith's presence, Cody. He's one of those monsters known as the press. Publishes the local daily newspaper and brought the first, and only, television station to Wickens, a CBS affiliate."

Lissa was plump, dark, big brown eyes, brown hair cut short and sassy, teeth that flashed almost as perfectly as Val's, round, pink-cheeked face with chronic little moisture swatches beneath her eyes.

She gave me a hug and peck on the cheek, a sigh as she stepped back, head tilted, looking me over. "Val the stinker . . . really got the pick of the litter."

Keith Vereen was smiling at her, offering his hand to me. He was tall, slender, slightly stooped, sandy-haired with quick, sharp blue eyes in a finely boned face. His movements suggested a carefully tuned conditioning and the reflexes of a cat.

"A real pleasure, Cody. But you're no stranger. Val's carryings-on about you in letters to her mother made you a friend quite awhile back.

"How about a drink, appetizer?" Keith suggested. We drifted

toward a buffet burdened with the wherewithal.

"Bourbon?" Lissa said. "I'll pour; want it neat, or with branch, soda, ginger ale?"

"A splash of branch is fine."

"How about a Sunday feature, Cody?" Keith said. "Isn't every day an assistant secretary of state surfaces in Wickens. I'd even ask Lissa to write it."

"No way," Lissa said. "Hunk like him . . . I couldn't be the least bit objective."

Our hands touched as I took the proffered drink. "You're a writer?"

"The best by-hell investigative reporter in the state of Louisiana," Keith said, "perhaps the South."

"Why stop there?" Lissa asked.

She didn't look like an investigative reporter; she looked like a jolly young woman with innocent devilment behind her eyes and pasta recipes in her head.

"She started on the *Sword,* which is what my grandpappy called the paper when he bought the first linotype machine. Unfortunately, we lost her in a short time to the *New Orleans Observer.* Been there how long now, Lissa?"

"Seven years, kiddo. Don't bother to ask my age."

"She's had offers from the *Washington Post, New York Times,* a news magazine or two," Val said in pride of her lifelong friend.

"They're not in New Orleans, lamb. They're in places where there's no old French market and the yokels don't know how to listen to Dixieland music."

Elva and George came in, beginning a pleasant hour. I felt so at home, I might have been born in Wickens.

Despite the comfort of the poster bed, I didn't sleep well. Finally, about two in the morning, I gave it up. I put on a robe and socks, and slipped downstairs to the kitchen. I filched makings, cold chicken roasted in a piquant Louisiana basting, French bread, shreds of jack cheese, and a generous slap of a Cajun version of slaw.

I carried the reuben out to the front porch. The night was nippy, but not cold. A breeze whispered in the pines and palm trees, the moon glinted behind scudding clouds, the faintest insinuation of primeval earth seeped from the swamps.

"You ought to have a cup of steaming coffee and chicory with that drooly goody. The chicory—it gentles everything, lulls you to sleep on a full stomach."

At the first soft murmur I'd turned. Lissa's round face, dimly seen, was smiling from a wicker chair in the darkness. Beside the chair was its wicker twin. I sat down, holding out the sandwich. "Want a hunk?"

"Sure." She reached, carefully wrestled off a modest share, sat back, taking a bite. "Very good."

"Want a whole one? You hardly got a mouthful."

"Better not." She bit into the morsel. "What's with you? Jet lag? The quiet against big-city ears?"

I shook my head. How could I tell her? *An awful premonition won't let me sleep . . . I've had them before, not often, never know when or how, but they're more real than the wailing of that night creature, which sounds like it's in bad trouble.*

"Oh, the excitement, I suppose," I said. "The day. Coming to Val's home, meeting you people, who are so very much exactly as you should be."

"So are you." She was silent a moment. She saw me looking in the direction where the night creature had screamed, one brief wail, abruptly cut off.

"It's a million years ago, not far down state road 61. But you've been in jungle even more deadly." She rustled, leaning slightly toward me. "You can keep from telling me what's on your mind, Cody. None of my business. So I won't ask."

"I won't volunteer."

"Touché. Well, I don't mind telling you why my bed was smothery, why I finally came down to look at the familiar yard and think about when we were kids, Val and I. Fact is, I need an ear . . . someone who won't sigh crossly and tell me I'm an emotional nit, acting like a stupid child."

"Give you my word. None of us sounds altogether brilliant when we need a sounding board."

"Truth is . . ." She took a breath. "Cody, I'm frightened. And if I tell you why, I'll sound like an underdone fool kid who got hold of some crack."

"Try me."

"It's this . . . the pattern."

"What pattern?"

"The appearances of the dead bodies in Mad Frenchwoman's Cove! But of course, you don't know any of it. I'm not yet making sense."

"No, you're not, Lissa. Why not try starting at the beginning?"

She eased back in her chair; she seemed small in it. It was a big barrel of a wicker, the top a little higher than her head, the arms great convolutions of wicker curved halfway around her.

"You've heard of the events of February 14, 1929, in Chicago, of course."

I thought for a second. "The Saint Valentine's Day massacre?"

"Yes . . . so it's known. Seven men waited for the arrival of a hijacked truckload of bootleg booze—six gangsters and an optometrist who enjoyed the company and lifestyle of gangsters. A mongrel dog was also present. Bugs Moran, the prime target in the gangland sortie, should have been there, but he was running late. As he approached the Clark Street warehouse to join the gangsters inside, he saw a big Caddy, police gong on the running board, pulling up and disgorging four men. Two were in police uniform, two in civvies. A fifth man, the driver, stayed in the car. Moran turned and made tracks while his seven pals were blasted with shotguns and submachine guns. Close range. Really gory. The gunfire attracted notice, but when two men in uniform herded two in civilian clothes out, it seemed just another Chicago episode in a time when such raids were commonplace. No one was ever convicted. Al Capone, having masterminded the tactic to wipe out members of a rival gang, had taken himself off to his Florida estate, and at the hour of the massacre was chatting with the Dade County solicitor."

"A perfect alibi," I remarked. "But why dwell on violence and murder on a day given to love?"

"Because there was another Saint Valentine's Day massacre, Cody. Way back in 1865."

"Close of the Civil War," I said.

"Yes. It made regional headlines, quickly forgotten, especially in the chaotic aftermath of war. But it's still in the history books, those multivolume things covering Louisiana history. Occasionally it crops up in Sunday supplement feature stories in one of the larger state newspapers."

"Who was massacred?"

"Seven young men, Yankee soldier boys sent in to help police a riverfront town in a region already neutralized and under Union control. They were invited to a Saint Valentine's Eve party by a beautiful young woman, Marie Louchard. On the way they were captured by a band of marauders, thieves, cutthroat killers posing as die-hard Rebs. They were herded onto a barge, hands bound, and dropped into the Mississippi. One by one their bodies washed ashore in Mad Frenchwoman's Cove. It's an inlet, and the river currents twist shoreward."

Lissa was still more than a hundred years from my fears for Valentina, but I had a foreboding that the threads were going to cross. I wanted Lissa to shut up, but I had to hear on.

And she continued, "The leader of the renegades was one Alberto Batione y Ochoa. He was of two families powerful at the time when the Spanish flag flew over the Cabildo in New Orleans, once the seat of Spanish government in Louisiana. Both families were notorious for their blood lust, sadism, and cruelties, and the genes certainly came to full expression in Alberto . . ."

She paused, taking a small breath. "Seven years ago, Cody, the first body washed up in Mad Frenchwoman's Cove. Young man. Hands bound. Cause of death, drowning. It was a run-of-the-mill report in the *Sword* and hardly made the other papers. Then the next year, another body . . . and the year following . . . always the same, a satanic valentine for Wickens. Along about the sixth year, the investigative reporter in me began to take notice, frame questions."

"And you discovered?"

"Nothing right away. Cases unsolved . . . During the course of a full year what's one more killing in a society rife with daily murders, rapes, muggings? The seven bodies in Mad Frenchwoman's Cove in life had been as unlike as peas and potatoes, one a street person, another a filling station attendant, a drug peddler, fellow who worked for an outdoor sign company . . . but my head wouldn't let go. And I came up with a link, Cody. Dear God, I went into the history of each victim, and I discovered that two were cousins, and I backtracked them, in a growing obsession with this thing. And would you know . . . every single one of the seven young men was descended from Alberto Batione y Ochoa. Cody, I swear . . . am I going nuts? The spirits of those seven Yankee soldier boys of 1865 have been about their revenge. Eye for eye, tooth for tooth . . . spirits real, or spirits imagined in an insane head . . . the result is as undeniable as men taking a trip to the moon."

"Seven," I said. "Seven Yankee boys, seven of Ochoa blood now accounted in Mad Frenchwoman's Cove."

"You fool," she said quietly. "You're trying to tell yourself that it's over. For some reason, you want to believe it. You're afraid for Valentina, Cody. I can see it in your eyes. I can smell your fear. I don't know how or why, but thank God you're in Wickens this Saint Valentine's. This year, if the pattern holds, this is the season for the pièce de résistance. The woman who betrayed the seven Union soldiers—Marie Louchard—is yet unatoned."

I pressed back away from Lissa's sweat-beaded face. "Hush!" I said thickly. "Don't say anything more."

"All right, Cody. As you say."

"No—you must." My hand caught her arm. "Valentina . . . Marie Louchard . . ."

"Five generations, Cody. Direct descent, through Valentina's paternal grandmother."

The night was a vacuum. Then Lissa shivered. "I'm cold," she said.

I was hardly aware when she rose and slipped away into the house.

I opened my eyes, and the world outside was deceptively pleasant: friendly sun, blue skies, a fluttering of birds outside the bedroom window.

The sun's brilliance suggested midmorning. Puffy-eyed, I stumbled into the shower. Sleep, when it came finally, had been deep, dark, a flight into temporary death.

Steady now. The little rituals: shower, shave, brush the teeth, get dressed, comb the hair.

While I made the automatic motions, I tried to cast my thought in the mold of Lissa. More than two years now since the fifth body had washed ashore in Mad Frenchwoman's Cove, quite a bit of rope for a reporter of Lissa's gifts. It wasn't difficult to comprehend what had sparked her first curiosity. Five corpses. All young males. All drowned. Same location, same time each year. Who were they, really? Did they have anything in common? And the common ancestry had hooked Lissa.

She had probably wanted to go at it full time, but a metropolitan editor involved in the large scene wouldn't have seen it that way. What you smoking these days, Lissa? What's this poppycock? Even if you devise a spook tale out of a riverfront town, so what? Louisiana abounds in spook tales, stories of voodoo queens, ghosts in the spreading live oak where Creole aristocrats fought duels, haunted mansions. If we're to go the sleazy tabloid route, why not go out to one of the rat holes today, buy a love potion or pin-stuck doll, and tell our readers about it? You should be in Baton Rouge, Lissa, telling me who is behind the sugar quota bill; you should be in Houston finding out where the oil brokers from Louisiana are meeting with their buddies in Texas; you should be tracing the ownership of the plot on which Parks and Recreation, City of New Orleans, is going to squander another million, sure as a piss ant crawls. Now get the hell to Baton Rouge, Lissa—and I can't pass up the old compliment that you're pretty when you're angry.

So it would have gone, whetting her interest the more, returning her spare time and thoughts again and again to Wickens.

When I came out into the upper hall, I heard the whirr of a vacuum cleaner downstairs. That would be Reba. She and Clyde, middle-aged couple, were the domestic staff, having a small home adjacent to the Marlowe place. Reba arrived each day and Clyde pruned, raked, fixed leaks, and painted as need arose, doing a little truck farming and fishing.

The vacuum was racketing in the living room, a counterpoint to Reba's work rhythm as she sang an old hymn. ("Oh, Beulah Land, sweet Beulah Land, as on the highest mount I stand . . .") Her tempo would get her through the living room in short order.

Seeing no one about, I went on to the secrets of the large, airy kitchen with its walk-in cooler, gas range, sinks of old-timey zinc, racked pots and pans of cast iron and copper. A work area centered the room and a sunny breakfast nook bay-windowed on the east.

Too late for breakfast, too early for lunch. I sure as hell had been out like a light once I tipped over the edge.

Hot coffee was in the urn, and I cut crusty Louisiana French bread for toast and found marmalade in the pantry.

I was munching, listening to the house, anxious to hear those little details Lissa might have left unsaid, when footsteps sounded and George appeared in the doorway.

A smile creased his hewn face. "Must have been the Louisiana air."

"Someone should have called me."

"Why? You got an appointment with the ambassador from Paraguay? How's the coffee holding out?"

"Tastes like it was just made."

He reached into the china cabinet for a big white mug that had his initial on it.

"Hate to eat and run, George." I dropped my napkin beside the marmalade-smeared saucer. "But I want to talk to Lissa."

He glanced as he turned the urn spigot. "She's not here."

"Oh?"

"She left about half an hour ago."

"Did she say where she's going?"

He shrugged. "Who asked? Whose business?"

He sat down opposite me at the breakfast nook table. "She did mention she wouldn't be here for lunch—popping down to New Orleans and back. Something about a detail in some records that had spewed up in her mind. Her words. Whatever it was, she seemed a little put out with herself that it had escaped notice before. 'Spewed up in her mind' . . . tendency to overwrite despite her brilliance, wouldn't you say? She told Elva she'd be back long before dinner. My guess is that she's gone off to buy a birthday–valentine gift for Valentina. Those two . . . they trinket-shop for each other as if they were buying for Saint Anne."

He was looking at me over the top of the coffee mug. "Anything wrong, Cody?"

Was anything right? I shook my head. Nothing for it now, except to wait until Lissa got back. I said, "You've known Val a long time."

"All her life. Her mother and I . . . everyone was sure we'd wind up married."

"What happened?"

His lips made an ironic smile. "Career . . . I was hell-set on the army. Dedication to the ambition, you might say, got me in West Point despite the muscularity between the ears. Elva was hell-set against it. Radical kid in those days. Flower child, Saint Joan of the armies of righteousness. The saps do run high when you're young, don't they? We had attitudinal difficulties, it's safe to say, estrangements based on noncompromise of principles, which are the worst estrangements of all, pigheaded stubbornness on the part of both, pride, and wounded hearts. I had my career and she ended up marrying Charles Marlowe. I'd like to call him a bastard, but he was a fine man, Cody. He passed on . . ."

"When Val was fifteen," I said. "She's told me about him. She was never close to him."

"It happens with kids sometimes. They were cut in different dispositions, but she respected him, and he never had a moment's trouble with her."

"Val would never give anyone trouble, George. If the relationship was like that, then excise the relationship, however painful."

"Like her mother," he said.

"You never married?"

His beefish shoulders lifted, dropped. "Mistresses. Not cheap. Lived with three women all told. The relationships were nicer than most run-of-the-mill marriages. Difference between me and a lot of officers, I didn't change mistresses at every post, with a wife back home. Very fond of all three, but the kind of love a man should have for a woman got stranded at the altar in Saint Louis Cathedral the day Elva married Charles Marlowe. I was a shavetail on duty in Panama that day."

"Did you see Elva often after that?"

He laughed, brief belly laugh. "Son, I came back here on my first leave after her marriage, spit and polish, sabers at the ready. Ah, youth . . . I was full of fire to duel old Charlie or something like that and drag Elva off by the hair. She kept us apart. And after that meeting with her, I knew she was too Catholic to divorce him. Sure, I saw her now and then during my career years, small town, old family ties. You don't move around much in Wickens without the bumping-into."

He reached across to slap my shoulder. "You can bet your last franc I see her often nowadays."

"Why don't you marry her, George?"

"Hell, I intend to. I think she keeps stalling because of Val."

My frown questioned.

He spread his hands. "It nettles me, I'll admit, but no throwing down of the gauntlet this time. I can wait. It's like she's got some kind of notion she shouldn't think solely of herself, but should wait to tie the knot until Val is safely married and the last shred of umbilical cord cut for good. What the devil's wrong with you, Cody? Val's the loveliest, most sensitive, intelligent woman on earth, and I can't believe you're a man with a stuck zipper. Heaven's sake, Cody, marry the girl and get her the hell out of our hair."

Before I responded, Reba came into the kitchen, pleasant, robust, giving me a sniff. "Had a special cut of country ham to go with the eggs and grits for you, Mr. Barnard, and you come sneaking down behind my back."

"I'm sorry, Reba."

She went to the dishwasher to remove crockery. "Now you know. No excuse."

George stood and stretched, lazily and contentedly. "Well, Cody, what's on for today? Name it, and I'll tell you if I'm amenable or any good at it."

"I really must talk to Lissa."

"Then I'll wander over to the country club and see if I can catch a foursome or try a hand at a penny-ante poker game. Come on over. You'll meet likable people."

"Thanks, George."

As he went out, I said to Reba, "The house is very quiet. Did Val and Elva go out?"

She nodded. "They went downtown to do some last-minute shopping for the valentine–birthday party. You'll have a ball! Real blowout every year, Val coming home and all, paper lanterns and people all over the lawn. Caterers are brought in so's me and Clyde and Elva ain't got a thing to do but have fun. Last year, Lissa hired a genuine Dixie band to come from New Orleans. Sakes alive, I wondered if those decrepit old blacks had played the processional for Noah to enter the ark. The old boys propped themselves up on the bandstand George had planked together on the lawn, and when that music started—day of miracles. Those fellows shed about thirty years apiece, first tune, and they got younger and stronger with every note. Lawdy, my blood is still singing from that music."

"Any Louchards at the party, Reba?"

She stiffened, then slowly slipped the last plate from the

dishwasher. "Where'd you hear that name?"

"Val's part Louchard, isn't she?"

"There ain't no more Louchards, Mr. Barnard," she said thinly. "The last to bear the name was Valentina's great-grandfather. He had but one daughter. The name ain't gonna be found in any Wickens phone books."

I didn't press Reba. She'd let me know I was on verboten ground. Marie Louchard's conspiracy to murder seven Yankee boys in 1865 was not a subject for conversation in a region where family trees still cast long shadows.

The respectful quality of my silence was the best ploy, though I'd used it inadvertently. Reba was thinking about it and as she stacked the dishes, she cleared her throat and said, "I reckon you'll be part of the family and have a right to know. So to save your folks trouble, I'll give you the Louchard bit—if you'll take it as the meaningless bit of scandal it is, let it go at that, and keep your mouth shut on any further question."

"Agreed, Reba." I looked at her with fresh interest. "Fire away."

"Ain't much firing, really. Marie Louchard, the ancestress you don't talk about, was a dilly in capital letters. At fifteen she was in a wealthy planter's pants long enough to rob him. She shilled for a riverboat gambler. She was come-on for a saloon keeper who rolled his passed-out patrons in a back alley. She was part of them hoodoo'ers for a while, would go to their bonfires and naked dances in swamp glens. She bedded with that cutthroat Alberto Batione y Ochoa, who was spawned by families worse than Attila and Hitler. She had a bastard boy, Rance Louchard, who was doubtless the seed of Alberto. He ended up on the gallows for cutting a trapper's throat and selling the pelts, but not before he'd sired a son, who sired a daughter, who was Valentina's grandmother. And that's the whole of it, Mr. Barnard."

"How did she end up, this dilly of an ancestress?"

"The story goes that she gave her bastard away, met a ship's captain, went to live in France, turned professional with her hoodoo dancing, making a great hit, toast of Paris. Her salon became the watering place for artists, writers, musicians, high-ranking politicians. She lived to a great age, passing peacefully in her château in the south of France."

"Some woman."

"And I guess ninety percent of it ain't fable. You want anything else?"

I shook my head, thanked her, and left the kitchen.

Once a stable, the garage was perhaps fifty yards off behind the house where the graveled driveway ended. A pickup truck was inside the sprawling frame building, keys in the ignition. Always wheels of some sort around, Val had said, so help yourself anytime you feel ambulatory.

I got in the truck, backed out, turned it, and drove off, trying to recall the street pattern between the Marlowe place and downtown.

The *Sword* occupied a three-story concrete-and-glass building in an area that had received city and private sector planning and reclamation money. Old structures had been razed to make way for a shopping arcade, off-street parking, a modern highrise, an arts center.

The state seal and motto were inlaid in the terra-cotta flooring of the spacious entry foyer. The main-floor office was a busy, sweeping array of desks devoted to advertising, bookkeeping, circulation. Wicket gates and a counter confined the public. A girl came to the counter, smiling and asking what she could do for me.

I told her who I was and asked if I could see Keith. She clicked a switch and intercommed with someone upstairs.

"I'm sorry, Mr. Barnard. Mr. Vereen is out. He's on the parks commission and an inspection of some sort was scheduled this morning. If you'd care to wait, the reception room is off the foyer, a TV, copies of the paper . . ."

"May I wait for Mr. Vereen in your library?"

"He may be out all day and just phone in. But if you like, the morgue is on the third floor. You can take the self-service elevator in the foyer. I'll tell Mr. Vereen's secretary where you are, and let Miss Kitterling know you're coming up."

"Thank you."

Miss Kitterling was a grayish, spare, pleasantly smiling woman in a long, brightly lighted warren of filing cabinets, tables strewn with clippings, packed bookshelves, and microfilm equipment.

An efficient woman, she soon had me seated at a small table whereon was a monitor screen, beside which she deposited the films I requested.

"I'll see if my computer gives me any further cross-indexing, Mr. Barnard, but I'm sure this is the batch of it."

I thanked her, and she retired to her long table and clipping shears, giving me a covert glance that expressed curiosity . . . an assistant secretary of state, personal friend of Mr. Vereen's, poring through files covering Saint Valentine's Day, unsolved murders of the past ten years.

I imagined she would have a go at the files herself, once the mysterious stranger was out of sight. She wouldn't find any answers, I finally admitted to myself. She wouldn't know what she was actually looking for. I knew vaguely, and I didn't find any answers.

The stories were routinely out of police records: DEAD MAN FOUND IN MAD FRENCHWOMAN'S COVE. DEAD WOMAN FOUND IN APARTMENT. MAN SOUGHT IN SHOOTING. GIRL STRANGLED IN BACK ALLEY.

I thought of the Atlanta child murders and how many little black boys had died before the city got the drift. Sometimes you do have to hit people over the head to get their attention. The Atlanta case had two critical elements: black boys, and a compressed time frame.

The Wickens situation lacked both. No visible relationship or common link between the victims—until Lissa, only Lissa had glimpsed a shred of light. No mounting certainty that next week or the week after would yield a dead body of prescribed race and color.

Just a body fished out of Mad Frenchwoman's Cove now and then, some of them coincidentally on Saint Valentine's Day. Start digging in that direction and you might find Yuletide, even Halloween victims.

Without critical elements, there was no hue and cry, no marshaling of special forces by police, not even the same detective quoted in consecutive years, except for the past two. His name was Homicide Detective Max Dufarge.

I thanked Miss Kitterling for her hospitality and asked the directions to police headquarters.

It was less than two blocks distant.

"Max is out, can I help you?"

"Out on a case?" I asked the burly desk sergeant.

He nodded. "That's his job, isn't it? Girl this time, right under our noses."

"Your noses?"

"Cruddy parking garage . . . girl strangled, body in her car . . . before this, too many muggings, senior citizens mostly, like we should patrol every level around the clock."

Phones were ringing; a lawyer was haggling bail for a client; two cops dragged in a wildly resisting drunk.

"This girl—have you identified her?"

The desk sergeant grimaced. "Max and his people just got over there and cordoned it off. She must have been killed within the hour. Max just radioed in for a make on a tag number and driver's license issued to a Lissa Aubunelli."

A captain was yelling at the sergeant from a frosted glass cubicle.

The sergeant muttered a curse under his breath. "Look, friend, the public is always curious. That's why we have TV. You can see all about it on the evening newscast."

Valentina reacted to the news with a frightful calm. "Lissa is dead," she said to no one outside herself. "I won't be seeing Lissa again,"

She looked then, at the faces, mine the closest. "I would like to go up to my room, Cody."

"Val—"

"I'll be okay. Just give me a small moment to accept it."

She went, quietly and quickly, up the broad stairs, and, watching from the bottom level, I heard her door close. I crept up and stood uncertainly. Then I heard her weeping beyond the closed door, and I knew she would come out, steady, dry-eyed, when she was quite ready.

George and Elva still stood in the lower hallway. George was stunned, but had presence—white faced, tight lipped, in control, the unflappable career army officer. Elva was rigidly steeled, tears in her eyes.

She shook off George's supporting arm. "I'll have to tell Reba and Clyde."

"How about Lissa's family?" I asked. "Shouldn't it be one of you, rather than a policeman knocking at their door?"

"She had no family, Cody," Elva said. "None other than us. Her parents were killed in a house fire three years ago. She had no brothers, sisters, grandparents—perhaps a distant cousin or two. We'll have to find that out." She slipped quietly toward the kitchen to look for Reba and Clyde.

George started to barrage me with questions, but driveway gravel showered outside and we heard a car door slam.

As we reached the front door, Keith burst upon the porch. The aristocratic cut of his lean face was all hard, flat planes. His blue eyes had darkened almost to black.

He jerked to a halt, looking from one to the other. "You—You've heard."

"Yes," George said, "Cody just now came with the news."

Keith let go a breath. "Then I'm not the messenger. Was certain I'd have to be. The news came across the mainframe printout, from our unit interfaced in the press room at headquarters. I got Dufarge on the wire, but as yet there doesn't seem to be much in the way of follow-up detail."

His movement was taut, uncomfortable. He pressed his buttocks against the banister, half-sitting, and brooded briefly. "Apparently another mugging in the gloom of the parking garage. Frigging city ought to sell it. Private owners would up the rate but provide security the city can't with its stretched-out manpower. Fatal mugging this time . . ." His thin lips tightened to disappearance. "And I might have stopped this one."

George glanced from Keith to me. My eyes were on Keith. "How?"

"Lissa called from New Orleans late in the morning. The call was relayed to my car during a parks' inspection. She said she wanted to see Max Dufarge and me as soon as she got back, and she was calling from the northern end of the parish, already out of the city proper."

"Did she say what it was about?"

Keith scathed me with a bitter look. "What would be the first thing a newspaperman would ask? She said I might possibly be bidding on a Valentine story. She'd been spare-timing a thing for a long time, and had the gist of it in place—except for the final identity. She'd eliminated a final false lead in New Orleans and said the answer was here in Wickens. She said it was time now to holler for help."

"Did she elaborate?"

"Not on the phone. She said Max and I would get it up to this point, all she had, before the day was out. She said she had enough to convince us it wasn't smoke and vapor, and we would move. Sounded a bit scary. But Lissa couldn't resist center stage; it was the trait that breathed fire into her most mundane story." An involuntary shiver went through him, delayed reaction. He looked a little sick, but pushed himself up. "How is Val?"

"Taking it," I said.

"Can I do anything?"

"Can anyone?" George asked.

"Have we got a shot of Jack Daniel's around the place?" Keith asked.

"We could all use a drink," George said, and led the way inside. He poured at the dining room sideboard and we went aimlessly into the living room, George carrying the bottle. We heard a door close in the back of the house. George tossed his drink, set the glass and bottle on the coffee table. "That will be Elva." He hurried out.

Keith sank into an overstuffed chair, pulled up again. "I could use another." He poured a second finger. "No ticket back for Lissa." He raised his eyes, saw my confused frown, and added, "Of course the statement is meaningless to you, Cody. But there was a ticket back in my case."

"Excuse me?"

He threw the drink down his throat. "Car accident. Terrible concussion . . . trauma . . . heart stopped . . . dead as last year's rose. A great medical team and that electric gadget they use to bang the old ticker started me up again. But for a minute or two, the reading of my will could have proceeded legally."

He looked at the shot glass, decided against a third, and eased the glass onto the table.

"I've tried to remember—but I couldn't at the time and the mists of eight years haven't helped—how it felt to die. You've heard the stories of people who cross over and are snatched back. A lot of them report a marvelous experience, a golden light, a feeling of joy and peace, a feeling of not wanting to be brought back, but to have the golden freedom of the light."

"How was it with you, Keith?"

"No golden light. I really have never been able to remember. I think it was dark, cold, a feeling of terrible anxiety because I was dying, dead. Maybe my linen was soiled when I got over there . . . Poor Lissa—I hope she got over there with her linen clean."

After the local evening newscast, the telephone began to

ring. It wouldn't stop. Elva kept answering, hearing the sympathetic expressions, consoling the shocked caller, answering the same questions. Finally she took the obvious measure and left the phone off the hook.

We talked to Homicide Detective Max Dufarge, who came accompanied by one of his men. We told him everything we knew.

We sat about the table. Food was on it. Perhaps we ate.

It was Saint Valentine's Eve and all the plans for the party had to be canceled, the caterer told by phone to send his bill but not himself, likewise the booking agent in New Orleans who handled Dixieland jazz groups.

Lissa Aubunelli was stretched out in a funeral home downtown, and we, finally, in our beds.

A moon milked palely in the darkness. The night was not quiet: the scratching of a night creature scurrying across the roof; the faraway striking of the grandfather clock in the lower hall; a skirl of night wind, creak of a house timber, a whisper of movement. Here in the house? Someone up, needing an aspirin? I rose to an elbow, listening. Nothing. I eased back and gradually my senses slipped into a halfway house of non-sleep.

The colors came in a single glimpse of tangled mangrove, saw grass, heat-blasted pines weeping dead, gray moss tendrils.

A narrow, rutted road with crushed-shell surface wormed painfully through the jungle. In a clearing off the road was a tumbledown clapboard shack. Beside the road were the ruins of a mailbox. Jagged holes had rusted through. The remains hung crookedly on a weather-eaten chain from a weather-eaten stanchion creatively fashioned from the iron tire of an old wagon wheel.

Zap!

The darkness was a wall.

I jerked on my pants and shoes. Across the hallway I hesitated for a beat of a second. Then I gripped the doorknob, flung the panel open, and I saw what I was afraid of seeing: an empty bed, sheet thrown back.

"Valentina!" My shout shattered through the house. I looked back and forth wildly in the hallway, ran down the stairs, two, three at a time.

"Valentina! Val!"

I was outside, seeing the vacancy of the porch, the land, the emptiness of the whole earth.

I ran back in. The house was awakening, lights flashing on, questioning voices rising.

George was charging down the stairs, in the direction of my voice.

Just inside the front door, I grabbed his arm. "Don't ask me anything! Just tell me— You've known this swamp country for years. Do you know a deserted shack with a mailbox mounted on a wagon-wheel iron rim?"

"Cody, what in the hell—"

"Damn you! Answer my question!"

"Of course I know. It's the old LeMoines place. Belonged to Keith Vereen's grandpappy. Hunters, fishermen still use it now and then, not that it's much shelter when a storm blows in. Now you answer a question for me. What's going on?"

"It's about Valentina, you long-winded bastard! She got up during the night. I know now that it wasn't my imagination or nerves. She slipped downstairs, and he was there, where he'd told her he would be, to talk to her about Lissa, a private thing, something Lissa had meant for her ears alone. What the filthy hell does it matter how he arranged it, the bait he used? He's got her. Nothing else matters. She's with him, George, the final one. The Louchard descendant. And I must get to the LeMoines place."

He was wearing pajama bottoms, barefoot. It was sufficient. "The keys are in the pickup."

He drove daredevil fast, but not recklessly, with the expertise instilled by terrains in many parts of the world.

"Tell me," he said.

I hung on to the seat, other hand braced against the instrument panel. "You won't believe me."

"Try me. I don't know how you came by this knowledge of the LeMoines place, or how I'm so certain you know that she's out there. But tell me—who did she meet?"

"Keith Vereen."

"You can't be serious."

"Very."

"Why did he do it?"

"Because he couldn't help himself."

"A man can always help himself, Cody."

"What if he's not entirely himself? What if he is traumatized in a car accident eight years ago and dies? What if seven residual life forces, psychic echoes, spirits, ghosts, whatever the hell you choose to call them, are present inside Keith, dwelling in a level just below his own sentience, when the doctors slam an electric charge and restart his heart?"

He didn't slow the pickup. Water showered, glitters in the night, as we slashed through a shallow ford.

"He was never the same after the accident, that much is for sure," George admitted.

"Call him spirit possessed, or simply mad. The result is the same. He was compelled to search out seven male descendants of the man who murdered seven Yankee soldier boys on a Saint Valentine's Eve a long time ago. He had to balance the scales, even the score."

"If any of this is true, Cody . . . if I'm not suffering a nightmare . . . that old massacre, involving Marie Louchard, it happened over a hundred years ago."

"They had time, those seven—eternity. But they had no instrument—until Keith's moment of death became a latchkey."

"And Lissa?"

"Getting too uncomfortably close. She didn't suspect Keith and forewarned him with a phone call. He simply drove out to U.S. 61, the only main road from New Orleans, and watched for her car. It was simple then to follow her into the parking garage, to say hello as she was getting from her car, to put his hands around her throat. She wouldn't have been able to make a sound."

The mailbox and rust-eaten wagon-wheel arch reared in the glare of the headlights. I was out of the truck, running, before George had fully stopped it.

I saw Keith's Mercedes parked in the weed-grown ruin of the driveway leading to the shack.

Then I saw the moving shadows, human figures, in the moon-frozen darkness just beyond and to one side of the shack.

He was carrying her across his shoulder. She wasn't moving. How hard had be slugged her?

"Valentina!"

I had outdistanced George, for all his conditioning. Keith turned slowly to face me.

"Stay back, Cody. Don't come any closer."

"Put her down, Keith. Back off. Please—you've known her all her life. She's your friend. She loved and trusted you."

"She's a Louchard, Cody. It's in the records. Go look at the records, as I did."

His *every* word had a different inflection. Seven inflections? Seven voices speaking through his lips?

"Kill the bastard!" George had reached my side. "Take him, Cody."

I had already decided it was the only way. A jump ahead of George, I was at Keith.

He stood unmoving.

A veil came, a gossamer shimmering through which Keith's image rippled and flowed. I gasped from a force that struck me.

I saw the moon spin, and knew that I had slammed onto my back. I heard bamboo rattling a fierce tempo. Wild palms bent and reared like slashing shadows. Night creatures were screaming, and a hard, quick wind showered jungle debris across my face, against the side of the LeMoines shack.

I realized that George was sprawled beside me, frothing incoherent sound.

"Stay back," Keith said. "She has Louchard blood in her veins. She is the guiltiest of all, and this is the moment reserved for her."

He turned and was starting to carry her away.

A bellow of anguish came from George's lips. "You fool! You mad fool! She is *not* Louchard, she's *my* bastard daughter. Not a part of the Louchard line. She was born nine months after a furlough—neither Elva nor I meant for it to happen. It was only that once. Charles Marlowe proved out infertile. Maybe he guessed, before the end, why he and Elva had not had other children. She's *mine,* you son of a bitch!"

The clearing seemed to suck a breath. Keith had heard. He hesitated, staring about as if for outside guidance.

This time my contact with him was hard, satisfying: he, I, and Valentina went down in a tangle. He thrashed, slipped free. His wild kick caught me on the cheek, breaking the skin. I heard viney tearings, and Keith was gone.

George was on his knees, gathering her up, cradling her against his chest, rocking in anguish.

"Oh, my baby! My little girl! . . ."
And she moaned softly.

As the jetliner entered the traffic pattern over the familiar grid of Washington National Airport, Valentina said quietly, "We're back, Cody."
"Yes."
"It's all over."
"Yes."
"Poor Keith"—her voice echoed a gentle pain—"making the river, trying to swim to freedom—or maybe not—washing up in Mad Frenchwoman's Cove."
"We agreed to let the past bury the past," I reminded her.
"And so we will. We'll close the door for keeps and take up life as we're meant to—after you tell me one thing. Just who am I, Cody?"
"You're the daughter of two wonderful people."
I touched her cheek. I imprinted every detail of her face in my mind forever.
"To borrow from Gershwin . . . You is my woman, Val."
Her lips parted just a little; her eyes deepened. "And I got to love one man 'til I die." A tiny crinkling at the corners of her mouth. "Aside from calling the Mississippi an old man, that poet fellow did have his perceptions."

Born in 1920 in North Carolina, Talmage Powell attended the University of North Carolina and has been a freelance writer since 1942. He has produced more than 500 short stories and twenty novels—mostly mystery and suspense—noted for their hard-edged prose and ingenuity. A frequent contributor to Alfred Hitchcock's Mystery Magazine, *his latest book,* Written for Hitchcock *(1989), is a collection of the best of these tales. "The Jabberwock Valentine" was first published in* Vicious Valentines *(1988), an original anthology.*

Childhood dreams unearth the past and lead to the future. . . .

TEN

Through the Ivory Gate

Mary Raymond Shipman Andrews

Breeze filtered through shifting leafage, the June morning sunlight came in at the open window by the boy's bed, under the green shades, across the shadowy, white room, and danced a noiseless dance of youth and freshness and springtime against the wall opposite. The boy's head stirred on his pillow. He spoke a quick word from out of his dream. "The key?" he said inquiringly, and the sound of his own voice awoke him. Dark, drowsy eyes opened, and he stared half-seeing, at the picture that hung facing him. Was it the play of mischievous sunlight, was it the dream that still held his brain? He knew the picture line by line, and there was no such figure in it. It was a large photograph of Fairfield, the southern home of his mother's people, and the boy remembered it always hanging there, opposite his bed, the first sight to meet his eyes every morning since his babyhood. So he was certain there was no figure in it, more than all one so remarkable as this strapping little chap in his queer clothes, his dress of conspicuous plaid with large black velvet squares sewed on it, who stood now in front of the old manor house. Could it be only a dream? Could it be that a little ghost, wandering childlike in dim, heavenly fields, had joined the gay troop of his boyish visions and slipped in with them through the ivory gate of pleasant dreams? The boy put his fists to his eyes and rubbed them and looked again. The little fellow was still there, standing with sturdy legs wide apart as if owning the scene; he laughed as he held toward the boy a key—a small key tied with a scarlet ribbon. There was no doubt in the boy's mind that the key was for him, and out of the dim world of sleep he stretched his young arm for it; to reach it he sat up in bed. Then he was awake and knew himself alone in the peace of his own little room, and laughed shamefacedly at the reality of the vision which had followed him from dreamland into the very boundaries of consciousness, which held him even now with gentle tenacity, which drew him back through the day, from his studies, from his play, into the strong current of its fascination.

The first time Philip Beckwith had this dream he was only twelve years old, and, withheld by the deep reserve of childhood, he told not even his mother about it, though he lived in its atmosphere all day and remembered it vividly days longer. A year after it came again; and again it was a June morning, and as his eyes opened the little boy came once more out of the picture toward him, laughing and holding out the key on its scarlet string. The dream was a pleasant one, and Philip welcomed it eagerly from his sleep as a friend. There seemed something sweet and familiar in the child's presence beyond the one memory of him, as again the boy, with eyes half-open to everyday life, saw him standing, small but masterful, in the garden of that old house where the Fairfields had lived for more than a century. Half-consciously he tried to prolong the vision, tried not to wake entirely for fear of losing it; but the picture faded surely from the curtain of his mind as the tangible world painted there its heavier outlines. It was as if a happy little spirit had tried to follow him, for love of him, from a country lying close, yet separated; it was as if the common childhood of the two made it almost possible for them to meet; as if a message that might not be spoken, were yet almost delivered.

The third time the dream came it was a December morning of the year when Philip was fifteen, and falling snow made wavering light and shadow on the wall where hung the picture. This time, with eyes wide open, yet with the possession of the dream strongly on him, he lay subconsciously alert and gazed, as in the odd unmistakable dress that Philip knew now in detail, the bright-faced child swung toward him, always from the garden of that old place, always trying with loving, merry efforts to reach Philip from out of it—always holding to him the red-ribboned key. Like a wary hunter the big boy lay—knowing it unreal, yet living it keenly—and watched his chance. As the little figure glided close to him, he put out his hand suddenly, swiftly for the key—he was awake. As always, the dream was gone; the little ghost was baffled again; the two worlds might not meet.

That day Mrs. Beckwith, putting in order an old mahogany

secretary, showed him a drawer full of photographs, daguerreotypes. The boy and his gay young mother were the best of friends, for, only nineteen when he was born, she had never let the distance widen between them; had held the freshness of her youth sacred against the time when he should share it. Year by year, living in his enthusiasms, drawing him to hers, she had grown young in his childhood, which year by year came closer to her maturity. Until now there was between the tall, athletic lad and the still young and attractive woman, an equal friendship, a common youth, which gave charm and elasticity to the natural tie between them. Yet even to this comrade-mother the boy had not told his dream, for the difficulty of putting into words the atmosphere, the compelling power of it. So that when she opened one of the old-fashioned black cases which held the early sun-pictures, and showed him the portrait within, he startled her by a sudden exclamation. From the frame of red velvet and tarnished gilt there laughed up at him the little boy of his dream. There was no mistaking him, and if there were doubt about the face, there was the peculiar dress—the black and white plaid with large squares of black velvet sewed here and there as decoration. Philip stared in astonishment at the sturdy figure; the childish face with its wide forehead and level, strong brows; its dark eyes straight-gazing and smiling.

"Mother—who is he? Who is he?" he demanded.

"Why, my lamb, don't you know? It's your little uncle Philip—my brother, for whom you were named—Philip Fairfield the sixth. There was always a Philip Fairfield at Fairfield since 1790. This one was the last, poor baby! And he died when he was five. Unless you go back there some day—that's my hope, but it's not likely to come true. You are a Yankee, except for the big half of you that's me. That's southern, every inch." She laughed and kissed his fresh cheek impulsively. "But what made you so excited over this picture, Phil?"

Philip gazed down, serious, a little embarrassed, at the open case in his hand. "Mother," he said after a moment, "you'll laugh at me, but I've seen this chap in a dream three times now."

"Oh!" She did laugh at him. "Oh, Philip! What have you been eating for dinner, I'd like to know? I can't have you seeing visions of your ancestors at fifteen—it's unhealthy."

The boy, reddening, insisted. "But, Mother, really, don't you think it was queer? I saw him as plainly as I do now—and I've never seen this picture before."

"Oh, yes, you have—you must have seen it," his mother threw back lightly. "You've forgotten, but the image of it was tucked away in some dark corner of your mind, and when you were asleep it stole out and played tricks on you. That's the way forgotten ideas do: they get even with you in dreams for having forgotten them."

"Mother, only listen—" But Mrs. Beckwith, her eyes lighting with a swift turn of thought, interrupted him—laid her finger on his lips.

"No—you listen, boy dear—quick, before I forget it! I've never told you about this, and it's very interesting."

And the youngster, used to these willful ways of his sister-mother, laughed and put his fair head against her shoulder and listened.

"It's quite a romance," she began, "only there isn't any end to it; it's all unfinished and disappointing. It's about this little Philip here, whose name you have—my brother. He died when he was five, as I said, but even then he had a bit of dramatic history in his life. He was born just before wartime in 1859, and he was a beautiful and wonderful baby; I can remember all about it, for I was six years older. He was incarnate sunshine, the happiest child that ever lived, but far too quick and clever for his years. The servants used to ask him, 'Who is you, Marse Philip, sah?' to hear him answer, before he could speak it plainly, 'I'm Philip Fairfield of Fairfield'; he seemed to realize that, and his responsibility to them and to the place, as soon as he could breathe. He wouldn't have a darky scolded in his presence, and every morning my father put him in front of him in the saddle, and they rode together about the plantation. My father adored him, and little Philip's sunshiny way of taking possession of the slaves and the property pleased him more deeply, I think, than anything in his life. But the war came before this time, when the child was about a year old, and my father went off, of course, as every southern man went who could walk, and for a year we did not see him. Then he was badly wounded at the battle of Malvern Hill; and came home to get well. However, it was more serious than he knew, and he did not get well. Twice he went off again to join our army, and each time he was sent back within a month, too ill to be of any use. He chafed constantly, of course, because he must stay at home and farm, when his whole soul ached to be fighting for his flag; but finally in December 1863, he thought he was well enough at last for service. He was to join General John Morgan, who had just made his wonderful escape from prison at Columbus, and it was planned that my mother should take little Philip and me to England to live there till the war was over and we could all be together at Fairfield again. With that in view my father drew all of his ready money—it was ten thousand dollars in gold—from the banks in Lexington, for my mother's use in the years they might be separated. When suddenly, the day before he was to have gone, the old wound broke out again, and he was helplessly ill in bed at the hour when he should have been on his horse riding toward Tennessee. We were fifteen miles out from Lexington, yet it might be rumored that father had drawn a large sum of money, and, of course, he was well known as a Southern officer. Because of the Northern soldiers, who held the city, he feared very much to have the money in the house, yet he hoped still to join Morgan a little later, and then it would be needed as he had planned. Christmas morning my father was so much better that my mother went to church, taking me, and leaving little Philip, then four years old, to amuse him. What happened that morning was the point of all this rambling; so now listen hard, my precious thing."

The boy, sitting erect now, caught his mother's hand silently, and his eyes stared into hers as he drank in every word:

"Mammy, who was, of course, little Philip's nurse, told my mother afterward that she was sent away before my father and the boy went into the garden, but she saw them go and saw that my father had a tin box—a box about twelve inches long, which seemed very heavy—in his arms, and on his finger swung a long red ribbon with a little key strung on it. Mother knew it as the key of the box, and she had tied the ribbon on it herself.

"It was a bright, crisp Christmas day, pleasant in the garden—the box hedges were green and fragrant, aromatic in the sunshine. You don't even know the smell of box in sunshine, you poor child! But I remember that day, for I was ten years old, a right big girl, and it was a beautiful morning for an invalid to take the air. Mammy said she was proud to see how her 'handsome boy' kept step with his father, and she watched the two until they got away down by the rose garden, and then she couldn't see little Philip behind the three-foot hedge, so she turned away. But somewhere in that big garden, or under the trees beside it, my father buried the box that held the money—ten thousand dollars. It shows how he trusted that baby, that he took him with him, and you'll see how his trust was only too well justified. For that evening, Christmas night, very suddenly my father died—before he had time to tell my mother where he had hidden the box. He tried; when consciousness came a few minutes before the end he gasped out, 'I buried the money'—and then he choked. Once again he whispered just two words: 'Philip knows.' And my mother said, 'Yes, dearest—Philip and I will find it—don't worry, dearest,' and that quieted him. She told me about it so many times.

"After the funeral she took little Philip and explained to him as well as she could that he must tell Mother where he and Father had put the box, and—this is the point of it all, Philip—he wouldn't tell. She went over and over it all, again and again, but it was no use. He had given his word to my father never to tell, and he was too much of a baby to understand how death had dissolved that promise. My mother tried every way, of course, explanations and reasoning first, then pleading, and finally severity; she even punished the poor little martyr, for it was awfully important to us all. But the four-year-old baby was absolutely incorruptible. He cried bitterly and sobbed out:

" 'Farver said I mustn't never tell anybody—never! Farver said Philip Fairfield of Fairfield mustn't *never* bweak his words,' and that was all.

"Nothing could induce him to give the least hint. Of course there was great search for it, but it was well hidden and it was never found. Finally, Mother took her obdurate son and me and came to New York with us, and we lived on the little income which she had of her own. Her hope was that as soon as Philip was old enough she could make him understand, and go back with him and get that large sum lying underground—lying there yet, perhaps. But in less than a year the little boy was dead and the secret was gone with him."

Philip Beckwith's eyes were intense and wide. The Fairfield eyes, brown and brilliant, their young fire was concentrated on his mother's face.

"Do you mean that money is buried down there, yet, mother?" he asked solemnly.

Mrs. Beckwith caught at the big fellow's sleeve with slim fingers. "Don't go today, Phil—wait till after lunch, anyway!"

"Please don't make fun, Mother—I want to know about it. Think of it lying there in the ground!"

"Greedy boy! We don't need money now, Phil. And the old place will be yours when I am dead—" The lad's arm went about his mother's shoulders. "Oh, but I'm not going to die for ages! Not till I'm a toothless old person with side curls, hobbling along on a stick. Like this!"—she sprang to her feet and the boy laughed a great peal at the haglike effect as his young mother threw herself into the part. She dropped on the divan again at his side.

"What I meant to tell you was that your father thinks it very unlikely that the money is there yet, and almost impossible that we could find it in any case. But some day when the place is yours you can have it put through a sieve if you choose. I wish I could think you would ever live there, Phil; but I can't imagine any chance by which you should. I should hate to have you sell it—it has belonged to a Philip Fairfield so many years."

A week later the boy left his childhood by the side of his mother's grave. His history for the next seven years may go in a few lines. School days, vacations, the four years at college, outwardly the commonplace of an even and prosperous development, inwardly the infinite variety of experience by which each soul is a person; the result of the two so wholesome a product of young manhood that no one realized under the frank and open manner a deep reticence, an intensity, a sensitiveness to impressions, a tendency toward mysticism which made the fiber of his being as delicate as it was strong.

Suddenly, in a turn of the wheel, all the externals of his life changed. His rich father died penniless and he found himself on his own hands, and within a month the boy who had owned five polo ponies was a hard-working reporter on a great daily. The same quick-wittedness and energy which had made him a good polo player made him a good reporter. Promotion came fast and, as those who are busiest have the most time to spare, he fell to writing stories. When the editor of a large magazine took one, Philip first lost respect for that dignified person, then felt ashamed to have imposed on him, then rejoiced utterly over the check. After that editors fell into the habit; the people he ran against knew about his books; the checks grew better reading all the time; a point came where it was more profitable to stay at home and imagine events than to go out and report them. He had been too busy as the days marched to generalize; but suddenly he knew that he was a successful writer, that if he kept his head and worked, a future was before him. So he soberly put his own English by the side of that of a master or two from his bookshelves, to keep his perspective clear, and then he worked harder. And it came to be five years after his father's death.

At the end of those years three things happened at once. The young man suddenly was very tired and knew that he needed the vacation he had gone without; a check came in large enough to make a vacation easy; and he had his old dream. His fagged brain had found it but another worry to decide where he should go to rest, but the dream settled the vexed question offhand—he would go to Kentucky. The very thought of it brought rest to him, for like a memory of childhood, like a bit of his own soul, he knew the country—the "God's Country" of its people—which he had never seen. He caught his breath as he thought of warm, sweet air that held no hurry or nerve strain; of lingering sunny days whose hours are longer than in other places; of the soft speech, the serene and kindly ways of the people; of the royal welcome waiting for him as for everyone, heartfelt and heart-warming; he knew it all from a daughter of Kentucky—his mother. It was May now, and he remembered she had told him that the land was filled with roses at the end of May—he would go then. He owned the old place, Fairfield, and he had never seen it. Perhaps it had fallen to pieces; perhaps his mother had painted it in colors too bright; but it was his, the bit of the earth that belonged to him. The Anglo-Saxon joy of landowning stirred for the first time within him—he would go to his own place. Buoyant with the new thought, he sat down and wrote a letter. A cousin of the family, of a younger branch, a certain John Fairfield, lived yet upon the land. Not in the great house, for that had been closed many years, but in a small house almost as old, called Westerly. Philip had corresponded with him once or twice about affairs of the estate, and each letter of the older man's had brought a simple and urgent invitation to come South and visit him. So, pleased as a child with the plan, he wrote that he was coming on a certain Thursday, late in May. The letter sent, he went about in a dream of the South, and when its answer, delighted and hospitable, came simultaneously with one of those bleak and windy turns of weather which make New York, even in May, a marvelously fitting place to leave, he could not wait. Almost a week ahead of his time he packed his bag and took the Southwestern Limited, and on a bright Sunday morning he awoke in the old Phœnix Hotel in Lexington. He had arrived too late the night before to make the fifteen miles to Fairfield, but he had looked over the horses in the livery stable and chosen the one he wanted, for he meant to go on horseback, as a southern gentleman should, to his domain. That he meant to go alone, that no one, not even John Fairfield, knew of his coming, was not the least of his satisfactions, for the sight of the place of his forefathers, so long neglected, was becoming suddenly a sacred thing to him. The old house and its young owner should meet each other like sweethearts, with no eyes to watch their greeting, their slow and sweet acquainting; with no living voices to drown the sound of the ghostly voices that must greet his homecoming from those walls—voices of his people who had lived there, voices gone long since into eternal silence.

A little crowd of loungers stared with frank admiration at the young fellow who came out smiling from the door of the Phœnix Hotel, big and handsome in his riding clothes, his eyes taking in the details of girths and bits and straps with the keenness of a horseman.

Philip laughed as he swung into the saddle and looked down at the friendly faces, most of them black faces, below. "Goodby," he said. "Wish me good luck, won't you?" and a willing chorus of "Good luck, boss," came flying after him as the horse's hoofs clattered down the street.

Through the bright drowsiness of the little city he rode in the early Sunday morning, and his heart sang for joy to feel himself again across a horse, and for the love of the place that warmed him already. The sun shone hotly, but he liked it; he felt his whole being slipping into place, fitting to its environment; surely, in spite of birth and breeding, he was southern born and bred, for this felt like home more than any home he had known!

As he drew away from the city, every little while, through

stately woodlands, a dignified sturdy mansion peeped down its long vista of trees at the passing cavalier, and, enchanted with its beautiful setting, with its air of proud unconsciousness, he hoped each time that Fairfield would look like that. If he might live here—and go to New York, to be sure, two or three times a year to keep the edge of his brain sharpened—but if he might live his life as these people lived, in this unhurried atmosphere, in this perfect climate, with the best things in his reach for everyday use; with horses and dogs, with out-of-doors and a great, lovely country to breathe in; with—he smiled vaguely—with sometime perhaps a wife who loved it as he did—he would ask from earth no better life than that. He could write, he felt certain, better and larger things in such surroundings.

But he pulled himself up sharply as he thought how idle a daydream it was. As a fact, he was a struggling young author, he had come South for two weeks' vacation, and on the first morning he was planning to live here—he must be light-headed. With a touch of his heel and a word and a quick pull on the curb, his good horse broke into a canter, and then, under the loosened rein, into a rousing gallop, and Philip went dashing down the country road, past the soft, rolling landscape, and under cool caves of foliage, vivid with emerald greens of May, thoughts and dreams all dissolved in exhilaration of the glorious movement, the nearest thing to flying that the wingless animal, man, may achieve.

He opened his coat as the blood rushed faster through him, and a paper fluttered from his pocket. He caught it, and as he pulled the horse to a trot, he saw that it was his cousin's letter. So, walking now along the brown shadows and golden sunlight of the long white pike, he fell to wondering about the family he was going to visit. He opened the folded letter and read:

"My dear Cousin," it said—the kinship was the first thought in John Fairfield's mind—"I received your welcome letter on the 14th. I am delighted that you are coming at last to Kentucky, and I consider that it is high time you paid Fairfield, which has been the cradle of your stock for many generations, the compliment of looking at it. We closed our house in Lexington three weeks ago, and are settled out here now for the summer, and find it lovelier than ever. My family consists only of myself and Shelby, my one child, who is now twenty-two years of age. We are both ready to give you an old-time Kentucky welcome, and Westerly is ready to receive you at any moment you wish to come."

The rest was merely arrangements for meeting the traveler, all of which were done away with by his earlier arrival.

"A prim old party, with an exalted idea of the family," commented Philip mentally. "Well-to-do, apparently, or he wouldn't be having a winter house in the city. I wonder what the boy Shelby is like. At twenty-two he should be doing something more profitable than spending an entire summer out here, I should say."

The questions faded into the general content of his mind at the glimpse of another stately old pillared homestead, white and deep down its avenue of locusts. At length he stopped his horse to wait for a ragged Negro trudging cheerfully down the road.

"Do you know a place around here called Fairfield?" he asked.

"Yessah. I does that, sah. It's that ar' place right hyeh, sah, by yo' hoss. That ar's Fahfiel'. Shall I open the gate fo' you, boss?" and Philip turned to see a hingeless ruin of boards held together by the persuasion of rusty wire.

"The home of my fathers looks down in the mouth," he reflected aloud.

The old Negro's eyes, gleaming from under shaggy sheds of eyebrows, watched him, and he caught the words.

"Is you a Fahfiel', boss?" he asked eagerly. "Is you my young marse?" He jumped at the conclusion promptly. "You favors de fam'ly mightily, sah. I heerd you was comin' "; the rag of a hat went off and he bowed low. "Hit's cert'nly good news fo' Fahfiel', Marse Philip, hit's mighty good news fo' us niggers, sah. I'se b'longed to the Fahfiel' fam'ly a hundred years, Marse—me and my folks, and I wishes yo' a welcome home, sah—welcome home, Marse Philip."

Philip bent with a quick movement from his horse and gripped the twisted old black hand, speechless. This humble welcome on the highway caught at his heart deep down, and the appeal of the colored people to southerners, who know them, the thrilling appeal of a gentle, loyal race, doomed to live forever behind a veil and hopeless without bitterness, stirred for the first time his manhood. It touched him to be taken for granted as the child of his people; it pleased him that he should be "Marse Philip" as a matter of course, because there had always been a Marse Philip at the place. It was bred deeper in the bone of him than he knew, to understand the soul of the black man; the stuff he was made of had been southern two hundred years.

The old man went off down the white limestone road singing to himself, and Philip rode slowly under the locusts and beeches up the long drive, grass-grown and lost in places, that wound through the woodland three-quarters of a mile to his house. And as he moved through the park, through sunlight and shadow of these great trees that were his, he felt like a knight of King Arthur, like some young knight long exiled, at last coming to his own. He longed with an unreasonable seizure of desire to come here to live, to take care of it, beautify it, fill it with life and prosperity as it had once been filled, surround it with cheerful faces of colored people whom he might make happy and comfortable. If only he had money to pay off the mortgage, to put the place once in order, it would be the ideal setting for the life that seemed marked out for him—the life of a writer.

The horse turned a corner and broke into a canter up the slope, and as the shoulder of the hill fell away there stood before him the picture of his childhood come to life, smiling drowsily in the morning sunlight with shuttered windows that were its sleeping eyes—the great white house of Fairfield. Its high pillars reached to the roof; its big wings stretched away at either side; the flicker of the shadow of the leaves played over it tenderly and hid broken bits of woodwork, patches of paint cracked away, windowpanes gone here and there. It stood as if too proud to apologize or to look sad for such small matters, as serene, as stately as in its prime. And its master, looking at it for the first time, loved it.

He rode around to the side and tied his mount to an old horse-rack, and then walked up the wide front steps as if each lift were an event. He turned the handle of the big door without much hope that it would yield, but it opened willingly, and he stood inside. A broom lay in a corner, windows were open—his cousin had been making ready for him. There was the huge mahogany sofa, horsehair-covered, in the window under the stairs, where his mother had read *Ivanhoe* and *The Talisman.* Philip stepped softly across the wide hall and laid his head where must have rested the brown hair of the little girl who had come to be, first all of his life, and then its dearest memory. Half an hour he spent in the old house, and its walls echoed to his footsteps as if in ready homage, and each empty room whose door he opened met him with a sweet half-familiarity. The whole place was filled with the presence of the child who had loved it and left it, and for whom this tall man, her child, longed now as if for a little sister who should be here, and whom he missed. With her memory came the thought of the five-year-old uncle who had made history for the family so disastrously. He must see the garden where that other Philip had gone with his father to hide the money on the fated Christmas morning. He closed the house door behind him carefully, as if he would not disturb a little girl reading in the window, a little boy sleeping perhaps in the nursery above. Then he walked down the broad sweep of the driveway, the gravel crunching under the grass, and across what had been a bit of velvet lawn, and stood for a moment with his hand on a broken vase, weed-filled, which capped the stone post of a gateway.

All the garden was misty with memories. Where a tall golden flower nodded alone from out of the tangled thicket of an old flowerbed a bright-haired child might have laughed with just that air of startled, gay naughtiness, from the forbidden center of the blossoms. In the moulded tan-bark of the path was a vague print, like the ghost of a footprint that had passed down the way a lifetime ago. The box, half-dead, half-sprouted into high unkept growth, still stood stiffly against the riotous overflow of weeds as if it yet held loyally to its business of guarding the borders. Philip shifted his gaze slowly, lingering over the dim contours, the shadowy shape of what the garden had been. Suddenly his eyes opened wide. How was this? There was a hedge as neat, as clipped, as any of Southampton in mid-season, and over it a glory of roses, red and white and pink and yellow, waved gay banners to him in trim luxuriance. He swung toward them, and the breeze brought him for the first time in his life the fragrance of box in sunshine.

Three feet tall, shaven and thick and shining, the old hedge stood, and the garnered sweetness of a hundred years' slow growth breathed delicately from it toward the great-great-grandson of the man who planted it. A box hedge takes as long in the making as a gentleman, and when they are done the two are much of a sort. No plant in all the garden has so subtle an air of breeding, so gentle a reserve, yet so gracious a message of sweetness for all of the world who will stop to learn it. It keeps a firm dignity under the stress of tempest when lighter growths are tossed and torn; it shines bright through the snow; it has a well-bred willingness to be background, with the well-bred gift of presence, whether as background or foreground. The soul of the box tree is an aristocrat, and the sap that runs through it is the blue blood of vegetation.

Saluting him bravely in the hot sunshine with its myriad shining sword points, the old hedge sent out to Philip on the May breeze its ancient welcome of aromatic fragrance, and the tall roses crowded gaily to look over its edge at the new master. Slowly, a little dazed at this oasis of shining order in the neglected garden, he walked to the opening and stepped inside the hedge. The rose garden! The famous rose garden of Fairfield, and as his mother had described it, in full splendor of cared-for, orderly bloom. Across the paths he stepped swiftly till he stood amid the roses, giant bushes of Jacqueminot and Maréchal Niel; of pink and white and red and yellow blooms in thick array. The glory of them intoxicated him. That he should own all of this beauty seemed too good to be true, and instantly he wanted to taste his ownership. The thought came to him that he would enter into his heritage with strong hands here in the rose garden; he caught a deep-red Jacqueminot almost roughly by its gorgeous head and broke off the stem. He would gather a bunch, a huge, unreasonable bunch of his own flowers. Hungrily he broke one after another; his shoulders bent over them, he was deep in the bushes.

"I reckon I shall have to ask you not to pick any more of those roses," a voice said.

Philip threw up his head as if he had been shot; he turned sharply with a great thrill, for he thought his mother spoke to him. Perhaps it was only the southern inflection so long unheard, perhaps the sunlight that shone in his eyes dazzled him, but, as he stared, the white figure before him seemed to him to look exactly as his mother had looked long ago. Stumbling over his words, he caught at the first that came.

"I—I think it's all right," he said.

The girl smiled frankly, yet with a dignity in her puzzled air. "I'm afraid I shall have to be right decided," she said. "These roses are private property and I mustn't let you have them."

"Oh!" Philip dropped the great bunch of gorgeous color

guiltily by his side, but still held tightly the prickly mass of stems, knowing his right, yet half-wondering if he could have made a mistake. He stammered:

"I thought—to whom do they belong?"

"They belong to my cousin, Mr. Philip Fairfield Beckwith"—the sound of his own name was pleasant as the falling voice strayed through it. "He is coming home in a few days, so I want them to look their prettiest for him—for his first sight of them. I take care of this rose garden," she said, and laid a motherly hand on the nearest flower. Then she smiled. "It doesn't seem right hospitable to stop you, but if you will come over to Westerly, to our house, Father will be glad to see you, and I will certainly give you all the flowers you want." The sweet and masterful apparition looked with a gracious certainty of obedience straight into Philip's bewildered eyes.

"The boy Shelby!" Many a time in the months after, Philip Beckwith smiled to himself reminiscently, tenderly, as he thought of "the boy Shelby" whom he had read into John Fairfield's letter; "the boy Shelby" who was twenty-two years old and the only child; "the boy Shelby" whom he had blamed with such easy severity for idling at Fairfield; "the boy Shelby" who was no boy at all, but this white flower of girlhood, called—after the quaint and reasonable southern way—as a boy is called, by the surname of her mother's people.

Toward Westerly, out of the garden of the old time, out of the dimness of a forgotten past, the two took their radiant youth and the brightness of today. But a breeze blew across the tangle of weeds and flowers as they wandered away, and whispered a hope, perhaps a promise; for as it touched them each tall stalk nodded gaily and the box hedges rustled delicately an answering undertone. And just at the edge of the woodland, before they were out of sight, the girl turned and threw a kiss back to the roses and the box.

"I always do that," she said. "I love them so!"

Two weeks later a great train rolled into the Grand Central Station of New York at half-past six at night, and from it stepped a monstrosity—a young man without a heart. He had left all of it, more than he had thought he owned, in Kentucky. But he had brought back with him a store of memories which gave him more joy than ever the heart had done, to his best knowledge, in all the years. They were memories of long and sunshiny days; of afternoons spent in the saddle, rushing through grassy lanes where trumpet flowers flamed over gray farm fences, or trotting slowly down white roads; of whole mornings only an hour long, passed in the enchanted stillness of an old garden; of gay, desultory searches through its length and breadth, and in the park that held it, for buried treasure; of moonlit nights; of roses and June and Kentucky—and always, through all the memories, the presence that made them what they were, that of a girl he loved.

No word of love had been spoken, but the two weeks had made over his life; and he went back to his work with a definite object, a hope stronger than ambition, and, set to it as music to words, came insistently another hope, a dream that he did not let himself dwell on—a longing to make enough money to pay off the mortgage and put Fairfield in order, and live and work there all his life—with Shelby. That was where the thrill of the thought came in, but the place was very dear to him in itself.

The months went, and the point of living now was the mail from the South, and the feast days were the days that brought letters from Fairfield. He had promised to go back for a week at Christmas, and he worked and hoarded all the months between with a thought which he did not formulate, but which ruled his down-sitting and his up-rising, the thought that if he did well and his bank account grew enough to justify it he might, when he saw her at Christmas, tell her what he hoped; ask her—he finished the thought with a jump of his heart. He never worked harder or better, and each check that came in meant a step toward the promised land; and each seemed for the joy that was in it to quicken his pace, to lengthen his stride, to strengthen his touch. Early in November he found one night when he came to his rooms two letters waiting for him with the welcome Kentucky postmark. They were in John Fairfield's handwriting and in his daughter's, and "*place aux dames*" ruled rather than respect to age, for he opened Shelby's first. His eyes smiling, he read it.

"I am knitting you a diamond necklace for Christmas," she wrote. "Will you like that? Or be sure to write me if you'd rather have me hunt in the garden and dig you up a box of money. I'll tell you—there ought to be luck in the day, for it was hidden on Christmas and it should be found on Christmas; so on Christmas morning we'll have another look, and if you find it I'll catch you 'Christmas gif' ' as the darkies do, and you'll have to give it to me, and if I find it I'll give it to you; so that's fair, isn't it? Anyway—" and Philip's eyes jumped from line to line, devouring the clear, running writing. "So bring a little present with you, please—just a tiny something for me," she ended, "for I'm certainly going to catch you 'Christmas gif'.' "

Philip folded the letter back into its envelope and put it in his pocket, and his heart felt warmer for the scrap of paper over it. Then he cut John Fairfield's open dreamily, his mind still on the words he had read, on the threat—"I'm going to catch you 'Christmas gif'.' " What was there good enough to give her? Himself, he thought humbly, very far from good enough for the girl, the lily of the world. With a sigh that was not sad he dismissed the question and began to read the other letter. He stood reading it by the fading light from the window, his hat thrown by him on a chair, his overcoat still on, and, as he read, the smile died from his face. With drawn brows he read on to the end, and then the letter dropped from his fingers to the floor and he did not notice; his eyes stared widely at the high building across the street, the endless rows of windows, the lights flashing into them here and there. But he saw none of it. He saw a stretch of quiet woodland, an old house with great white pillars, a silent, neglected garden, with box hedges sweet and ragged, all waiting for him to come and take care of them—the home of his fathers, the home he had meant, had expected—he knew it now—would be some day his own, the home he had lost! John Fairfield's letter was to tell him that the mortgage on the place, running now so many years, was suddenly to be foreclosed; that, property not being worth much in the neighborhood, no one would take it up; that on January 2nd Fairfield, the house and land, were to be sold at auction. It was a hard blow to Philip Beckwith. With his hands in his overcoat pockets he began to walk up and down the room, trying to plan, to see if by any chance he might save this place he loved. It would mean eight thousand dollars to pay the mortgage. One or two thousand more would put the estate in order, but that might wait if he could only tide over this danger, save the house and land. An hour he walked so, forgetting dinner, forgetting the heavy coat which he still wore, and then he gave it up. With all he had saved—and it was a fair and promising beginning—he could not much more than half-pay the mortgage, and there was no way, which he would consider, by which he could get the money. Fairfield would have to go, and he set his teeth and clenched his fists as he thought how much he wanted to keep it. A year ago it had meant nothing to him, a year from now if things went his way he could have paid the mortgage. That it should happen just this year—just now! He could not go down at Christmas; it would break his heart to see the place again as his own when it was just slipping from his grasp. He would wait until it was all over, and go, perhaps, in the spring. The great hope of his life was still his own, but Fairfield had been the setting of that hope; he must readjust his world before he saw Shelby again. So he wrote them that he would not come at present, and then tried to dull the ache of his loss with hard work.

But three days before Christmas, out of the unknown forces beyond his reasoning swept a wave of desire to go South, which took him off his feet. Trained to trust his brain and deny his impulse as he was, yet there was a vein of sentiment, almost of superstition, in him which the thought of the old place pricked sharply to life. This longing was something beyond him—he must go—and he had thrown his decisions to the winds and was feverish until he could get away.

As before, he rode out from the Phœnix Hotel, and at ten o'clock in the morning he turned into Fairfield. It was a still, bright Christmas morning, crisp and cool, and the air like wine. The house stood bravely in the sunlight, but the branches above it were bare and no softening leafage hid the marks of time; it looked old and sad and deserted today, and its master gazed at it with a pang in his heart. It was his, and he could not save it. He turned away and walked slowly to the garden, and stood a moment as he had stood last May, with his hand on the stone gateway. It was very silent and lonely here, in the hush of winter; nothing stirred; even the shadows of the interlaced branches above lay almost motionless across the walks.

Something moved to his left, down the pathway—he turned to look. Had his heart stopped, that he felt this strange, cold feeling in his breast? Were his eyes—could he be seeing? Was this insanity? Fifty feet down the path, half in the weaving shadows, half in clear sunlight, stood the little boy of his lifelong vision, in the dress with the black velvet squares, his little uncle, dead forty years ago. As he gazed, his breath stopping, the child smiled and held up to him, as of old, a key on a scarlet string, and turned and flitted as if a flower had taken wing, away between the box hedges. Philip, his feet moving as if without his will, followed him. Again the baby face turned its smiling dark eyes toward him, and Philip knew that the child was calling him, though there was no sound; and again without volition of his own his feet took him where it led. He felt his breath coming difficultly, and suddenly a gasp shook him—there was no footprint on the unfrozen earth where the vision had passed. Yet there before him, moving through the deep sunlit silence of the garden, was the familiar, sturdy little form in its Old-World dress. Philip's eyes were open; he was awake, walking; he saw it. Across the neglected tangle it glided, and into the trim order of Shelby's rose garden; in the opening between the box walls it wheeled again, and the sun shone clear on the bronze hair and fresh face, and the scarlet string flashed and the key glinted at the end of it. Philip's fascinated eyes saw all of that. Then the apparition slipped into the shadow of the beech trees and Philip quickened his step breathlessly, for it seemed that life and death hung on the sight. In and out through the trees it moved; once more the face turned toward him; he caught the quick brightness of a smile. The little chap had disappeared behind the broad tree trunk, and Philip, catching his breath, hurried to see him appear again. He was gone. The little spirit that had strayed from over the border of a world—who can say how far, how near?—unafraid in this earth-corner once its home, had slipped away into eternity through the white gate of ghosts and dreams.

Philip's heart was pumping painfully as he came, dazed and staring, to the place where the apparition had vanished. It was a giant beech tree, all of two hundred and fifty years old, and around its base ran a broken wooden bench, where pretty girls of Fairfield had listened to their sweethearts, where children destined to be generals and judges had played with their black mammies, where gray-haired judges and generals had come back to think over the fights that were fought out. There were letters carved into the strong bark, the branches swung down whisperingly, the green tent of the forest seemed filled with the memory of those who had camped there and gone on. Philip's feet stumbled over the roots as he circled the veteran; he peered this way and that, but the woodland was hushed and empty; the birds whistled above, the grasses rustled below, unconscious, casual, as if they knew nothing of a child-soul that had wandered back on Christmas day with a Christmas message, perhaps, of goodwill to its own.

As he stood on the farther side of the tree where the little ghost had faded from him, at his feet lay, open and conspicuous, a fresh, deep hole. He looked down absent-mindedly. Some animal—a dog, a rabbit—had scratched far into the earth. A bar of sunlight struck a golden arm through the branches above, and as he gazed at the upturned, brown dirt the rays that were its fingers reached into the hollow and touched a square corner, a rusty edge of tin. In a second the young fellow was down on his knees digging as if for his life, and in less than five minutes he had loosened the earth which had guarded it so many years, and staggering with it to his feet had lifted to the bench a heavy tin box. In its lock was the key, and dangling from it a long bit of no-colored silk, that yet, as he untwisted it, showed a scarlet thread in the crease. He opened the box with the little key; it turned scrapingly, and the ribbon crumbled in his fingers, its long duty done. Then, as he tilted the heavy weight, the double eagles, packed closely, slipped against each other with a soft clink of sliding metal. The young man stared at the mass of gold pieces as if he could not trust his eyesight; he half thought even then that he dreamed it. With a quick memory of the mortgage he began to count. It was all there—ten thousand dollars in gold! He lifted his head and gazed at the quiet woodland, the open shadowwork of the bare branches, the fields beyond lying in the calm sunlit rest of a southern winter. Then he put his hand deep into the gold pieces, and drew a long breath. It was impossible to believe, but it was true. The lost treasure was found. It meant to him Shelby and home; as he realized what it meant, his heart felt as if it would break with the joy of it. He would give her this for his Christmas gift, this legacy of his people and hers, and then he would give her himself. It was all easy now—life seemed not to hold a difficulty. And the two would keep tenderly, always, the thought of a child who had loved his home and his people and who had tried so hard, so long, to bring them together. He knew the dream-child would not visit him again—the little ghost was laid that had followed him all his life. From over the border whence it had come with so many loving efforts it would never come again. Slowly, with the heavy weight in his arms, with the eyes of a man who had seen a solemn thing, he walked back to the garden sleeping in the sunshine, and the box hedges met him with a wave of fragrance, the sweetness of a century ago; and as he passed through their shining door, looking beyond, he saw Shelby. The girl's figure stood by the stone column of the garden entrance. The light shone on her bare head, and she had stopped, surprised, as she saw him. Philip lifted his hat high, and his pace quickened with his heartthrob as he looked at her and thought of the little ghostly hands that had brought theirs together; and as he looked the smile that meant his welcome and his happiness broke over her face, and with the sound of her voice all the shades of this world and the next dissolved in light.

"'Christmas gif',' Marse Philip!" called Shelby.

*Born on April 2, 1860, in Alabama, Mary Raymond Shipman Andrews studied law under her husband, William Andrews, later Justice of the New York Court of Appeals. Her first literary success was the independently reprinted short story "The Perfect Tribute" (1906), in which President Lincoln hears a wounded Confederate prisoner's opinion of the Gettysburg Address; it sold more than 600,000 copies. Her works include humorous fiction about men (*The Eternal Masculine*, 1913) and a biography of Florence Nightingale (*The Lost Commander*, 1929). She died in 1936. "Through the Ivory Gate" was first published in the June 1905 issue of* Scribner's.

After the colonel lost his wife, he lost his wits. . . .

ELEVEN

A Tragedy of South Carolina

Sarah Morgan Dawson

Then why did she not keep the pigs from his cotton patch? He had warned her! No man of his race ever failed to keep his word! By the eternal powers of mud and the state of South Carolina, he was a gentleman! He never said a thing he did not mean! This thing had gone on long enough. Again and again he had said, "Sure as you let those hogs of yours in my cotton, I'll blow your brains out!" Did they believe him? Well, they knew now whether he kept his word or not! Thank themselves for playing with fire once too often! Why did he not kill the pigs? Well, he had not thought of that! He had remembered he had to keep his word. By the powers of mud, a gentleman has to think of that first!

But this was in his twilight, whiskey-strengthened meditation on the broad piazza.

When the sun had been overhead, hours ago, he was standing there looking at Scipio, who had fallen asleep bolt upright, sustained by the handle of his hoe, which had ceased to turn the soil. The colonel had retired to the house to fortify himself with his midday toddy. Scipio took the next best thing, from his point of view—a nap. As the colonel, mellowed by the subtle influence of the old corn whiskey, stepped out on the sunlit piazza, those depraved pigs, before his very eyes, were ravaging his one hope of earning a living. Scipio, with a jerk that made the hoe scatter the soil, awakened at the ringing cry, "Here, you, Scipio!" He sprang forward briskly.

The colonel advanced with compressed lips and resolute stride. His hands grasped a gun. "Come along!" was his brief command.

Scipio followed, neither demurring nor questioning. Indeed, a bolder man than Scipio would have shrunk from inquiring the meaning of that deadly and intense silence. The colonel's fixed eyes and martial stride inspired caution. A clear, young voice rang out on the silence.

"Pa-a!"

The colonel half turned, without looking at the speaker. Waving the hand that was not clutching the gun, he tenderly cried, "You go back, Lorena! I'll come back, by and by!"

"Well, pa-a! What you goin' to shoot?"

"Hogs, child!"

"I'll go, too!"

"No you won't! You go just where I tell you: right in that house. And stay there, too!"

She was a strange, frail, elflike child; tall, slender, on the debatable land between childhood and girlhood. Her threadbare, outgrown garments accentuated, in rents, the poverty sufficiently proclaimed by the naked feet and long stretch of stockingless legs. The mass of black hair hanging raggedly over her shoulders betrayed the absence of a mother's care. The pose and tone of this fresh young creature bespoke a freedom and self-reliance rarely found in one of so few years. Her mother had passed away within her brief span of memory. Young as she was, she remembered the patient endurance, the poverty, toil, and humiliation that had been the portion of that mother in those latter days. "Befoh de wah," the colonel had been the owner of more lands and of nearly as many "subjects" as fall to the lot of some European kings. The bride he had enthroned in his ancestral home was envied by all the maidens of the land, because of the rare fortune that had come to her. No matrimonial candidate of the country could rank with the colonel. The wife never forgot this when poverty and degradation banished from the fine old house every sound of mirth and almost every trace of pardonable pride. It was her misfortune to fade with his waning fortunes. Loyally she ministered, as servant, to him who had crowned her queen of his princely home. But her fragile physique was ill suited to rough fare and coarse work. She sank visibly and without a murmur. She would have held herself as unworthy, had she failed to conceal from him the burden under which she was crushed. The end was sudden, fortunately. She died in a superhuman effort to accomplish some menial task beyond her strength.

Only then did the colonel fully understand what her life had been. Henceforth, he was more than ever silent, and more than ever devoted to the one living child. His library, which had been his delight in days of luxury, was still his favorite retreat. But external contact with books now sufficed him. Rarely were they touched, save by the child who lay on the well-trodden carpet, striving to unravel their secrets. Her singular inspiration in drawing was his chief interest. Untaught, she had mastered the art of reproducing her childish fancies with wonderful ability.. Her father was her sole companion. She was not aware that the demon drink did not always leave him in a state for ideal intercourse. Drunk or sober, she never saw the difference. And he had the grace to save his deeper potations for the night, when they would kill him more speedily and make him less offensive. Through the day, he merely drank enough to deaden himself to the memory of the galling poverty that had blasted his life. All the tenderness lavished on his wife was now centered on the child. She followed him afield; she ran beside him as he hunted the game that occasionally varied their common fare. In earliest youth she learned to light his pipe, bring his whiskey, and to discharge the household duties within her limits. The toil of others was the play of this little one. Apart from the whole unheeding world, father and child clung to each other. They neither knew nor cared for other interests. Had she died, he would have avenged himself on an unjust omnipotence by rushing unbidden into the awful mysteries of the unseen. In the elementary instructions unconsciously bestowed upon the child he had never included the knowledge of a Heavenly Father. Long ago she had ceased to repeat the half-forgotten prayers her mother had taught her. If the name of God suggested anything to her mind, it was chiefly as a potent curse of her father's when things went wrong in the field. And so the little weed grew with its own peculiar use and beauty, neither knowing nor caring that development, fruition, and decay were the inscrutable laws illustrated in its obscure sphere.

Hearing the beloved father order her to the house, she turned without demur and busied herself with her daily duties.

Meanwhile, the stern, silent man stalked on, bearing his gun, and followed by Scipio, who reluctantly dragged behind. It was but two hundred yards to the next house, a rough log structure which stood bleak and somber in its few acres of neglected land. The poor dwelling consisted of two rooms, divided by a broad, open passage. A single mud chimney relieved the dark outline; a thin wreath of smoke arose in delicate waves in the limpid atmosphere. On this balmy day, it could only be a kitchen fire that was needed within.

The mistress of this lowly home was standing on the porch. Three rough steps led down to the littered ground. She had stepped from the room that served as kitchen, bedroom, parlor, and workroom. Glancing through the rude opening that served as a window, she had seen the colonel and his dusky attendant in their singular progress. Curiosity prompted her to leave the double rasher of bacon frying in the skillet and made her hasten out to watch them pass. Her son, a gaunt, tall youth of twenty, collapsed, rather than crouched on the hearth to take her place. No word of explanation passed between them. His lank yellow hair crowned him as the stubble crowns the neglected field. The coarse homespun shirt of dubious tint served alike as coat and shirt. Certainly they are never worn together. One broken and patched suspender held his recalcitrant butternut trousers as much in place as they ever would be. A pair of suspenders was never owned in its entirety by any one of his caste. "Galluses" they called them; if originally purchased, they could only have been to divide between father and son, or near neighbors; they twain were never again one flesh.

The youth raked hotter embers on the sweet potatoes banked in the ashes that ever lay half a foot deep in the yawning fireplace. A few more minutes, and the last crisp brown shade would touch the frying bacon. Already the hoecake was firmly crusted on the side presented to the live coals opposite the board on which it was spread. The primitive table with its yellow earthenware stood near the fire. The loom, with its half-finished cloth, was at one end of the room, and the bed, with its dingy appurtenances, was at the other. Halfway between these two prominent pieces, knelt the young "cracker" on the hearth. His protruded tongue was held upside down between his discolored teeth as he thrust his iron fork in the hoecake, the bacon, or the potatoes, to test their fitness for serving. Absorbed in this critical examination, he hardly heeded when his mother suddenly called, "Teddy!" Turning the last slice of bacon in its dripping fat, he laid the fork on the ashes and reluctantly arose to join her. As he shambled to the porch through the open hallway, once more his mother cried, "Teddy!"

No one ever called him again—not even to dinner!

The bacon sizzled angrily in its neglect; fretted and puckered up its edges, and burned away to crisp, black ashes. The hoe-cake baked through to the board, which slowly and sullenly charred and crumbled in hot resentment. The sweet potatoes, but now luscious with their hidden sugar exuding on the skin in soft candy, stiffened, hardened, and burned in their stifling bed, unseen and untasted.

For the colonel had kept his word as a gentleman, "by the eternal powers of mud and the state of South Carolina!"

When Teddy's mother had abandoned her cooking duties to her son, she had stepped out wearing that calico sunbonnet, without which this peculiar class of women are never seen. Sometimes strips of pasteboard serve to give those shapeless hoods an evanescent form. But these soon collapse and dangle helplessly around the face. The next device is to wear them loosely folded over backward, and drawn forward to fall in any random plait that calico can assume. So decked, the southern "cracker," or "sand-hiller," is apparently unconscious of the lack of any other garment, at home or abroad. These bonnets are worn afield, to keep off heat, cold, sun, rain. They are worn in the house, to be prepared for any of these possibilities in their constant visits to the outer air. Whether it be a stroll to the woodpile, or to the pigsty, or to the "branch," or to the corner where the daintiest bit of clay lies hidden for the dirt-eater's delectation, the sunbonnet crowns the woman from the cradle to the grave.

So Teddy's mother stepped from the hearth to the porch, the sunbonnet that shielded her from the fire still falling around her eyes. From under its shadow she glanced at the colonel, who was now some paces from the wooden steps, Scipio respectfully halting in the rear.

"Them hogs of yourn," said the colonel, adopting the vernacular familiar to Teddy's mother, "have got in my cotton again."

She looked at him in silence. To her dull mind it must have seemed unimportant where they "got," provided they got enough to fatten them for killing. It did not matter to her; she planted no cotton herself. Indeed, she planted nothing that required care.

The colonel was very quiet—frightfully so, had she been

intelligent enough to see the danger signal. Then he said deliberately:

"I told you I'd blow your brains out if you let your hogs in my patch again. I'm going to keep my word. Here, Scipio, shoot that old hag! Quick, fool, before I brain you!"

"'Fore God, colonel, I kint! O Lawd! Maussa, don't mek po' Scip shoot buckra same like 'possum! You kin shoot bes', colonel! Shoot, please, maussa! Let Scip go!"

The colonel saw crimson. Purple veins distended his temples; crimson veins swelled in his eyeballs; a Niagara of curses burst from his livid lips. His hand was raised with the gun pointed at the Negro who groveled at his feet.

"Teddy!" cried the motionless woman, just as she would have said, "Teddy, dig some more 'taters!"

"Take it, you fool, or I'll shoot you! Shoot and be—"

"Teddy!" monotonously repeated the mother the second time.

Teddy had shuffled out, one hand grasping his sagging trousers, the other shading his fishy eyes from the noontime glare. In a flash he had seen more than living man can boast; for the swift bullet that pierced his mother's body had sped through his yokel heart. Together they fell on the rough flooring, he already seeing with eyes that were not of the flesh; and she, poor soul, doomed to a brief space of horror and pain—a sense of awful isolation and merciful oblivion at last.

The colonel turned stoically away, mindful to take his gun from Scipio's trembling hands. He gave neither look nor regret to the dead, nor yet to the death in life lying in a long, ghastly, straggling line along the porch and gaping passage. Scipio's slouch became grotesque as he followed his master home. Fear suggested flight; but the innate instinct of the former slave recognized that the colonel was his refuge and the arbiter of his fate. His ashen face expressed abject terror and a passive irresponsibility to leave "consequences" to higher natures; for, even in his mortal panic, he felt that he and the gun had nothing to do with the murder. It was the colonel who had "gone off!" And the colonel was the biggest man in the county: twice as big as the sheriff and the jailor. The colonel would "fix it."

Within a few steps of home the colonel halted. Scipio shifted from one foot to the other, an ebony image of degradation and helplessness. The colonel was strangely touched by this silent appeal. "Scipio," he said kindly, almost tenderly, "there will be some talk about this and I don't want you to get in trouble. You know the canebrake; and if you don't get victuals enough, you know where to find more. You are welcome to all you can take of mine. But canebrakes are not always safe. Travel on; better go when you can than run when you must. You are too good a Negro to waste on a hanging, and you have done nothing to deserve hanging—only some people are born fools and think they can carry things as they please! It is all right; you had it to do. Don't worry about it any more than I shall. I have no money; and money won't help you. Take my flask, though; you'll need that. And be off while the coast is clear."

"Thankee, colonel! I'll go. 'Tain' like I had a fambly. I kin git up an' git. No one ain' gwine find me. Goodby, colonel! Thankee kindly!"

The colonel gazed calmly at the retreating form of the lithe Negro who swung lightly along the untraced path to the canebrake. Fresh life had clearly been awakened in his downtrodden breast by the prospect of travel and new scenes unconnected with any prospect of toil.

Lorena came dancing from the house.

"Did you shoot the pigs, pa-a?"

"Yes, both."

"Why, there was lots of them, pa-a! Two ain't shakes to what's in the patch now!"

"The worst are done for; the rest don't matter," said the colonel, indifferently.

She caught the gun to relieve him of the burden. Quickly he held it above her grasp.

"Look out; you'll get hurt!"

"O pa-a! Would you take me for a pig?" she laughed.

Echoing the laugh tenderly, he led her by the hand to the place where the gun habitually rested, and then to the frugal dinner she had prepared for his return.

The disheveled chicken with the disjointed leg had grown weary of the social void in its haunts. There had been no implied invitation to potato peelings and hoecake crumbs. The land around was too poor to offer spontaneous hospitalities of attractive character. Chickie felt that an unwonted gloom had settled on its limited prospects. At best, life held no charms for her. "Cracker" chickens are so imbued with the shiftlessness and indolence of their owners that they speedily lose even the instinct of laying eggs. Poultry can hardly be said to be "cultivated" in such circles. No energy remains. Enough chickens to pick the casual worm from the neglected path, or clear the refuse from the family living rooms—enough to spare for the hawks and the wild things that prowl in the night—these amply content the modest aspirations of the "cracker." If they ever vary the monotony of bacon and cornbread by an occasional ration of chicken, no stranger has yet witnessed the orgy.

The frowzy little pullet fluttered up from step to step, ever pausing for a remark from the mother and son who lay supinely motionless in the rays of the sinking sun. Within the compass of her chicken life, familiar as she was with their idleness, never had she known them to be as lazy as this. Clucking and peeping in a shrill falsetto, vainly she interrogated them as to their eccentricity. Bright eyes blinking, head askew, feathers apparently developed during a stiff gale which had impelled her ever forward, she circled around and around the twain in irritating inquiry. Suddenly, a satisfactory reply seemed vouchsafed. The raw dough of the hoecake still clung to the dead woman's hands. Going from the hearth to her death, there had been no thought of the toilet observances all too rare among "crackers." The chicken accepted the dough as an answer to prayer for enlightenment and sustenance. It solaced itself pecking the stiff cold fingers clean of every trace of meal. While thus actively engaged a man passed by. Attracted by the extraordinary situation, he drew near the porch. To glance, to shudder, to fly was the work of half a minute. Nor had he run far when he met another "one gallus" man, hands in pocket, slouch hat drawn over his eyes, sauntering toward him.

"Bill! Teddy an' his ma-a is lyin' there dead. Murdered!"

The other nodded. "Knowed it sence noon. Been awaitin' to see who's goin' to tell on the colonel."

"The colonel! Did he do it?"

"N-o-o-o! Yes! Leastways, he made Scipio do the shootin'. I was outside the fence, an' I took keer to lay low. Jim an' Pete was along. They've done gone. Reckon I'll go, too."

"Well, we won' git our heads blowed off for tellin' on Scipio!"

"Tell an' be blowed, if you've a min' to. I'm goin' to min' my own business an' git out! I ain't fool enough to stay here an' tackle the colonel."

"Bill! You won' leave 'em there, an' all these pigs an' things a-roamin' in the night?"

"Well, you go tell the sheriff, kin' er keerless like, he better ride out this way. He'll think it means whiskey, an' he'll ride fast enough. I'm off for a run up the country." And even as he spoke he strode past the frightened man. The latter sauntered to town and intimated to the sheriff that some interest might attend a ride out that road. The story was whispered as he went along. When the sheriff arrived in the fast-falling twilight, pine torches flared their banners of crimson and yellow and smoke over the dreary scene. Hemmed in by the living half-circle, the faces of the dead seemed to mock and mow in answer to fearful comments and vain queries. Those who pressed too near, in their curiosity, or urged by eager neighbors, struggled back to place a barrier of life between themselves and the dead.

From his broad piazza, where he sat smoking and meditating on the events of the day, the colonel saw the fitful light and wavering forms so near. If anyone wanted him they knew where to find him.

Presently the sheriff walked up the avenue and respectfully accosted him. The colonel received him as though this were his reception evening and the sheriff his first and most honored guest. The sheriff began painfully.

"Of course, colonel, it's all nonsense them fellows is talkin'; but you'll not think hard of me for askin' you—"

"Anything you like, sheriff! Take your time. Anything!"

The sheriff, with a gasp, seized the other horn of the dilemma. "They say, colonel, that Scipio killed Teddy and his ma-a yonder."

"Indeed!" said the colonel.

"Yes, sir; and I hope you don't min' our ketchin' an' hangin' him so close to your house, sir?"

"Oh! Hang him, by all means, if you catch him!" said the colonel cordially.

"An' you won't take no offense, colonel? 'Most on your place; one of your hands, too! It's hard on me, colonel, to have to do things displeasin' to you! You know my duty—"

"No one knows better than I, sheriff! Do what you think best.

Have a drink? Well! Here's to you sheriff!"

Drink was never far from the colonel's hand. It was only decorum with him to drink with any chance visitor, and any number of them, night or day. So with the glow of the corn whiskey in their veins, he and the sheriff considerately told each other as little as the law required under the awkward circumstances. Each was ready to declare that the other was a "perfect gentleman," warranted to evince no conscientious scruples in critical moments. The colonel had merely sanctioned the lawful prosecution of Scipio—if he could be found, and if guilt attached to him. The sheriff thanked him effusively and returned to the seething crowd around the two cadavers.

"Where's Scipio?" he called in a voice mellow with recent whiskey.

Silence was only broken by the thick utterance of Negro whispers. Again he called, "Come here, Scipio!"

A skinny old Negress drew near.

"Law, maussa! Scipio done dead long time. 'Fo' freedom come."

"Who are you?" roared the sheriff.

"I Scipio ma-a! He ain't never live here, no how," she sturdily asserted. The black faces remained unshaken in their gravity. Some of the white men laughed aloud, even in the presence of death, at this astounding invention.

"We'll find him when we want him," said the sheriff curtly. "But first, we'll have an inquest. Any of you got an opinion about this here murder—if it is a murder?"

"No, sir!" "I ain't!" "'Taint no murder!" "Serve 'em right!" "Nuffin' but po' white trash!" "Buckra." "Does de jury git pay same like de courthouse?" These, simultaneously, from many voices.

"Well, all you who don't know and don't keer, step up an' form the jury."

"Mebbe dey is playin' 'possum," suggested a wary African.

"Dey's dead sure 'nuff!" replied another, stirring the old woman tentatively with his distorted shoe end.

"Who am dat say Scipio shoot 'em?"

There was an implied menace in this question which led to silence. No man cared to make himself responsible for the rumor in the face of unknown possibilities. White men stood stolidly; Negroes shifted restlessly, eager for a pretext for a row.

"If Scipio ain't here, an' no one ain't see him shoot, den Scipio ain't do it."

"Bress God! Dat so!" groaned the religious element.

"An' if Scipio ain't shoot, dey ain't shoot!" logically deducted an old ebon solon.

"Amen! Dat so, Lawd! Black man, white man, can't tell by de bullet who pull de trigger."

This audaciously irrelevant insinuation was greeted with a gasp of amazement. Mindful of late hospitalities, the sheriff was equal to the emergency.

"See here, Joe Saunders! An' you, Pompey; an' you fellows there! You ain't got nothin' to do with who did it, nor why it was done! That's none of your business; you've only got to say they were shot. The law does the rest."

On this simple basis, the jury was rapidly impaneled. As quickly the stereotyped verdict was formulated: "Came to their death by gunshot wounds inflicted by a person or persons unknown to the jury."

Time flies rapidly, even with those who chide its droning. But to Lorena, transformed into an ideal nymph of seventeen, time had brought no solace nor prosperity. She still roamed the woods, barefooted, driving cows which neither increased nor profited. Her father, her books, her sketches, these formed her world. Her drawing was inspired. She had no training, no theories to follow; she obtained results as the bird learns to sing, as the bee learns to make honey. On that plane, there was no room for improvement.

The colonel kept aloof from the world and sought no sympathy. But the girl's isolation weighed heavily upon him. Still more and more he resorted to the grave of his beloved wife, as though she could give him the help he dared not ask of heaven and would not ask of men. But he ever returned home bowed down by a burden that only increased with years.

Though he never spoke of it, whispers were afloat of a ghastly woman with a calico sunbonnet drawn over her eyes, who daily, in the gloaming, walked around the colonel's once beautiful home. It was not a pleasant topic; but there were those who averred that they had seen the gruesome vision. Under the seal of secrecy, scores likewise confessed that they, also, had met a woman in that peculiar guise, silent and intent on her mission. No one could question the colonel; but no one could doubt that he, also, was conscious of her presence. He never complained, whatever the mortal stress laid upon him. Year after year, he endeavored to wrest from the earth the return other men could so confidently expect—always meeting with loss, or at best, a scanty return. And ever, in the twilight, as he sat on the wide piazza, while Lorena prepared the meager supper, his meditations were disturbed by the quiet apparition of a woman, who glided out of the surrounding shadows and came toward him. The form was the homely one so familiar to him in life. The routine never varied. Up to where he sat, then around and around the house—the face in the limp sunbonnet felt rather than seen. While he remained without, she walked her weary round; when he entered the library, she peered into each window as she passed. The monotonous tramp continued until he fled from the house. She never spoke. She seemed merely a typical "cracker," indifferent to surroundings, shielded by the calico sunbonnet that drooped over her eyes. Her face was ever turned on the colonel, though she uttered no word.

The colonel stoically accepted this as one of the incomprehensible hostilities with which an inscrutable fate had long pursued him. When the monotony became intolerable he withdrew from the piazza, where he had passed his evenings for a lifetime, and retreated to the library. But in the twilight within he still listened acutely for the familiar step on the crisp leaves or on the rain-soaked earth. He learned to shrink nervously from the faint sound and from the shadowy form that flitted past each window, the face with the unseen eyes always turned fixedly toward him. Finally, he learned to close the great shutters before sunset. It was unendurable suspense waiting for the unwelcomed form that never failed to glide by. His ear, grown doubly acute, learned all that his eyes refused to look upon, so that his soul loathed life and chose rather strangling and death. He dreaded the day; but the night was still more awful. He would leave the house when Lorena slept, and walk all night, never resting, save when he could throw himself on his wife's grave. Earth held no other refuge for him. By and by, he intuitively understood that the woman in the sunbonnet was familiar to all who passed him by. No one dared tell him; yet he knew that she was so notorious that no one cared to pass his house after sunset. He only grew more reticent and more lonely.

After some years of stoic endurance, the strain could no longer be borne. The colonel nailed the doors and windows of his ancestral home and abandoned the place to ruin. He moved to a poor cottage on the outskirts of a large village some miles away. Isolation was still their portion. Poor as they were, he would take almost nothing from his beloved home. The associations which he sought to escape were too closely entwined with all that house contained. Nameless treasures, ancient furniture that had survived the wreck of fortune—all were left to molder in the deserted house. Lorena made no protest. The books dearest to her he transferred to the cottage. One drawing, which revealed her singular genius, he carried away with him. This erratic sketch which so impressed him, long survived him. It remains a singular memento of the family history. He wanted no other token from that once happy home. His whole mind was absorbed by the one image he sought to flee—the ghastly woman in the sunbonnet. Remorse needed no external suggestion to feed the fire that ever burned in his heart.

Far from the home he loved, in this new and humble shelter, fate might well have sent some respite to the broken and desolate man. But a nemesis who never relented stalked beside him when he fled from his past, and ruthlessly she scourged him to the bone. She was neither triumphant nor aggressive. She merely conveyed the impression that somewhere from the remote depths of that limp calico cavern, her dead eyes were fixed on him. When he could endure no more, the colonel stalked in grim despair to the grave of his wife, where the woman in the sunbonnet never came. Exhaustion always brought him merciful sleep on that desolate mound of earth. The villagers whispered of the new sentry-round followed by the silent woman who watched over the colonel in the gloaming.

Five years more of this unsought and undesirable companionship proved the limit of endurance for the colonel. The last time came for him as it comes for all. Whether, that night, the eyes finally gleamed from the depths of that shabby bonnet, or whether she had summoned him to confront them elsewhere, cannot be known. Only, the night came when he kissed Lorena with more than usual tenderness, and, as she left the room with the step of a young goddess, followed her with loving gaze. Presently he passed out of the cottage for the last time. He was not alone. He carried the gun which Scipio had so ably handled on that memorable day. And as he walked down the path, clutching the gun with an iron grip, the woman in the sunbonnet followed him. Where he went—what he felt—what he saw—remains untold.

It was Lorena who traced him to her mother's grave in the early morning. Often she had found him there, oblivious of all pain and sorrow, pillowed on the only refuge he had known in weary years. She caroled on her way, through field and woods, knowing where she would find him sleeping. The voice he so loved would awaken him with no startling consciousness of new torment to be faced.

Stooping over, the more gently to arouse him, she tripped on a gun lying by his side. With a stifled cry the girl fell on the still heart of the desolate suicide.

She did not long survive him; nor did she make her moan to heaven above or earth beneath. She held aloof, as ever, from the compassion that would gladly have encircled her. For a brief space, she roamed the woods and old haunts alone. Silent now, she lived her life of isolation, refusing all proffer of companionship or sympathy. And one morning those who pitied her from afar found her lying at the foot of a slight precipice, her faultless face with its inscrutable smile turned to the sky. One beautiful arm was thrown over her head; the dead hand grasped trailing vines and wildflowers that delicately traced a shrine around the exquisite form. There was no indication of struggle, no evidence of pain. Was it accident? Was it design? Did a demon force or did a spirit lure her to her doom? Who knows?

They carried her to the deserted cottage, and there they stood astounded before the sketch her father had loved best of all. It was hanging just over the couch where she lay in her final sleep. Years before, in her elfin girlhood, she had with unconscious and prophetic hand sketched her young divinity that was to be and its pathetic end.

The picture represented a girl in the dawn of womanhood, of rarest beauty, lying dead at the base of the crag they had just seen. The faultless arm was tossed upward, a long spray of vines and wildflowers had encircled the radiant sylphlike form. In awestricken whispers they noted every strange detail of the singular coincidence. Nor did any false sympathy murmur, "Would she could have tarried with us!" If ever a hope had crossed her piteous life, it could only have gleamed from the unknown beyond the grave.

Near a well-known town of today, the old ancestral residence of the colonel stands deserted and shunned. No one loiters near it or cares to fathom the mysteries within. The faded carpets and dusty furniture and books may still be discerned through the slats of the window shutters which were so firmly nailed by the colonel, when he hoped to escape the memory of the past. What was once luxury, is now the haunt of uncanny things that scurry through the obscurity and decay. No one dares penetrate within the silent house. It is the haunt of the woman in the sunbonnet, keeping watch and ward over the phantom of her murderer. Only a soul as vacuous as hers, as idle and as lonely, would brave the lion in his den! Only the tranquil ghost of the woman in the sunbonnet would venture to encounter the shade of the colonel in that moldering house! Today he is still shrinking, yet eagerly listening for the unfaltering footstep that hounded him to suicide.

Sarah Morgan Dawson was the wife of Francis Warrington Dawson, an English immigrant who spent most of his life in Charleston, South Carolina. He served as a captain in the Confederate Army during the Civil War and was editor of Charleston's The News and Courier *until his murder in 1889. Their son became a well-known foreign correspondent and author, who spent much of his adult life in Paris. He became paralyzed in 1920 from an assassination attempt. Sometime after 1900 Mrs. Dawson moved to Paris to be with her son and died there in 1909. "A Tragedy of South Carolina" was first published in the November 1895 issue of* Cosmopolitan.

When a man spends the night with a prostitute, he loses more than his wallet. . . .

TWELVE

Sleeping Beauty

Robert Bloch

"New Orleans," said Morgan. "The land of dreams."

"That's right," the bartender nodded. "That's the way the song goes."

"I remember Connee Boswell singing it when I was just a kid," Morgan told him. "Made up my mind to hit this town some day and see for myself. But what I want to know is, where is it?"

"It?"

"The land of dreams," Morgan murmured. "Where'd it all disappear to?" He leaned forward and the bartender refilled his glass. "Take Basin Street, for instance. It's just a lousy railroad track. And the streetcar named Desire is a bus."

"Used to be a streetcar, all right," the bartender assured him. "Then they took 'em out of the Quarter and made all the streets one way. That's progress, Mac."

"Progress!" Morgan swallowed his drink. "When I got down here today I did the Quarter. Museum, Jackson Square, Pirate's Alley, Antoine's, Morning Call, the works. It's nothing but a tourist trap."

"Now wait a minute," the bartender said. "What about all the old buildings with the balconies and grillwork, stuff like that?"

"I saw them," Morgan admitted. "But you pass one of those fine old green-shuttered jobs and what do you see sitting right next door? A laundromat, that's what. Laundromats in the *Vieux Carré*. They've killed off your old southern mammy and installed an automatic washer in her place. All the quaint, picturesque atmosphere that's left is hidden behind the walls of a private patio. What's left to see are the antique shops on

Royal Street, filled with precious items imported from faraway Brooklyn."

The bartender shrugged. "There's always Bourbon Street."

Morgan made a face. "I hit Bourbon tonight, before I came here. A big neon nothing. Clip joints and strip joints. Imitation Dixieland played for visiting Swedes from Minnesota."

"Careful, Mac," said the bartender. "I'm from Duluth myself."

"You would be." Morgan tackled a fresh drink. "There isn't a genuine native or a genuine spot in the whole place. What's the song say about Creole babies with flashing eyes? All I saw was a bunch of B-girls out of exotic, mysterious old Cincinnati."

The bartender tipped the bottle again without being asked. "Now I get the drift, Mac," he muttered. "Maybe you're looking for a little action, huh? Well, I know a place—"

Morgan shook his head. "I'll bet you do. Everybody knows a place. Walking north, before I crossed Rampart, I was stopped three times. Cab drivers. They wanted to haul me to a place. And what was their big sales pitch? Air conditioning, that's what! Man waits half his life, saves his dough for a trip down here, and the land of dreams turns out to be air conditioned!"

He stood up, knocking against the bar stool.

"Tell you a secret," Morgan said. "If Jean Lafitte was around today, he'd be a cab driver."

He lurched out of the tavern and stood on the sidewalk outside, inhaling the damp air. It had turned quite foggy. Fog in the streets. Fog in his brain.

He knew where he was, though—north of Rampart, east of Canal and the Jung Hotel. In spite of the fog, he wasn't lost.

All at once Morgan wished he *was* lost. Lost on this crazy, winding little side street where the grass pushed up between the brick paving-stones and all the houses were shuttered against the night. There were no cars, no passersby, and if it wasn't for the street lamps he could easily imagine himself to be in the old New Orleans. The *real* New Orleans of the songs and stories, the city of Bolden and Oliver and a kid named Satch.

It had been that way once, he knew. Then World War I came along and they closed down Storeyville. And World War II came along and they turned Bourbon Street into a midway for servicemen and conventioneers. The tourists liked it fine; they came to the Mardi Gras parades and they ate at Arnaud's and they sampled a Sazerac at the Old Absinthe House and went home happy.

But Morgan wasn't a tourist. He was a romantic, looking for the land of dreams.

Forget it, he told himself.

So he started to walk and he tried to forget it, but he couldn't. The fog grew thicker—both fogs. Out of the internal fog came phrases of the old songs and visions of the old legends. Out of the external fog loomed the crumbling walls of the Saint Louis Cemetery. Saint Louis Number One, the guidebooks called it.

Well, to hell with the guidebooks. This was what Morgan had been looking for. The real New Orleans was inside these walls. Dead and buried, crumbling away in decayed glory.

Morgan found the grilled gate. It was locked. He peered through the bars, squinting at foggy figures. There were ghosts inside, real ghosts. He could see them standing silently within—white, looming figures pointing and beckoning to him. They wanted Morgan to join them there, and that's where he belonged. Inside, with the other dead romantics—

"Mister, what you doing?"

Morgan turned, stumbling back against the gateway. A small man peered up at him, a small white-haired man whose open mouth exuded a curious, sickish sweet odor.

One of the ghosts, Morgan told himself. *The odor of corruption—*

But it was only alcohol. And the old man was real, even though his face and his eyes seemed filled with fog.

"Can't get in there, mister," he was saying. "Place is closed for the night."

Morgan nodded. "You the watchman?" he asked.

"No. Just happened I was wandering around."

"So was I." Morgan gestured at the vista beyond the gateway. "First, damned thing I've hit in this town that looked real."

The old man smiled, and again Morgan caught the sickish sweet odor. "You're right," he said. "All the real things are dead. Notice the angels?"

"I thought they were ghosts," Morgan admitted.

"Maybe so. Lots of things inside there besides statues. See the tombs? Everybody's buried above ground, on account of the swamps. Them as couldn't afford a tomb, why they just rented a crypt in the cemetery wall. You could rent by the month if you liked. But if you didn't pay up—out came Grandpa! That is, if the snatchers didn't get him first."

The old man chuckled. "See the bars and chains on the doors?" he asked. "Rich folk put them up. Had to protect their dead from the body snatchers. Some say the grave robbers were after jewels and such. Others claim the darkies needed the bones for voodoo. I could tell you stories—"

Morgan took a deep breath. "I'd like to hear some of those stories," he said. "How about going somewhere for a drink?"

"A pleasure." The old man bowed.

Under ordinary circumstances, Morgan would have found the spectacle slightly ridiculous. Now it seemed appropriate. And it was appropriate that the little man led him down twisting streets into ever-thickening fog. It was appropriate that he steered him at last into a small, dingy bar with a single dim light burning in its curtained window. It was appropriate that the stranger ordered for them both without inquiring what Morgan would have.

The bartender was a fat man with a pockmarked face which bore no expression at all as he set glasses down before them. Morgan stared at the cloudy greenish liquor. It looked like a condensation of the fog, but it gave off the odd, sickish sweet smell he had come to recognize.

"Absinthe," the old man murmured. "Not supposed to serve it, but they know me here." He raised his glass. "To the old days," he said.

"The old days."

The drink tasted of licorice and fire.

"Everybody used to know me then," the stranger told him. "Came to Storeyville in nineteen-and-two. Never did pick up the accent, but I've been a professional southerner ever since. A real professional, you might say." He started a chuckle that ended up as a wheeze. "Throat's dry," he explained.

Morgan beckoned to the bartender. The green liquor climbed in the glasses, then descended. It rose and fell several times during the next hour. And the old man's voice rose and fell, and Morgan felt himself rising and falling, too.

It wasn't a panicky feeling, though. Somehow it seemed quite natural for him to be sitting here in this lonely little bar with a shabbily dressed old lush who gazed at him with eyes of milky marble.

And it was natural for Morgan to talk about how disappointed he was in New Orleans, about wishing he'd been here to see the Mahogany Hall and the Ivory Palace—

"Storeyville," the old man said. "I can tell you all you want to know about that. Said I was a *professional* southerner." He wheezed again, then recovered himself. "Had six chickens on the block," he said, "Wouldn't think it to look at me now, but I was a mighty handsome lad. And I made out. Had my own rig, nigger coachman and all. When autos came along, I got me a *chauffeur.* Wore spats every day of the week." He lifted his glass. "Six chickens, a high-class house. Professor in the parlor, mirrors all over the walls in every room upstairs. Bartender on duty twenty-four hours a day, and the biggest call was for champagne. Customers came from far away as Memphis, just to see the oil paintings."

"No air conditioning?" Morgan mumbled.

"What's that?"

"Never mind. Go on."

"Called it the Palace," the old man murmured. "And it was. When the girls came down in their evening-dresses, with their hair done up and their eyes kind of sparkling behind their fans, they looked like queens. And we treated our customers like kings. Things were a lot different in the trade, then. Us fancy operators, we knew how to show a man a good time. We didn't hustle 'em in for a quick trick and push 'em out again. Gave a sociable evening, a little refinement, a little refreshment, a little romance."

He sighed. "But the army closed Storeyville. Jazz bands went north, professors got jobs in shoeshine parlors, and I sold the oil paintings. Still, I was luckier than most. I'd made my pile. Even hung onto the Palace, but closed everything up except for my own room downstairs. Nobody around today except me and the Red Queen."

"The Red Queen?"

"Told you I was a professional. Just because the lid clamped down, that didn't mean all us oldtimers got squashed. I've kept going, on the q.t., understand? Sort of a sentimental gesture, if you follow me. Never more than one chicken now, but that's enough. Enough for the few who still appreciate it, who still want a taste of the old days, the old ways—"

Morgan burned his throat on the drink. "You mean to tell me you're still—in business?" he asked. "You've got a girl, the same kind who used to work in Storeyville in the old days?"

His companion nodded solemnly. "Trained her myself," he murmured. "Wears the old dresses, old-fashioned stuff, not like the chippies over in the big houses. Got her room fixed up like it was forty-five, fifty years ago. Like stepping into the past, and she treats you right, you know? I'm pretty careful who I let in these days, but there was something about you, I said to myself when I saw you—"

Morgan stood up. "Come on," he said. He produced his wallet, flung a bill on the table. "I've got dough. Been saving it up just for this trip. How much is this going to cost me?"

"She'll set the price," the old man told him. "For me this is only—well, you might call it a hobby."

Then they were out in the night again, and it seemed to Morgan that the fog was thicker, the streets darker and narrower than before. And the absinthe burned, and he alternately stumbled forward and hung back; eager for the past recaptured and wondering why he was seeking a nameless destination with a drunken old pimp.

Then they came to the house, and it looked like any other ancient house in the fog, in the absinthe haze. The old man unlocked the door, and he stood in the dark, high-ceilinged, mahogany-paneled hallway while the gas jet sputtered on. The old man's room was off to the right; the big double doors of what used to be the parlor were tightly closed. But the huge staircase loomed ahead, and Morgan blinked as his companion reeled over to it and cupped his hands, shouting, "Company!"

His voice echoed and reechoed down the long hall, reverberating off the walls and the doorways, and Morgan got the feeling they were all alone in the dim circle of light from the gas jet, that the old man was crazy, that this was indeed the land of dreams.

But, "Company!" the old man shouted again, his face contorted, his voice angry and insistent. "Damned woman," he shrilled. "Sleeps her life away. I've had trouble with her before about this. Thought I'd taught her a lesson, but maybe I'll have to teach her again"—and once more he shouted up the stairway.

"Company!"

"Send him up."

The voice was soft, musical and thrilling. The moment Morgan heard it, he knew he hadn't made a mistake. Crazy old man, crazy old house, crazy errand—but there was the voice, the warm and wanton invitation.

"Go ahead," the little man urged. "Right at the head of the stairs, her room is. You won't need a light."

Then he went into his room and Morgan climbed the stairs, feet moving over frayed carpeting, eyes intent on the doorway looming above the landing. When Morgan reached the door he fumbled for the knob in the darkness, standing there for a long moment as he tried to enter.

Quite suddenly the door opened inward, and there he was in the big bedroom, with twenty crystal chandeliers tinkling their welcome, twenty velvet carpets offering cushioned caresses to his feet, twenty ornate vanities spreading a pungent powder-and-patchouli perfume from their littered tops.

Twenty great canopied beds straddled the center of the room, and twenty occupants waved him forward. The light blazed down on the redness; the rich, reflected radiance of twenty Red Queens. They had red hair and red lips and red garters and red nipples. Twice twenty white arms opened to enfold him in an embrace that was all illusion.

Morgan reeled forward through a thousand rippling reflections from the mirrored walls and ceiling, trying to find the real bed and the real Red Queen. She laughed at him then, because he was drunk, and she held out her hand to guide him, draw him down beside her. And her touch was fire, and her mouth was a furnace, and her body was a volcano gushing lava, and the mirrors whirled wildly in a long red dream of laughter and delight.

He must have put on his clothes again and tiptoed downstairs around dawn; he couldn't remember. He didn't recall saying goodbye or paying the girl or seeing the old man again, either, nor could he recollect walking back into the Quarter. The absinthe had left him with a splitting headache and a bitter aftertaste in his mouth, and now he moved like an automaton, turning into the first place he saw.

It was a small oyster bar, but he didn't want the traditional dozen raws—he needed coffee. The fog was gone from the morning streets, but it lingered inside his skull, and Morgan wondered vaguely how he'd managed to find his way back to familiar surroundings. He stepped up to the counter and reached for his wallet.

His pocket was empty.

His hand began a search, up and down, forward and back. But his wallet was gone. His wallet, his identification, his license, his three hundred dollars in cash.

Morgan couldn't remember what had happened, but one thing was obvious. He'd been rolled. Rolled in the good old-fashioned way by a bad old-fashioned girl.

In a way it was almost funny, and in a way it served him right. He knew that, but somehow he failed to see either the humor or the justice of it all. And when it came to justice—

Morgan gave up all thoughts of coffee and went to the police. He started to tell his story to a desk sergeant, told a little more of it to a polite lieutenant, and ended up telling the whole thing over again to a plainclothes detective as he walked with him down Rampart Street, heading east.

The detective, whose name was Belden, didn't seem to be polite at all. Morgan freely admitted he'd been drinking last night, and even found the first little bar he had patronized. The bartender Morgan had talked to was off duty, but the day man gave the detective his home phone, and Belden called him from the tavern and talked to him. The bartender remembered seeing Morgan, all right.

"He said you were drunk as a skunk," the impolite Belden reported. "Now, where did you go from there?"

"Saint Louis Cemetery," Morgan said. But to his chagrin, he couldn't find his way. In the end, Belden led him there.

"Then what?" Belden demanded.

"Then I met this old man—" Morgan began.

But when Belden asked for an exact description, Morgan couldn't give it to him. And Belden wanted to know the old man's name, and where they'd gone together, and why. Morgan tried to explain how he'd felt, why he had agreed to drink with a stranger; the detective wasn't interested.

"Take me to the tavern," he said.

They prowled the side streets, but Morgan couldn't find the tavern. Finally he had to admit as much. "But I was there," he insisted. "And then we went to this house—"

"All right." Belden shrugged. "Take me to the house."

Morgan tried. For almost an hour he trudged up and down the winding streets, but all the houses looked alike, and their sameness in the sunlight was different from their distinctiveness in darkness. There was nothing romantic about these shabby old buildings, nothing that savored of a midnight dream.

Morgan could see that the detective didn't believe him. And then, when he told him the whole story once again—about the old man training his girl in the Storeyville tradition, about the mirrored room upstairs and the red garters and all the rest of it—he knew the detective would never believe. Standing here in the bright street, with the sun sending splinters into his reddened eyes, Morgan found it hard to believe himself. Maybe it *had* been the liquor; maybe he'd made up the part about the old man and all the rest. He could have passed out in front of the cemetery, someone might have come along and lifted his wallet. That made sense. More sense than a journey to the land of dreams.

Apparently Belden thought so too, because he advanced just that theory as they started walking back.

Morgan found himself nodding in agreement, and then he turned his head suddenly and said, "There it is—that's the tavern we went into, I'm sure of it!"

And it *was* the tavern. He recognized the pockmarked man who had served them, and the pockmarked man recognized him. And, "Yes," he told Belden. "He came with the old one, with Louie."

The detective had his notebook out. "Louie who? What's his last name?"

"This I cannot tell you," the bartender said. "He is just an old man, he has been a long time in the neighborhood. Harmless but—" The bartender made a twirling gesture close to his forehead.

"Do you know where he lives?" Belden asked.

Surprisingly enough, the bartender nodded. "Yes." He muttered an address and Belden wrote it down.

"Come on," he said to Morgan. "Looks as if you were giving me a straight story after all." He uttered a dry chuckle. "Thought we knew what was going on down here, but I guess the old boy fooled us. Imagine, running a panel house undercover in this day and age! That's one for the books."

A surprisingly short walk led them to the building, on a street scarcely two blocks away. The house was old and looked untenanted; some of the front windows were caved in and the drawn green shades flapped listlessly in the hot morning breeze. Morgan didn't recognize the place even when he saw it, and he stood on the doorstep while Belden rang the bell.

For a long while there was no answer, and then the door opened just a crack. Morgan saw the old man's face, saw his rheumy red eyes blinking out at them.

"What you want?" the old man wheezed. "Who are you?"

Belden told him who he was and what he wanted. The old man opened the door a bit wider and stared at Morgan.

"Hello," Morgan said. "I'm back again. Looks like I mislaid my wallet." He'd already made up his mind not to enter charges—the old boy was in enough hot water already.

"Back?" the little white-haired man snapped. "What do you mean, you're back? Never set eyes on you before in my life."

"Last night," Morgan said. "I think I left my wallet here."

"Nonsense. Nobody here last night. Nobody ever comes here anymore. Not for over forty years. I'm all alone. All alone—"

Belden stepped forward. "Suppose we have a look around?" he asked.

Morgan wondered if the old man would try to stop him, ask for a search warrant. Instead, he merely laughed and opened the door wide.

"Sure," he said. "Come on in. Welcome to the Palace." He chuckled again, then wheezed. "Throat is dry," he explained.

"It wasn't so dry last night," Morgan told him. "When we drank together."

The old man shook his head. "Don't listen to him, mister," he told Belden. "Never saw him before."

They stepped into the hall and Morgan recognized it. The dark paneling looked dingy in the daylight, and he could see the dust on the floor. There was dust everywhere, a thick coating on the wood of the double doors and a lighter deposit on the small door leading to the old man's room.

They went in there, and Belden began his search. It didn't take long, because there weren't many places to look. The old man's furniture consisted of a single chair, a small brass bed, and a battered bureau. There wasn't even a closet. Belden went over the bed and mattress, then examined the contents of the bureau drawers. Finally, he frisked old Louie.

"One dollar and fourteen cents," he announced.

The old man snatched the coins from the detective's hand. "See, what'd I tell you?" he muttered. "I got no wallet. And I don't know anything about the mark, either. I'm clean, I am. Ask down at the station house. Ask Captain Leroux."

"I don't know any Captain Leroux," Belden said. "What's his detail?"

"Why, Storeyville, of course. Where do you think you are?"

"Storeyville's been closed for almost forty-five years," Belden answered. "Where do you think *you* are?"

"Right here. Where I always been. In the Palace. I'm a professional man, I am. Used to have six chickens on the block. Then the heat came on strong, and all I had left was the Red Queen. She sleeps too much, but I can fix that. I fixed it once and I can fix it again—"

Belden turned to Morgan and repeated the twirling gesture the pockmarked bartender had made.

But Morgan shook his head. "Of course," he said. "The wallet's upstairs. She has it. Come on!"

The old man put his hand on Morgan's shoulder. His mouth worked convulsively. "Mister, don't go up there. I was only fooling—she's gone, she beat it out on me this morning. I swear it! Sure, she copped your leather all right. Up to her old tricks. But she did a Dutch on me, you won't find her—"

"We'll see for ourselves." Belden was already pounding up the stairs, and Morgan followed him, the dust rising from the stairtreads. Morgan started to choke. His ears began to hurt, because Belden hammered on the door at the head of the stairs.

"You sure this was the one?" he panted.

Morgan nodded.

"But it couldn't be, man—this door isn't locked, it's sealed. Sealed tight."

Morgan didn't answer him. His head throbbed, and his stomach was beginning to churn, but he knew what he must do. Shouldering the detective aside, he thrust the full weight of his body against the door.

The ancient wood groaned, then splintered around the rotten

doorframe. With a rasp of hinges, the door tottered and fell inward.

A cloud of dust billowed out, filling Morgan's lungs, blinding him. He coughed, he choked, but he groped forward and stepped into the room.

The twenty chandeliers were gone, and the twenty carpets and the twenty vanities and the twenty beds. That's because the mirrors hung cracked and broken in their frames. Now there was only one of everything—one cobwebbed chandelier, one ragged and moldering patch of carpet, one vanity whose littered top gave off a scent of dead perfume and musty decay, and one canopy bed with its yellowed hangings mildewed and shredded.

And the bed had only one occupant. She was sleeping, just as the old man whined now while he peered over Morgan's shoulder. Always sleeping, and maybe he'd have to fix her again like he did once years ago. Morgan saw that she was still wearing the red garters, but aside from that he wouldn't have recognized her. One skeleton looks just like another.

"What the hell kind of a joke is this?" Belden wanted to know.

The old man couldn't tell him, because he was alternately whining and complaining, and then he was weeping in a high, shrill voice—something about the Red Queen and the old days and how he hadn't meant to do it, and only he could awaken her on the nights when Company came calling.

Morgan couldn't tell him, either. He couldn't tell him about the land of dreams, or the land of nightmares either.

All he could do was walk over to the bed, lift the rotting skull from the rotting pillow, reach his hand underneath, and pull out his brand-new, shiny leather wallet.

Robert Bloch, a prolific master of heart-stopping terror, sold his first story within two months of his high school graduation. Born in Illinois in 1917, Bloch's best early work is collected in The Opener of the Way *(1945). His 1949 novel* Psycho, *made into the second most profitable black-and-white film in movie history, led Bloch to a Hollywood career as a film and television writer. Winner of the Screen Guild Award (1960) and a Mystery Writers of America (MWA) Edgar Allen Poe Award (1961), Bloch served as MWA's president in 1970–71. His latest works include the novel* Psycho House *(1990) and a two-volume collection of his short stories. "Sleeping Beauty" first appeared in the March 1958 issue of* Swank *under the title "The Sleeping Redhead."*

The boys say they dumped their dead cousin's body in the river, but Granny says Maid Mary took the baby to heaven. . . .

THIRTEEN

The Burlap Bag

Davis Grubb

The room of the house was warm, for the Christmas morning itself was unseasonably warm. Liza fanned herself with a cardboard fan from the undertaker's establishment they had visited the day before. She stared out the window by the scuffed, warped door at the melting expanse of snow which stretched to the river.

She wore five petticoats, three sweaters from the relief people, army socks, and a heavy pair of man's work brogans. Yet, as was she, her clothes were immaculate as she tilted to and fro rhythmically in her rocker.

On her old face was all of her past. Wars had been fought, won and lost, battles and sieges had raged across the contours of that face, leaving it trampled some, shell-scarred a bit, and rutted with the wheels of life's jostling caissons. Yet there was still upon the face fortitude, even merriment, which was unvanquished, even virgin, a face still capable of bristling outrages and incontinent and outrageous joys. Snows seemed to have fallen on the territory of that face, too, snows of yesteryear drifted in her piled white hair.

She stared now across the poorly furnished room at her latest sorrow, her daughter Lovey's stillborn infant. The dead child lay like a small, translucent figurine cast in beeswax, in a cheap, small, pine coffin which rested upon two sawhorses, the legs of which were wrapped in pale blue satin bunting.

It was all for the best, the old woman mused, rocking all the faster, for Lovey—like her sister Dovey, who was knifed to death by her lover in a speakeasy called the Blue Moon—was a whore in a Baltimore Street whorehouse, and, had the child been born alive and kicking, the relief people would surely have taken it and put it Lord knows where. Liza flung her face around to regard the dead baby for an instant and then, unable to endure the spectacle any longer, rose and stole to the wall where her dulcimer hung, fetched it back to the rocker, laid it across her knees and began playing and singing in a young, high, keening voice:

> Oh, my lover he roves, he trips the groves,
> He trips both groves and valley.
> Scarce in the dew, there could I view,
> The tracks of my loved Molly!

The irrelevancy of the lyric to the occasion, Death or Christmas either one, troubled her not the slightest. And with no further glance at the infant's coffin, cheap yet somehow as elegant as a satin lined candy-box, she went on in her clear, sweet voice:

> Last night I made my bed so wide,
> Tonight I'll make it narrow:
> With a pretty baby by my side,
> And a dead man for hits father!

Attracted by singing, for she sang less and less these days, the two little boys of the dead Dovey came into the room for they gloried in her songs, so full of gypsies and kings and gore.

It was a large country boardinghouse they lived in, down the Ohio River a mile from Glory. Somewhere from afar in the upper recesses of the great ragged building came the drunken laughter of one of the boarders and the crash of a festive bottle against the wall.

Twins seemed to run in that family. Wilfred and Pretty Boy, he had been christened that in memory of the poor boy Floyd, were five. They were, oddly enough, considering their parents, reasonably bright and curious and mischievous. They came now to the woman's side, resting their small fingers on the wicker of her old rocker and breathing in her clean smell of camphor and arnica and the rose petal sachet bags she stitched and filled every autumn and packed among her things.

"Grandma?" asked Pretty Boy. "Sing us the Cherry Tree Ballat."

Liza shook her head and fetched from the unfathomable

deeps of her skirts and sweaters and petticoats a small can of snuff.

"The Cherry Tree Ballat," asked Wilfred. "Hit's Christmas, Grandma, and you done sing hit ever' year since we was borned."

"But this Christmas," said the old woman, "hit's not the same, children. With that poor dead child yonder in its pine coffin. And Lovey sleepin' off a bad drunk in that house on Baltimore Street."

She shook her head fiercely, not smiling and then abruptly smiling: that smile which is the vainglorious reflex of the poor.

"What kind of Christmas morn is this!" she cried out then, laying the dulcimer on the carpetless floor beside her rocker. Lovey off drunk and whorin'! That poor stillborn baby yonder in hits coffin, and she'll not show up when the county and the preacher come to take it this afternoon. And what's worstest of all, not a Christmas toy in sight for you two younglings!"

She smiled at the children.

"Fetch me my burlap bag from the pantry," she said. "Hit's like as not about to turn afreezin' tonight for there's a west wind from across the river. And I must go up and gather coal on the railroad tracks for the stove."

The burlap bag meant a great deal to her. Freight trains, swaying and clashing past along the river route spilled goodly sized lumps from the high heaped hoppers and these were the family's sole means of warmth and fuel for cooking. Now the children paid her no mind.

Pretty Boy snuffled his runny nose and sleeved at it.

"How come we never got no toy this year, Grandma?" he asked candidly. "Was we bad this year gone by?" "No, lambs, no," cried the old woman, ruefully. "You been angels the live-long year!"

She let her gaze stray then into the snow, pristine and unsullied, beyond the window glass which was so old it was wrinkled.

"There warn't no money for toys," she said. "Because ever' penny of the Christmas relief check hit went to buy that poor dead babe hits little coffin and a gown and a bit of fancying cloth and them two sawhorses hits coffin rests upon."

She thrust her rough brogans hard against the floor and set her bulging wicker chair rocking faster than ever. The children wandered off. Liza was heedless of them now: her griefs and shames had overtaken her now and for an instant she was a little mad, like an ancient Ophelia, and then she rallied; flung her head back again; still a little mad, yet stubbornly fending off her feelings and chanting into the hushed air of the stuffy, sealed room:

> Last night I made my bed so wide
> Tonight I'll make it narrow!
> With a pretty baby by my side—

Then she stopped and coughed, wheezing a little with her asthma like a sound from a broken concertina, and settled back in her rocker for a little nap before she fetched the burlap bag herself and went into the cold and gathered the coal along the rocky ballast of the railroad tracks. Sorrow and misfortune always made her either furious with outrage or drowsy, and the thought of the dead infant and no toys for Dovey's bastard younglings, this was all too much. She slept now in her chair, heedless of them, dreaming of her beauty and youth at Raven's Rock.

Pretty Boy, the bolder of the two children, sidled over to the small, garishly ruched coffin and looked at the motionless infant. Wilfred came presently to his side, full of the same thought.

Liza was deep asleep now, and snoring like a paper nest of wasps in the eaves of a stable, and Pretty Boy had the dead infant out of its coffin now and fetched it off to a place that was warm by the black iron stove, for the room was growing chilly as the coals in the fire clinkered down. His twin witnessed this audacity with envious awe. One finger was sucked guiltily into his lips.

"Grandma she'll git awful mad, Pretty Boy, if she wakes and catches us," he said. "And what if Aunt Lovey was to come home unespected?"

"She's in that house on Baltimore Street," Pretty Boy said. "A-whorin'."

Pretty Boy glared back stubbornly, holding the dead infant tight in his grip, its long white burial gown draped over his arm.

"I don't aim to harm it none," he said. "Scuff it up or git it dirty. I just want to play with it for a while."

"How come?" asked Wilfred.

"You don't see no other toys around this Christmas mornin', do you?" he whispered savagely, resentfully.

He pondered it a moment, ferreting out better reasons.

"In some ways," he observed. "Hit's better than a fake play-toy. This here baby doll—hit's real."

Wilfred still sucked on his finger, the only clean one, full of awe and admiration and many other emotions for the bold brother. He watched as the latter attempted to stand the dead child on its tiny bootied feet and ended by propping it against the wall.

"When we git done playin' with it a spell," he said, "we'll put it back. And neither Grandma nor Lovey need never know."

He scowled thoughtfully, inventively, at the object.

"We could play store with it," he said. "And sell it things. If we had somethin' to sell."

Wilfred, emboldened now, approached a few feet closer to Pretty Boy by the stove and the dead infant propped against the soiled, mildewed wall. He had propped it hastily so that it tilted a little drunkenly to leeward. Wilfred, halting in his emboldened approach, thought of a fresh objection, with a sidelong and uneasy glance at the snoring old woman, the mute dulcimer by her side.

"Playin' with hit thisaway, Pretty Boy," he said. "We'ns might catch somethin' from hit."

"Catch what, if I may ask?"

"I don't know. Catch hits—its deadness."

Pretty Boy scoffed and seized the dead child up again.

"Hit never died at all," he said. "For hit was borned dead. It never even breathed nor cried nor caught a sight of the sun. So there couldn't be nothin' to catch."

Pretty Boy propped the long-gowned corpse against the wooden box where they kept the coal. Wilfred grew more uneasy by the minute and gasped when the dead child, abruptly, slipped from its erect posture and fell, striking the harsh, scrubbed floor with a muffled thump. Liza murmured a snatch of a ballat in her sleep at the faint and distant disturbance.

To the dismay now not only of Wilfred but of Pretty Boy the shock of the fall had opened one blue eye so that it stared up at the boys. This development so unnerved Wilfred that he sat down suddenly, cross-legged, on the floor, as though his legs had failed him. He sucked on the one clean finger again.

"Jist look, Pretty Boy," he said. "Like hit war awatching us. Knowing. Thinking. Wishing a curse onto us maybe."

Pretty Boy snorted contempt at this thesis, fetching the body up from the floor, brushing off some coal dust and carrying it to the bench by the front door. With some effort he bent the tiny legs at the hips and set it upright there. The open eye seemed more acutely cognizant and indicting than before. Yet Pretty Boy ignored this. Wilfred felt the gathering coldness in the room as the glowing cinders in the coal stove dwindled and diminished. That one open eye seemed to give to the face a kenning and arcane knowing beyond the understanding of either of the children.

"There now," Pretty Boy commanded. "You jist sit there, baby, and don't you dasn't move. I'm the county health doctor and I come to make you well."

He pondered this, staring, and came up with a more appropriately ecclesiastical improvisation.

"No," he said. "I take that back. I hain't the county doctor at all. Set there like a good baby while I tell you who I really am."

His voice fell to an earnest and in no sense blasphemous whisper.

"I'm Lord Jesus," he said. "And you're Sir Lazarus, the Knight, and I done come to raise you from the dead."

Wilfred, a child of more secular leanings, found no consolation in this.

"Do me a big favor, Pretty Boy," he said then. "Either make that one eye be closed again or else open the other one. Hit just plumb gives me the willies with that one astarin' at us'ns thataway."

Pretty Boy endeavored to comply. The lid of the other eye only opened halfway and would fall back halfway when he pulled it all the way open. The adjustment worsened matters considerably.

"Now!" said Wilfred in a harsh whisper. "Now you done it."

"Hit's better. And hit war your idea anyways, dern you, Wilfred!"

"Lordy, if Grandma don't ever give us both a hiding now!" Wilfred whispered, tears of terror glittering in his eyes. "We went and done it now, Pretty Boy."

"We'll get it straightened out and back in hits coffin ere she ever wakes," Pretty Boy said, calmly. "You know how sound Grandma's little naps are."

"That's just it," said Wilfred. "Her naps. They're little. You never know when she'll wake up spritely as a fox!"

"She's good for another five minutes," Pretty Boy said, appraising the old woman with a measuring stare. "We still got time to git it fixed up proper."

Wilfred got to his legs now and went and sat on the saltbox with frayed carpeting tacked on it that served the room as a stool. Pretty Boy glared at him, forlornly. And there was a glitter in his erstwhile cynical eye now, too.

"Hit's better," he sobbed, "than no playtoy at all, hain't it? Well hain't it, damn you? This hyere—hit's Christmas morning."

Wilfred ignored this sentiment, his gaze mesmerized by the one open eye and the half-open eye, both seemingly fixed on him.

"One eye all wide and starey," he murmured. "And the other one sort of squintin'. Looking like it was about to make us both be dead like hit is, too."

Pretty Boy waved his hand, having gotten a grip on himself again.

"Hit don't think nothin'," he said. "Dead things they can't think, you derned fool."

Wholly skeptical of this, Wilfred picked his nose, defeated now by the whole dilemma.

Wilfred was by no means the more adventuresome of the two.

Pretty Boy, himself a little unnerved now, struggled desperately with the lids. He got the left eye shut again—almost, let us say. Yet the right eye, the staring one, was now slightly crossed. The dead child's countenance had now assumed an expression beyond mere malevolence or necromancy; it seemed more than a little crazed, as though its mind had been unbalanced by what they were putting it through. Without a moment's more of hesitation Pretty Boy seized up the disarranged body and stalked stealthily back to the coffin with it. But it didn't quite fit now. The small legs under the cheesecloth gown were crooked and stiff at the hips and resisted Pretty Boy's panicked attempt to straighten them. A tiny soft bone cracked somewhere within. And the body was even more resistant to its resting place in the Long Home. Pretty Boy with moist, trembling hands seemed now to be struggling in even combat with the tiny body, and losing. At last he turned and crossed the room and sat on the bench, staring at Wilfred.

"See if you can fix hit," he whispered, hopelessly, knowing better than to ask.

"In a pig's ass I will," said Wilfred. "I'm shed of the whole thing."

"Well, what'll we do then?" Pretty Boy sobbed. "Grandma'll wake directly. Lovey she might come home. The people from the welfare and that preacher from the Salvation Army acomin' this afternoon. Jist look at that thing, Wilfred. Hit's plumb ruinet. And we—"

"We, hell," whispered Wilfred furiously. "Hit was your idea and I never had nary a hand in a bit of hit."

Wilfred, if the truth be told, was radiant with mean and scurvy righteous-mindedness that he had had no part in the cosmetic havoc his brother had wrought upon the hapless infant body. Pretty Boy sat still on the bench, as if striving to rid himself of visions of unspeakable eventualities. He spat upon the floor and glowered out the window at the virgin snow that stretched down the slope to the railroad tracks and beyond that to the river banks.

"We jist got to think of somethin'," he sobbed, trembling as if in a fever, the sweat standing in beads on his forehead though by now the room had grown quite chilly.

"I don't mean to brag nor nothin'," Wilfred said at last. "But I got the whole fishing line untangled."

"How? What—?"

"Grandma's burlap coal bag," Wilfred said.

"What about it?"

"We take the baby out of the coffin," Wilfred said. "Put hit in that bag—weight hit down with them four big heavy chunks of coal yonder in the coal box, tie hit at the top with a piece of rope—"

"You don't mean go drop hit in the river?" Pretty Boy whispered.

"Sure," Wilfred said. "Like Aunt Lovey did that litter of kittens oncet."

"Well, then what will we tell them when Grandma wakes up and they all come and the baby hit hain't there?"

"We'll tell them Gypsies come sneaking in," Wilfred said.

"Ever'body knows Gypsies loves roasted babies."

Pretty Boy considered this.

"How come them Gypsies never woken up Grandma?"

"Gypsies is soft treddin'," Wilfred said. "And they held knives at our throats to keep us quiet whilst they made off with the poor little body."

Pretty Boy considered this.

"Grandma'll sure raise a ruckus," he said. "She puts a lot of store in that burlap coal bag."

"She can easy get another one."

"Yeah, but you know her. She gits somethin' and hit's the only one in the world. Nothin' can replace hit."

There was no further contention. Pretty Boy fetched the burlap bag from the pantry, carried it to the coal box, took out four or five heavy lumps, dropped them in the bag and carried it to the coffin. Then, wholly lacking in decorum or solemnity, he tucked the dead child in. They found a length of clothesline, cut off a yard and tied the bag at the top. Then, creeping across the old and squeaking wood of the floor, opened the front door softly, left with their burden and made their way down the snow which, having fallen in the night, bore, as yet, no footprint. On the way Pretty Boy almost lost his grit.

"Grandma," he said. "She's sure to suspicion us when she finds that burlap bag gone. I tell you she puts a lot of store in that bag. Fetches coal home in it every day."

"I'll think of something to tell her," Wilfred said. "I thought of this, didn't I? Don't you reckon I can figure out a fib about the burlap bag?"

"Couldn't we just save the bag?" inquired Pretty Boy, still apprehensive. "And just dump the body in the river?"

Wilfred stared at him contemptuously.

"Pretty Boy," he said. "Sometimes I suspicion you're as simpleminded as Lovey."

"Well, could we?"

"Sure," Wilfred said. "And have some of them shanty boat trash down river see it floating past and drag it in with a gaff and fetch it back to the house in worse shape than you got it into now. Or maybe have it float all the way down to Dam Number 20 and have the lockmaster find it. And fetch it to the county courthouse."

Pretty Boy pondered still.

"Don't dead things sink just natural?"

"Hell no. Now come on. Get some sand in your craw. Let's get this done and over with and be up in our rooms when Grandma wakes."

They came to the river's edge, where the cattails grow in the spring and the catfish leap on moonlit nights like dark dolphins in some Silurian ocean which once that land had been. Pretty Boy wasn't up to it. It took Wilfred to haul off and fling the burden as far as he could out into the deeper part of the river, beyond the shoals, and both stood watching as it disappeared, a few bubbles bursting as they rose from it, and then the river moved on unruffled and unrevealing.

From afar then, from the town of Glory now, came the clear clarion of bells from a dozen churches, each a different timbre and voice, each praising the day and the child and its mother, Maid Mary; their stumbling bronze and iron chanting telling the hushed, expectant air of the approaching magi and the star and the mother—Maid Mary—and the speaking beasts of stable and stall, and poor bewildered Joseph, cuckold of God as the old ballads irreverently yet reasonably infer. They were back in the big room by then and Liza was awake. She smiled at them. And the distant, unbridled ecstasy of the chanting bells set her off. She flung back her face, sang out loud:

> Lulee Lulay! Lulee Lulay!
> The Babe hit is born this Christmas Day!

Conscience can be conquered. Rationalized. Stifled. Forgotten. But seldom in the minds of children. It was Wilfred who, weeping as hard as Pretty Boy, came forth to the old woman's chair to make the fearsome confessions. When he was done the old woman was unperturbed, indifferent. She seemed not even to hear them.

"Whilst I was nodding in my rocker," she said. "I had a dream. No—hit war more than a dream, darlings. Hit war a vision!"

The children waited.

"I dreamed—I seed it—Maid Mary acoming down to take up poor Lovey's stillborn babe from hits coffin," she said. "And she stood there whilst she made it whole again and quick again—not dead. And bore it with her like moonbeam through the ceiling."

She sighed.

"Lord, she was purty," she said. "And I seed her—feeling not fittin'—but I purely couldn't take my eyes away. Golden hair clean to her bare heels and a long gown of dark blue with the crescent moon beneath her little bare feet and stars, like fireflies, shining through her gown."

She looked at the boys and smiled.

"Now what's all this folderol you two been tellin' me about takin' the dead babe from hits coffin yonder and playing with it like a playtoy till hit war all bent out of shape and soiling its poor cheap little burial gown and then dropping hit in the river?"

"Hit's gospel truth, Grandma," said Pretty Boy, not crying now, having gotten it out of him and ready for whatever chastisement lay ahead.

The old woman smiled radiantly, a countenance behind whose flesh seemed to stand the unwavering flames of waxen tapers, whiter than the snow, whiter than the moon, somewhere burning deep behind the life-scarred, yet translucent and uncannily youthful, flesh of the ancient and embattled face, the face of one of those, His despised poor. She poked each of them in the ribs with a gnarled forefinger.

"Now no more sich blathering nonsense," she said. "I've got to git me down there on that railroad track and get the big lumps afore them shanty boat trash down in the cattails along the shore beat me to it. Now git! This room's like an ice house."

The children grew stiff as marionettes. Presently Liza grumbled and was off out the front door by herself.

In an amazingly short while she was back with the bag bulging with chunks of good bituminous coal. She went to the stove, emptied the bag into the coal box, tossed it back onto the pantry stool, chose a few goodly sized lumps to lay upon the still glowing clinkers. Then she fetched, from its stone jug, a half a tin cup of coal oil, sloshed it in, and shut the black iron slotted door. She turned and looked then at the children an instant before she hobbled across the room and sank into the self-shaped comfort of the creaking wicker rocking chair.

"You can't understand now," she said, "what done come to pass this strange Christmas day. Maybe when you're growed you will, maybe. And then again maybe it will never be made manifest to you. But I tell you true—hit war no dream. I seen her plain. Heard the dead babe turn quick and commence to cry for the breast of her."

And she clapped her old hands thrice and snatched up her dulcimer from the floor by the chair and thrumming it merrily began to sing the younglings' favorite, "The Cherry Tree Carol."

Abruptly she stopped her singing and turned her luminous face upon them.

"God save us each!" she cried. "Hain't it a mercy and a goodness to know in our hearts that hit was us'ns Maid Mary chose to fetch a playmate to the lonely, little Lord?"

Yet neither child took heed nor hark to song nor words from Liza. They stood again, having crept there once more, timorously, to the pantry door and stared at it on its stool. The same one. The only one in the house. Liza's coal sack. And beside it the length of clothesline they had bound it with at the top. And both rope and bag bone-dry.

When Davis Grubb was born in West Virginia in 1919, his family had lived in the South for 200 years. His first novel, The Night of the Hunter *(1953), was a major success. Charles Laughton, Robert Mitchum, and Lillian Gish turned it into an even more successful film in 1955. Other well-known works include* The Voices of Glory *(1962), a massive biography of a Southern town, and the superb collection* Twelve Tales of Suspense and the Supernatural *(1964), which includes many stories used on the "Alfred Hitchcock Show." Grubb died in 1980. "The Burlap Bag" was first published in* The Siege of 813 *(1978), a collection by the author.*

A court-martialed soldier returns from the grave for a shot at revenge. . . .

FOURTEEN

Two Military Executions

Ambrose Bierce

In the spring of the year 1862 General Buell's army lay at Nashville, licking itself into shape for the campaign that resulted in the victory at Shiloh. It was a raw, untrained army, although some of its factions had seen hard enough service, with a good deal of fighting in the mountains of western Virginia and in Kentucky. The war was young and soldiering a new industry, imperfectly understood by the young American of the period, who found some features of it not altogether to his liking. Chief among these was that essential part of discipline, subordination. To one imbued from infancy with the fascinating fallacy that all men are born equal, unquestioning submission to authority is not easily mastered, and the American soldier in his "green and salad days" is among the worst known. That is how it happened that one of Buell's men, Private John Bennett Greene, committed the indiscretion of striking his officer. Later in the war he would not have done that; like Sir Andrew Aguecheek, he would have "seen him damned" first. But time for reformation of his military manners was denied him: he was promptly arrested on complaint of the officer, tried by court-martial, and sentenced to be shot.

"You might have thrashed me and let it go at that," said the condemned man to the complaining witness; "that is what you used to do at school, when you were plain Will Dudley and I was as good as you. Nobody saw me strike you; discipline would not have suffered much."

"John Greene, I guess you are right about that," said the lieutenant. "Will you forgive me? That is what I came to see you about."

There was no reply, and an officer, putting his head in at the door of the guard tent, explained that the time allowed for the interview had expired. The next morning, when in the presence of the whole brigade, Private John Greene was shot to death by a squad of his comrades. Lieutenant Dudley turned his back on the sorry performance and muttered a prayer for mercy, in which he himself was included.

A few weeks afterward, as Buell's leading division was being ferried over the Tennessee River to assist in succoring Grant's beaten army, night was coming on, black and stormy. Through the wreck of battle the division moved, inch by inch, in the direction of the enemy, who had withdrawn a little to reform its lines. But for the lightning the darkness was absolute. Never for a moment did it cease to rain, and never when the thunder did not crack and roar were unheard the moans of the wounded among whom the men felt their way with their feet, and upon whom they stumbled in the gloom. The dead were there too—oh, there were dead a-plenty.

In the first faint gray of the morning, when the swarming advance had paused to resume something of definition as a line of battle, and skirmishers had been thrown forward, word was passed along to call the roll. The first sergeant of Lieutenant Dudley's company stepped to the front and began to name the men in alphabetical order. He had no written roll, but a good memory. The men answered to their names as he ran down the alphabet to "G."

"Gorham."

"Here!"

"Grayrock."

"Here!"

The sergeant's good memory was affected by habit:

"Greene."

"Here!"

The response was clear, distinct, unmistakable.

A visible movement, an agitation of the entire company front, as from an electric shock, attested the startling character of the incident. The sergeant paled and paused. The captain strode quickly to his side and said sharply, "Call that name again."

Apparently the Society for Psychical Research is not first in the field of curiosity concerning the unknown.

"John Greene."

"Here!"

All faces turned in the direction of the familiar voice; the two men between whom in the order of stature John Greene had commonly stood in line squarely confronted each other.

"Once more," commanded the inexorable investigator, and once more came—a trifle tremulously—the name of the dead man:

"John Bennett Greene."

"Here!"

At that instant a single rifle shot rang out from the obscurity, away to the front beyond the skirmish line, followed, almost attended, by the savage hiss of an approaching bullet, which, passing overhead, struck audibly, punctuating as with a full stop the captain's exclamation, "What the devil does it mean?"

Lieutenant Dudley pushed through the ranks from his place in the rear.

"It means this," he said, throwing open his coat and displaying a visibly broadening stain of crimson on his breast. His knees gave way; he fell awkwardly and lay dead.

A little later the regiment was ordered out of line to relieve the congested front, and through some misplay in the game of battle was not again under fire. Nor did John Greene, expert in military executions, ever again signify his presence at one.

Born in Ohio in 1842, Ambrose Bierce volunteered for the Union Army in 1861. After the war he took up newspaper work, with biting political pieces as his forte. Appointed editor of the San Francisco News Letter *in 1868, he soon published his first short story.* Tales of Soldiers and Civilians *(1891) helped launch his national reputation. Bierce disappeared in Mexico in 1913 while covering its civil war. The circumstances of his death have never been learned. "Two Military Executions" was first published in the November 1906 issue of* Cosmopolitan.